BRITNEY FARR

Searching for Refuge

Book one in the Search Series

Britney Farr

First published by Britney Farr 2020

Copyright © 2020 by Britney Farr

All rights reserved. No part of this publication may be reproduced, stored or transmitted in any form or by any means, electronic, mechanical, photocopying, recording, scanning, or otherwise without written permission from the publisher. It is illegal to copy this book, post it to a website, or distribute it by any other means without permission.

This novel is entirely a work of fiction. The names, characters and incidents portrayed in it are the work of the author's imagination. Any resemblance to actual persons, living or dead, events or localities is entirely coincidental.

Britney Farr asserts the moral right to be identified as the author of this work.

First edition

ISBN: 978-1-7351256-0-2

Editing by Beth Dorward
Cover art by Lance Buckley
Proofreading by Catherine Buckles

This book was professionally typeset on Reedsy.
Find out more at reedsy.com

This book is dedicated to my grandmother Shirley (1933-2018) for always believing that I could do great things with my life. "When you're famous, can I have your autograph?" How about a book dedication instead?

This book is also dedicated to my supportive husband, Jeff, who pushed me to go after my dream and never once doubted me. I love you.

Contents

Preface	iii
Chapter 1	1
Chapter 2	18
Chapter 3	29
Chapter 4	46
Chapter 5	66
Chapter 6	90
Chapter 7	121
Chapter 8	136
Chapter 9	161
Chapter 10	173
Chapter 11	187
Chapter 12	199
Chapter 13	207
Chapter 14	212
Chapter 15	220
Chapter 16	232
Chapter 17	247
Chapter 18	254
Chapter 19	268
Chapter 20	289
Chapter 21	294
Epilogue	301
A Free Novella Just for You	304

About the Author 305
Also by Britney Farr 307

Preface

And the beast was given a mouth uttering haughty and blasphemous words, and it was allowed to exercise authority for forty-two months. It opened its mouth to utter blasphemies against Sabaoth, blaspheming his name and his dwelling, that is, those who dwell in Heaven. Also it was allowed to make war on the Notzrim to conquer them. And authority was given it over every tribe and people and language and nation, and all who dwell on Earth will worship it, everyone whose name has not been written before the foundation of the world in the Book of Life of the Lamb who was slain. If anyone has an ear, let him hear . . .

Chapter 1

"Run, keep moving."

"I'm moving as fast I can."

"Shhh! They'll find us if we're not quiet."

"They're going to find us if we don't move."

The darkness of night veiled the land, making it nearly impossible to see the desolate landscape that was ravaged by massive meteors.

A dense gray fog clung to the air and dampened the clothes of the four travelers as they shuffled their way behind the dilapidated building.

"Why don't you let me lead?" Amina retorted.

"No, I know where we are." Josiah's deep voice responded through gritted teeth.

"Well, then move. They're going to catch up."

"I'm moving. Again, it's a bit dark." Josiah's voice was edgy, yet unrattled.

"Will you two stop bickering and move?" Aiden hissed. His voice resembled that of the woman's, only deeper and more anxious.

They moved slowly through the darkness as rubble slid out from under their feet, causing them to stop, regain footing, then keep moving. They groped at a fallen brick wall to help stabilize them. It was a tedious but necessary act.

In the distance, voices shouted. If the group didn't hurry, they'd soon be caught.

"Shall I turn on a light so we can move faster?" a raspy fourth voice asked. She sounded older than the others.

Suddenly a small light beamed out from the darkness, revealing the woman's ragged clothing and a large rucksack on her back. Immediately a man's hand reached out and squelched the light.

"No, no light. We show light and we—"

"I saw something, over there!" a voice in the distance shouted. Flashlights bounced faster in their direction.

The other woman swore under her breath.

"Sorry, I didn't think—"

"Too late now."

"Let's go." Josiah snapped.

The group moved faster. Footing didn't matter anymore; they needed speed and feet like a goat. They moved as quickly as possible until suddenly their feet slipped from under them and one by one, they slid down a long embankment, toppling onto one another as they reached the bottom.

They pushed their way off each other and back onto their feet to keep moving. They were now in the open dirt field filled with deep craters.

"We're almost to the entrance."

"How do we get there without them seeing?"

"I could set off a deterrent flare," the older woman suggested.

"Good, do it."

They waited in the darkness. A quiet hiss, then a pop sounded. Out in the distance, at least a hundred yards east

CHAPTER 1

of their location, they saw a flare light glowing on the ground, giving the illusion of people holding flashlights.

A voice yelled. "Look, they're over there!" The flashlights, along with the pursuers, faded into the distance.

Once the group was certain the coast was clear, they crawled out of the crater and continued their fast-paced journey through the field, using the craters and scattered boulders as cover.

"Stop, I found the entrance," Josiah reassured the group.

It wasn't long before they heard the grating sound of scraping metal and a dim light shined revealing a manhole that had been camouflaged by a large boulder on hydraulics. They each climbed in, the lid tightly sealed, and the rock lowered and locked itself back in place before anyone noticed it had ever been touched.

Down below the group was able to relax. The younger of the two women, Amina, dropped her rucksack and moved to the wall where she ran her hands along the cement until she felt a small metal electrical box. She flipped a switch. A string of lights illuminated above them leading in both directions revealing the decommissioned sewer tunnels.

Amina turned back to the rest of the group. Her dark brown eyes flashed with confusion and a hint of fear. "What the just happened?" She stood still, but she clenched and unclenched her fists, trying to ease the adrenaline still pumping through her body. She hoped no one noticed she was shaking all over.

"That's what you'd call a close call, little sis." The younger of the two boys smirked. He pushed his chestnut-colored hair out of his face.

"A little too close if you ask me. And don't call me little sis, Aiden. We're the same age or did you forget?"

Aiden straightened his back and puffed his chest out, trying to make himself taller than the five-foot-seven he was. "Yeah, but I came out first."

His sister smacked him playfully in the stomach. "That's beside the point. We were still born on the same day, you nitwit."

"Alright, enough you two," Josiah said. He was behind them, next to the other woman. He had a long narrow face and his big brown eyes held a softness to them as he put his arm around the woman's shoulders, concern painted on his face.

Seeing the woman's light blue eyes glistening, Aiden frowned. "Maya, are you alright?"

She shook her head. "I am so sorry." Her voice trembled as she held back tears. "I could have killed us."

The other man, Josiah, spoke calmly. "You have nothing to be upset about."

Amina tried to hold back her own emotions and anxiety. "She's right though, we could've been killed up there."

Josiah looked at Amina sharply. "But we weren't and we're safe." She glared at Josiah before she walked to her rucksack and slung it over her shoulder. Josiah turned to Maya and spoke gently. "And you helped make that happen, right?" Maya nodded. "Good. Then put it behind you and let's go. We have food to deliver."

"Thank you, Josiah. You are most forgiving."

"You're welcome, Maya." With that, Josiah started down the tunnel.

As their footsteps echoed in the tunnel, Amina marinated on the situation. Being spotted by the military police, called the Myriad, changed everything. For nearly nine years they had gone undetected. As they had to venture further away

CHAPTER 1

from home, the risk grew exponentially, but seeing footmen so close to a tunnel entrance troubled her.

"Josiah, aren't you at all concerned about this?" Amina inquired. "I mean, it's one thing to be seen while still in the store or on the streets, but we were close to home. I think we need to do something about it, heighten security or carry weapons of our own."

Josiah was quiet for a moment, continuing to look forward as they walked. Finally, he spoke quietly. "Of course, I'm concerned about this, but we don't need to overreact."

"I'm not overreacting," she asserted, her voice coming out more strained than she expected. "I'm pointing out an issue that we can't ignore. You know the Myriad are out for our blood and they'll do anything to find and kill us. We need to be proactive about this."

"Why? They didn't get in. We're still safe." Josiah shrugged as if to say this was a moot conversation.

Amina pressed him more, ignoring his seemingly lax attitude. "But for how long? What happens the next time we or some other team is seen? What if it happens at an entrance and they find it and get in? How can you be sure we're safe?"

"I trust the coalition and their security measures. Now stop worrying."

Amina opened her mouth but closed it again. They could've been killed or worse, their home could've been invaded. Yet Josiah seemed unphased.

As the group turned a final corner, the tunnel ended and dropped off ten feet into a large cylindrical space. In the center was a massive firepit burning fiercely. The fire rose high above everyone, casting enough light to reveal a large twenty-five-foot cement dome full of people. This fire was smokeless.

In the beginning of their tunnel existence, scientists worked around the clock to find a way to vent the smoke. Eventually, they discovered a compound solution that would mysteriously vaporize any signs of smoke when poured onto the burning wood.

Dispersed between the people were piles of clothes, bags, blankets, and various other items. It was like an unmanned flea market.

Along the walls of the dome were several openings. Most were small alcoves people had made into homes while a few of the larger ones were tunnels leading to more dwellings that were set up in the exact same way, a dome-shaped room with a firepit, tents, and piles of junk littered about. It was a dump, but it was home.

The tunnels had become their safe haven about one year after the Great Desolation began. It was the only oasis for those who chose not to align themselves with the new world leader, Teivel, but rather to align themselves with the ancient faith of Sabaoth. Those who dedicated their life and received Sabaoth's mark called themselves the Notzrim, and they were considered enemy number one in Teivel's eyes.

Amina was the last to climb down the ladder leading into the dome they called Dwelling Three and over to the massive firepit. Voices mixed with clanging metal, water dripping overhead, and the crackling fire echoed, making the place a constant buzz of noise.

As Amina and the others continued their way to the center of the dwelling, she could see the faces of people light up. She knew the only reason they were happy to see her and the others was because they had food to disperse, but Amina didn't mind, she liked feeling needed.

CHAPTER 1

Food was scarce these days. Early on, many had brought in an abundance of food and resources to share. The leaders of the underground, called the elders, along with the help of their scientists, also found a way to grow a limited variety of fruits and vegetables. The problem was people didn't realize how long they'd be hiding. As time dragged on, the food supply dwindled, and the scientists couldn't keep up with the growing demand for fresh food. It was left up to small volunteer teams to go above ground at night and find whatever food they could scavenge from abandoned stores and homes.

Standing beside the firepit was a woman dressed in a black uniform, bulletproof vest, and gun holster. The group made it to the firepit and Josiah stopped to talk to the officer while the others spread out.

"Time for grub!" Aiden shouted, his voice bouncing in every direction.

More dwellers made their way over and formed lines in front of each scavenger in order to conduct their usual business of trade.

As much as Amina wished she could just give the food to everyone for free, she knew that wasn't possible. There were too many items she needed and this was the best way to get them. The scavengers were mostly interested in little necessities that would help them with their next raid such as batteries, knives, jackets, or shoes.

On occasion, a very grateful Notzrim would present a larger trade: a radio, cookware, or even better—a book. Books had become a precious commodity and highly coveted. Especially if it was a copy of the Sacred Book. Supposedly, all the Sacred books and anything related to Sabaoth were burned, but every so often one would appear and would be shared among the community.

Amina mindlessly passed out food, making her trades. It was all the same items and routine. She had been in the tunnels for five years, and the monotony of life was getting to her, but it was safe.

Next in line was a little girl, no older than ten. She was barefoot and her dress was caked with dirt. The little girl smiled, showing her missing bottom front tooth.

Amina smiled and her mouth dropped open with surprise. "Why Miss Lily, you've lost a tooth." The little girl's sweet smile widened as she nodded her head. "Is a new one growing in?" She nodded again and then pulled her lip down and opened her mouth wide. Amina glanced into the girl's mouth. She saw the smallest bit of white popping through the gums. "Very nice."

The little girl let go of her lip, and with her dirt-stained hands, she presented her trade: a copy of *The Wizard of Oz*. It was terribly worn and several pages were falling out of the binding, but it was obvious the book had been cherished and loved.

Amina's eyes widened again, but this time with true shock and delight. She delicately took the book from Lily and ran her hand across the embossed title. She looked at the girl. "Are you sure you want to give this to me? You might not get another book for a very long time." The little girl nodded with misty eyes. Amina cupped Lily's face with one hand. "Thank you."

Amina gently placed the book beside her with the rest of her loot before pulling out a bag of croutons, banana chips, and a can of beans from her rucksack. She handed Lily the food and chuckled a bit as she tried to juggle it in her tiny arms.

"One more thing." Amina pulled out a small tootsie roll.

CHAPTER 1

"This is just for you." Amina tucked the candy into Lily's pocket. Lily smiled big. "You're very welcome. Thanks for the book." The little girl giggled and then walked away. In all the time Amina had known Lily, she never spoke. But what she lacked in speech, she made up for in personality, and Amina adored the little girl and her smiles.

The last person in her line did not appear as easy to please. He was gruff-looking with broad shoulders, bulky arms, and a long beard and mustache. If it weren't for the forlorn look in his eyes, he'd be intimidating.

"Morning, Tempe. How goes it?" Amina asked cheerfully.

"Is it morning already? I've lost track of days and time and everything else for that matter."

Amina tried to stay positive despite her own struggles. "He'll be here any day now; I'm sure of it." She plastered a fake smile on her face, hoping he would believe it.

"You say that every time, but it hasn't happened yet."

"Keep hoping. It will happen as it is written, and we cannot lose hope."

At least, wasn't that what Aiden was always telling her? She hoped her words would encourage Tempe. He was often depressed, along with so many others who continued to hope for something that seemed would never come to fruition.

Amina paused before changing the subject. "So, what do you have for me today?" Amina asked cheerfully.

Tempe pulled out a brown wool blanket large enough for two people. "It's just been washed too. They have soap in Dwelling One."

"This is great." Amina took the blanket and set it on top of her pile. "And thanks for the tip about the soap." She pulled out food for Tempe's family of five. "Eat well, be nourished."

"We'll never be nourished with this little bit of food." Tempe shook his head and walked away.

Amina peered into her bag and found only one item left for herself. She sighed with disappointment, but she still tried to be grateful for the can of Spam left over. *I hate Spam.*

"Hey, Amina. I need some food." The voice was quiet but forceful.

Amina felt her muscles tighten and she straightened, preparing herself for whatever might come next.

Across the way, she saw a tall lanky man making his way toward her. He didn't look like he had much fight in him, but his voice was desperate. *Where had he come from?*

"Sorry Gavin, I'm all out." She did not respond well to boorish behavior, but she knew she had to try and stay calm or risk a fight. Turning to the other scavengers she shouted, "Anyone got food left?"

"I'm out!" Aiden shouted along with the other two.

Amina frowned and turned back to the man. "Until tomorrow. Sorry." Amina quickly turned away from the man and squatted down to collect her things and get away. Turning someone away could go one of two ways. Amina hoped he would just yell and scream as he walked away, kicking barrels and throwing things. He didn't.

Amina felt a firm hand grab her arm hard and yank her to her feet. She was soon face-to-face with the livid man. His face was crimson and Amina felt his fingers bruising her skin. Out of the corner of her eye, she could see others watching the commotion.

"Now listen here. I've gone without a decent meal for the past two days because you scavengers don't seem to ever have enough by the time I get here. I can't go another day on just

CHAPTER 1

watery tea and lettuce. I know you keep food for yourself, so give it to me." He gave her a little shake as if the jolt would scare her into compliance.

Amina took a slow breath to keep herself calm, but her voice took on a new edge as her blood boiled. She spoke slowly. "You are out of line, sir. We can only come back with so much and you will have to wait till the next round or go to another dwelling."

"I can't wait that long. Did you not hear me?!" The man threw Amina to the floor roughly and darted for her bag. Amina had had enough. She quickly stood up and was about to grab the man to throw him back, but at that same moment, Aiden saw the commotion and rushed over like a ferocious lion. He hurdled the trash can in his way and tackled the man to the ground. Rolling around, Aiden gained control and pinned the man's arms down so he couldn't move. "No one hurts a woman, especially when it's my sister! You got it?"

At this point, a small crowd had formed around them and the coalition officer pushed her way through and hovered over Aiden.

"Is there a problem here?" she inquired.

Aiden looked from the officer to Gavin. "I don't believe there is, ma'am."

Gavin shook his head. "No, no problem. I'm sorry. Please forgive me. It must be the lack of food that's getting to me."

The officer eyed the two men skeptically before walking away, dispersing the crowd as she went.

Aiden got off the man and helped him up. "I know you are hungry, brother, but you can't turn on us. It's already chaos up there, don't bring it down here too. Now, what did you have to trade?"

"Glow sticks."

Aiden smiled. "Well, it just so happens that I need glow sticks more than I need my single can of corn." Aiden walked to his sack to get the can. While he was gone, Gavin walked to Amina sheepishly.

"Please forgive me."

"You're forgiven. I know what it's like to be so hungry you lose focus."

Aiden returned with corn and made the trade. "Now I don't want to see this happen again or I'll have to report you."

"Of course. Thank you." Gavin took his corn and darted to the nearest ladder.

"Are you alright?" Josiah asked as he sat down in the dirt and pulled out a can of Spaghetti O's and a knife.

Amina shot him an offended look. "Of course I am. I can handle myself. Although, Aiden doesn't seem to think so," she said a little more sarcastically.

"I know *you* can handle yourself," Aiden defended, "I just get worried about how *they* react." He motioned toward the other people in the dwelling.

"What, desperate?"

"And crazy. It's not always safe, no matter what people might say."

"And if the elders didn't think I could handle it they wouldn't have appointed me to the team."

"You're my little sis, I have to look out for you."

Amina rolled her eyes. "Again, we're the same age."

"No, I literally meant, little." Aiden stuck his hand out to indicate how much shorter Amina was to him. "You're shorter than me."

"By like two inches," Amina defended. Aiden always knew

how to press her buttons. "But even if I am, I can still whip you any time." Amina threw her hands up and got into a fighting position egging Aiden on with soft punches to his arm and chest. Aiden sparred with her for a moment until he grabbed Amina around the waist and hoisted her over his shoulder. Amina squealed playfully and flung herself backward forcing Aiden to let go. She landed in a handstand and then somersaulted to her feet.

"Alright, you two, why don't you come eat," Josiah said as he started to open his can of Spaghetti O's.

Amina threw her arm around Aiden's shoulders as they both walked back to the firepit and sat down.

The four of them bowed their heads and Josiah prayed. "Our great and mighty Sabaoth, giver and sustainer of life, thank you for this food we have to eat today. Despite our circumstances, you care for us and you provide for us. Might we always be grateful to you for all you provide us each and every day until Mashiakh's return. Mashiakh, come quickly. Amen."

Amina opened her eyes, rifled through her sack, and pulled out the can of Spam. "You want to share since you gave yours away?" she asked Aiden.

Aiden glanced at her can. "Spam? Why didn't we give Gavin that and I could've kept the corn?"

Amina chuckled as she opened her can with a knife. "As much as I hate it too, I'd rather have the protein."

Aiden made a disgusted face as he took the can from Amina and sniffed it. "If that's what you can call it." He grabbed a fork out of his sack and slowly ate the Spam, scrunching his nose with every tiny bite.

Amina chuckled at his over-exaggerated expressions.

"Would you like a clothespin?"

Aiden glared at her. "This Spam is rank. Here you eat the rest," Aiden complained as he handed Amina the can.

Amina investigated the can and found most of it gone. "Is that why you left me less than half?"

"What? That is totally half right there."

Amina took the fork and finished eating the Spam. It was indescribably salty but food was food. "Aiden, do you have water to wash this down?"

Aiden rummaged through his sack again and found a canteen. "I don't think there's much left, but you can have it." He handed her the canteen and she downed it, washing away the taste of unidentifiable processed meat.

At that moment, a tall muscular man wearing cargo pants and a shirt with no sleeves came running up to the group with a black trash bag. He dropped it in front of the group. "Merry Christmas!"

They all looked at each other a bit confused. Not that it was uncommon for Terrance to say odd things, but it wasn't every day that Terrance had a giant trash bag.

Aiden tried to open the bag but Terrance quickly swatted his hand away. "Not so fast there, bucko."

Amina shook her head. She would've thought it actually was Christmas by the way Aiden bounced excitedly. "What's got you grinning like a Cheshire, Terrance?"

Casually Terrance sat down. "Oh not much, just that I went to see Old Lady Sheila and she had a boatload of goods." Terrance grabbed the bag and dumped it out on the ground revealing clothes, socks, blankets, towels, and a whole lot more.

Amina did her best not to look as awe-struck as her brother,

CHAPTER 1

but she couldn't help but gawk.

"Have at it."

Aiden dove into the clothes without hesitation. "Oh man, do I need some new clothes, mine smell like something died."

Amina and the others joined him in the rummaging. It was a solid collection of both men's and women's clothes: jeans, leggings, cotton shirts, tank tops, leather vests, you name it. They had all been patched, washed, and made to look as new as possible. Once they went underground, "new clothing" meant hand-me-downs and re-purposed clothing people traded. Old Lady Sheila was the one to manage all the clothing trades and was the underground's head seamstress. Terrance was her nephew, so he always had first pick.

Josiah stuck his hand out and Terrance shook it. "Thank you, Terrance. It's really appreciated."

"There's more there than a porcupine's got needles. I don't even know what some of it is. I figure the next time I need something, y'all could help me out."

Amina glanced at Josiah when she heard Terrance's comment. Josiah was never keen on making deals, especially if he felt he couldn't keep it.

Amina kept looking through the items but listened, ready to jump in and mediate if necessary.

Josiah crossed his arms. "That depends on what you're wanting."

"Oh calm yourself. You don't need to get your panties in a wad. I just mean supplies. Y'all get so much through your trading and people don't seem to want to trade with me much."

"I wonder why," Aiden said as he stood to try on a leather jacket he found.

"Shut up." Terrance pushed Aiden causing him to lose his

balance and fall into the pile of clothes.

"I can't promise anything, but I will try," Josiah decided.

"That's all I'm asking brother."

Amina was uneasy with Terrance's request. Terrance wasn't always the one to be found on the honor roll. Many times Amina had caught him sneaking around with contraband or stirring up trouble all in the name of peace, or so he'd say.

When the crew finally found what they wanted, Terrance scooped everything back into his bag. "Well, I'm off to the next dwelling to deliver goodies." With a final salute, he threw the bag over his shoulder and headed out.

Aiden watched him leave. "He's like Santa Clause, only skinnier and less jolly."

Amina shook her head. "You're ridiculous. I don't even know what to do with you sometimes."

"Just love me." Aiden grinned from ear to ear; Amina laughed.

"I'm taking off," Josiah spoke up. He grabbed his sack and slung it over his shoulder. "I'll see you tomorrow."

Amina nodded. "Sure thing, Josiah."

Maya stood up, looking ragged. "I should get some rest as well. Blessings to you both." She turned and slowly walked away. The attack had rattled her; it had rattled them all.

Before Maya got too far, Amina called after her. "Maya, wait a minute." Amina walked over, frowning. "I want to apologize, for earlier. You were trying to help, and I was inconsiderate. I'm sorry."

Maya smiled as she took Amina's hand. "You weren't wrong. I need to be careful up there but thank you Amina for your apology. I forgive you." Maya hugged Amina before walking away, even though she had to know Amina was not much of a

CHAPTER 1

hugger.

Amina walked back to her things and noticed Aiden still hanging around. "So, what are you doing the rest of the day?" she asked.

"I am going to see Paul and Mo."

Amina held up a small rag doll. "Great. I found this mixed in with Terrance's things. Will you give it to Emily for me?"

"You could come with me and give it to her yourself."

Amina turned back to her bag and finished packing. "I-I've got things to do. I'm going to head over to Dwelling One. They have soap and I need a shower." Amina gathered her new gifts and shoved them into her already full rucksack.

Aiden placed a hand on Amina's. "There's nothing so important that it can't wait. You need to see your family, they're important."

Amina stood, avoiding his gaze. Family was important to her, and she loved her family, but her aunt made her uncomfortable. She was a reminder of her mother—someone she really didn't want to think about ever again. "I do see them, twice a month, you know that."

Aiden pleaded with her silently until she acquiesced.

"Fine." She breathed, shoving the last item into her sack.

Chapter 2

Amina and Aiden made their way through the twists and turns of the tunnels until they reached Dwelling Five where even more people were bustling about, anxious to get their day started. As they wandered down the metal stairs that led to the floor of the dome and through the crowd of people with makeshift carts, wagons, and oversized bags, Amina spotted a small group of mostly children sitting around an elderly man near the central firepit.

Everyone listened, enthralled with the man's animated voice and facial expressions. As he spoke, he flailed his arms about wildly, which only made the younger children laugh hysterically and spout tears.

When Amina and Aiden were in earshot, Amina tuned into the man's silvery voice like a trance.

"Imagine what would happen if you went to a friend in the middle of the night, while he was dead asleep, and you start pounding on his door." The man wildly knocked on an invisible door. "He won't wake up. So, you ring the doorbell over and over and start shouting desperately, 'Friend, lend me some food. An old friend traveling through just showed up, and I don't have a thing on hand.'" The storyteller paused a moment to let this absurd situation sink in before he continued. "Well,

CHAPTER 2

let me tell you, the friend hears you now, and he's not happy." At this point, the storyteller stood up, furrowed his brow, and walked in place as he continued. "He gets out of bed grumpy as can be and stomps to his window to yell back, 'What's wrong with you? Don't bother me. The door's locked; my children are all down for the night; I can't get up to give you anything.'" The storyteller paused again and his face softened. He spoke tenderly but still with great conviction. "But let me tell you, even if he won't get up because he's a friend, if you stand your ground, knocking and waking all the neighbors, he'll eventually get you whatever you need to make you go away." The crowd laughed.

Amina stood there, perplexed. The story seemed so familiar, and yet, she couldn't place it.

Aiden leaned over and whispered, "Is that from the Sacred Book?"

A light went on. *Of course, that's it.* "Yeah. It sounds a little different, but I'm pretty sure it is."

"That's what I thought. We should stay and see if he tells another."

As the crowd quieted their laughter, the old man sat again to share the lesson.

"My friends, there is great wisdom in being persistent. Especially when we persist in asking for good things." The man pointed to the sky. "Mashiakh to work in our lives and come quickly." His gaze moved from person to person. "Do not lose hope, He is always listening to us. Do not cease your prayers, He is still communing with us. And stop falling into the lies that He is not working. He is always working. He is always in control." His eyes met with Amina's and seemed to burn a conviction deep inside her. She looked away as she felt

19

a tingling in the pit of her stomach.

The man smiled, and dispelling his serious tone, said, "Well, my friends, that is all for this morning. May Sabaoth bless you and keep you, may He make his face to shine upon you, and may you go in peace. Amen."

A resounding "Amen" echoed through the dome.

While much of the crowd wandered back to their respective places, many lingered, thanking him for his teaching or asking questions.

Amina stood frozen, lost in her thoughts. The man's story and stare pierced her insecurities as if he could see right through her facade.

"I thought no one taught anymore." Aiden pondered, shaking Amina out of her daze.

Amina shrugged. "I guess we've been living in the wrong dwelling. C'mon, let's find Paul and Mo."

Amina grabbed Aiden's arm and pulled him away from the crowd and toward their aunt and uncle's tent. As they were walking away, they heard a young girl's voice cry out from behind. "Cousin Amina!"

Amina turned just in time to see a tiny eight-year-old girl with long dirty blond braids and freckles all over her face come running toward them with the biggest smile. When she reached her cousin, she held up her arm to reveal a beaded bracelet. "Look what I made."

Amina took Emily's hand and inspected the colorful bracelet. "This is a beautiful bracelet."

"Should I make you one too? Mommy is letting me take apart her old jewelry to make my own."

"Isn't that thoughtful? I would love one." Amina picked her up and gave her a big hug.

CHAPTER 2

"Okay, I will and I'll use green beads because that's your favorite color."

"That's perfect."

"Where have you been? You've been gone a long time."

Guilty, Amina drooped her shoulder and frowned. "I know. I've just been rather focused on my job."

Emily put her finger on Amina's nose. "Well don't let it happen again."

Amina mimicked Emily with her own finger on Emily's nose and said in a goofy yet serious voice, "I won't."

In truth, Amina had no real excuses for not coming to see her family more often. Emily put a smile on her face and her uncle, being one of the elders in the underground, always had interesting news to share. They weren't the problem. It was her aunt that made Amina hesitate. She looked so much like Amina's mom, and it made it hard to be around her. Amina knew it wasn't her fault and Mo tried so hard to be sensitive to the situation, but Amina couldn't help herself. Any time she was around Mo she found herself projecting her bitterness onto Mo.

Emily laughed as Amina put her down, and that's when Emily noticed Aiden standing there quietly.

"Aiden, cat got your tongue?" Amina asked.

Aiden tried to talk but nothing came out. His eyes widened as he grabbed at his throat and face, looking for the problem. His eyes bulged with exaggerated concern.

Emily laughed each time Aiden tried to talk but pretended that his tongue wouldn't move. He eventually pulled his tongue out of his mouth and stretched it as far as he could, this really got Emily belly laughing.

Amina couldn't help but smile at her brother's antics. He

was so good with children and could always get them to laugh. Amina appreciated his lighthearted attitude.

Playing along with Aiden's joke, Amina leaned down and picked up a small piece of rubber. "I think if you throw this the cat will chase it."

Emily furrowed her brow and leaned back a little. "There's no cat."

"Don't you see him? The one that's got Aiden's tongue? He's big and gray with yellow eyes."

Emily giggled again and threw the piece of rubber as far as she could. Aiden mimed being released from the invisible cat. He bent over and breathed heavily. "Phew, you saved me. I thought that cat would never leave." Aiden grinned. He ran and grabbed Emily, pulling her into a twirling hug, and then swung her up onto his shoulders as the trio started walking.

"Where's your mom and dad?" Amina asked.

Emily put her finger to her nose and looked up. "Ummm . . . probably at home, but I don't know because I was playing with Josie and then we went to listen to Father Stephen share another story."

"Yeah, about that, how long has he been teaching stories?"

Emily shrugged. "I dunno, a long time? Why? You never heard him before?"

Amina shook her head. In fact, it had been many years since she had heard anyone share the sacred teachings. When the war began and the ability to gather became illegal, most churches stopped meeting. Occasionally, a home study would pop up, but they were under wraps.

Amina had to rely on her own memory, a few extraneous books she and Aiden had brought with them into the tunnels, and her own handwritten journal of sacred passages.

CHAPTER 2

Aiden lifted Emily off his shoulders as they approached a large burgundy canopy. Emily opened the flap and ran inside with the other two following close behind. The tent was just large enough for about eight people, but it only housed three. There were pillows and wooden crates strewn about as furniture and several rugs to keep the dirt at bay. In one section of the tent was a small kitchenette, and at the far end was another flap leading to the bedroom. The place was much nicer and homier than Amina's tent, but that was typical of many homes.

When the Notzrim first started hiding in the tunnels, many tried to bring as many possessions as possible to make life comfortable. Even now, after the Notzrim faith had been banned and they were forced to fortify themselves in the tunnels, many did whatever they could to live as comfortably as possible by sneaking above ground to steal and bring back new items. Eventually, the elders banned going above ground for everyone except the food scavengers. Even still, new items would occasionally pop up for trade.

"Mama, papa, I brought visitors!"

A petite woman in her mid-fifties stepped out from behind the bedroom flap. Her dirty blond hair was pulled back into braids like Emily's, and she had matching freckles on her cheeks. She wore a long green skirt that flowed as she walked and a long-knitted sweater.

She smiled when she saw her niece and nephew. "Well look who we have here." The woman walked over and hugged them both. Her body felt frail beneath Amina's arms. "It's nice to see you two. Especially you, Amina, I don't get to see you very often."

Amina glanced suspiciously at Aiden; he shrugged innocently. *How often did he come to visit without her?*

Focusing back on her aunt she replied, "I know it's been a while. Sorry about that Aunt Mo."

Mo walked over to the kitchenette and pulled a boiling pot of water off the tiny camping stove. "I'm just glad you're here now. Family is important to me and I like to see them often." Mo placed a single leaf into each of the small bowl-like cups and poured the water. "So, to what do we owe the pleasure?" Amina and Aiden sat on the pillows as Mo handed a cup to each of them.

"What do you mean?" Aiden blew on his tea. "Can't we just come and visit our favorite aunt and uncle?"

"And cousin," Emily chimed in, plopping herself next to Aiden. She leaned her head on his arm.

"And cousin."

Mo sat on one of the pillows. "Certainly, you can, but most of the time you're only here during our bi-monthly get-togethers. Especially with this one." She gestured to Amina. "Don't get me wrong. I love when you come to visit. It's just you don't tend to come just for the sake of coming."

Amina stared into her cup. It wasn't like she didn't care about her family, but there were other things going on. She couldn't sit around and socialize all day long; she'd rather be out providing and taking care of others.

"I said I was sorry. What else do you want?" *Was she purposely trying to make this visit even more uncomfortable?*

She shook her head. "I would like to see you more, that's all. It's comforting to have my sister's children here. You remind me of her so much and it makes the pain of her leaving a little more bearable."

Amina winced at that comment. That was the last person

she wanted to be compared to. "She made her choice," Amina mumbled.

"I know, but it doesn't make me miss her any less." Mo took a small sip of tea.

Changing the subject, Amina said, "Well, sorry to disappoint, but we did come with a purpose. We have clothes and a few blankets we thought you three could use." Amina opened her bag and started pulling out the few items she and Aiden had set aside.

Mo's eyes lit up. "That's not disappointing at all. I always welcome clean clothes. We've had these for a least a month."

"I also came across this." Amina pulled out the small doll and handed it to Emily. Emily audibly gasped and squealed with excitement as she reached out for the raggedy doll like a precious jewel.

"She's so pretty!" Emily hugged the doll tight and swayed back and forth.

"I'm glad you like her. There aren't many dolls hanging around. You be sure to keep her safe."

"I will." Emily looked at her mom. "May I go show Josie?"

Mo smiled. "Go ahead."

Emily kissed her mom on the cheek, waved goodbye, and was out of the tent all in one whirlwind of energy.

Aiden took a sip of tea. "So, where's Uncle Paul?"

"Training."

"Training for what?" Amina inquired.

"One of the coalition officers, Jared I believe, started a self-defense class. Your Uncle thinks it's a good idea to be prepared for a fight if it comes to that."

Aiden leaned in, placing an arm on his knee. "Really? I'm impressed. I never saw Uncle Paul as much of a fighter."

Mo pursed her lips. She looked like she wanted to say something but refrained. Instead, she explained. "He's not. He just wants to be prepared for whatever might happen. Things aren't getting any easier and it's getting closer and closer to the end." Mo bit her bottom lip. "I don't like the idea of it, but I can't believe that as we get closer to the end that we will be completely protected down here. This place isn't exactly a fortress."

Finally, someone on Amina's side. "That's exactly what I've been thinking lately. Aiden and I were spotted this morning in the field coming back and-"

Mo's eyes widened with concern. "You were spotted? Are you alright? Did you report it?"

Amina waved her hand as if batting a fly. "We're fine and I'm sure Josiah said something. The point is the Myriad are getting closer to home and I'm afraid it's only a matter of time before they find us."

"And you have a plan, don'tcha sis?" Aiden tried to look Amina in the eyes, but she refused to look at him. "It's okay if you don't. You don't always have to try and rescue everyone."

Amina tried to smile but she really wished she had a plan. It was plaguing her, like an itch she couldn't scratch. "I know that. I'm not superwoman, but I don't like sitting back and doing nothing. There has to be a way to better protect our home. We're not the first crew to be spotted and we won't be the last. If we're not careful, no one is going to make it to the end alive."

"We could leave," Mo suggested.

"What like the five of us? What about everyone else?"

"I have heard there is a small group gathering to discuss an exodus. Maybe it's time we seek refuge somewhere else."

CHAPTER 2

Amina took a sip of her tea. It was weak, with more water than actual tea. "And where are they planning on going? It's a war zone out there and we're enemy number one. They wouldn't last a day."

"I don't think they've figured that out yet, but there must be somewhere better than here, right?"

Amina shrugged. "Doubtful. Unless you're well trained in combat and willing to fight, you'd be better hiding out." Of course, she thought leaving might be the best way to go, but it meant giving up the familiar. It meant taking unknown risks to go to an unknown location with a false hope that it would be safer for them than the tunnels. When in reality nowhere was safe.

Mo was quiet. She bit her lip again as she swirled the last bit of tea in her cup.

"Is there something you're not telling us, Aunt Mo?" Aiden pressed. He too must've sensed Mo was hiding something.

Mo smiled, shaking her head. "No, it's nothing. I just worry about what's going to happen to us is all. A typical worrywart."

Amina glanced at Aiden who shook his head. Neither of them was convinced, but they dropped it and moved on to lighter topics. As they carried on their conversation, Amina found herself enjoying the time with her aunt. She was kind and remarkably joyful despite her worries.

The twins spent a good hour chatting with Mo, the longest Amina had ever spent without Paul being there too.

Aiden glanced at the tent flap. "When will Uncle Paul be back? I want to learn more about this self-defense class."

Amina and Mo both responded with surprise. "You do?"

He looked between the two women. "Yeah, what's wrong with that?"

Mo put up her hands. "Nothing, just surprising. You don't strike me as the fighting type either."

"Not unless he's fighting me." Amina playfully jabbed Aiden in the side.

He pushed Amina's arm away. "I'm not, but Uncle Paul might have a point about being prepared if things go south."

"Well, after his training he had a prayer meeting with the other elders, so who knows when he'll be back." Mo grabbed the now empty cups and walked to her kitchenette. "I'll let him know you stopped by."

Amina stood. "We should go. I still want to get to Dwelling One and get some soap before it's all gone."

Mo's eyes lit up. "They have soap?"

"That's what I heard. I'll bring some to you if I can."

"That'd be wonderful." Mo walked over and hugged Aiden and Amina one more time. "Thanks for coming by, it means a lot to me." Amina could tell she was sincere.

Chapter 3

Amina jolted awake. Outside she heard a man desperately yelling for help. Without thinking, Amina rushed out of her tent searching around the open space. Seth bounced around frantically, dripping with sweat and breathing heavily.

"Medic! Medic! Someone please, I need a medic!"

There weren't many awake, but a few groggy faces curiously popped out of their tents.

Amina jogged over to Seth to quiet him down before he woke the whole dwelling.

Seth grabbed Amina by the shoulders. His voice blared, making Amina's ears ring slightly. "Amina! Someone is badly injured. We need help!"

"Okay, calm down. I'll see what I can do."

Just as Seth and Amina were heading toward an exit, Josiah and Aiden showed up.

"What's going on?" Josiah asked earnestly.

"I'm not totally sure. Someone's hurt and needs help." Amina turned to Seth, hoping he'd say something. His eyes darted in every direction but theirs.

Josiah nodded "Where is he?"

Seth came out of his stupor just long enough to register Josiah's words. "Southeast entrance. Hurry!"

"Okay, Aiden. Go grab your first aid bag and meet us there."

"Don't you think it'd be better to get Mo or another nurse?"

"Not until we know what's going on."

Aiden knitted his brow but did as he was asked. He sprinted to his tent while Seth led Amina and Josiah to the injured man.

As they swiftly made their way through the tunnels, Amina prodded. "Who is he? How did this happen?"

"I don't know who he is. We were on our way back from a raid and one of our guys tripped over something. He thought it was just trash, but then we heard a groaning noise. I don't recognize him, but it's dark and the guy's really beat up."

"Is he Notzrim?" Josiah inquired.

Seth avoided Josiah's look as he kept moving. "I don't know, maybe, but probably not."

Amina stopped, paralyzed by his words. "You brought an outsider in here? Do you know how potentially dangerous, even fatal, to the whole system that could be?" A mixture of fear and anger rose inside her.

"I know, but what kind of Notzrim would I be if I had left a man in need?"

"He could be Myriad," Josiah insisted. "This could be a trap."

Seth shook his head desperately. "You won't think that once you see him. Please, help," he begged.

Neither responded. Amina was ready to walk away and let someone else handle the problem, but Josiah responded. "Okay."

Amina dragged her feet as she reluctantly followed the others. *What were they getting into?*

At the southeast entrance, Amina saw the rest of Seth's crew. There were two men, one standing and pacing around like an anxious cat, the other was using the wall as support as he wiped his mouth with his shirt. Then there was a woman, who knelt near the injured man, applying pressure to the wounds.

Amina approached them quickly to get a better look at the man. He appeared to be in his early thirties, but it was hard to tell. His clothes were torn and caked in dirt, blood, and sweat. There were numerous cuts and bruises covering his entire body. Most appeared to be surface wounds, however, there were some more alarming gashes across his abdomen and left arm. The woman had applied a tourniquet on his arm and was holding a blood-soaked jacket over his abdomen. Amina was uncertain that either of those was helping. The man grew paler by the minute, and he was starting to shiver.

Amina knelt beside Tallulah. Her scared green eyes locked with Amina's and her voice quivered as she spoke. "The wounds are deep, he's losing a lot of blood." Smelling the blood mingled with sweat made Amina's stomach churn and she thought she might be sick. She had to get up and walk away.

In that moment Aiden arrived. "So, what do you—" As soon as Aiden got a good look at the victim he recoiled. "Ooh geez, get a look at this guy."

"Focus Aiden," Amina breathed, still trying to calm her stomach. "Can you help him?" She looked earnestly at her brother and that's when she saw her. Aunt Mo was standing beside Aiden with her nurse's bag. Before Amina could respond, Mo rushed to the man and set to work.

Amina crossed to Aiden and lowered her voice. "What is she doing here? I thought I said not to get her yet?"

"I know, but none of us are nurses. I know some first aid but not enough." Aiden peered over Amina's shoulder at the man lying lifeless on the ground. "And by the looks of it, it was a good idea I asked her to come. He looks wrecked. Who is he?"

"We don't know. He could be one of us, but he could also be Myriad. That's why I didn't want anyone else here until we knew what was going on," Amina snapped.

"Too late now, she's here, so deal with it." Aiden huffed past his sister and over to his aunt.

Amina pressed her hand against her forehead. It felt as if things were slowly spiraling out of control.

"His pulse is weak, and he's lost a lot of blood. I can stabilize him, but he needs a doctor," Mo explained calmly.

Amina took in a slow breath, refocusing on the situation at hand. "Okay, stabilize him and then we'll get him over there." Amina turned and found Josiah eyeing Seth and his crew, silently scrutinizing them. He hadn't said anything, but Amina could see his brain ticking. "Can you help me take him?" Josiah didn't respond. "Josiah!"

Still watching the others, he stated flatly. "No, we're not taking him to the medical ward, not until I have my questions answered, like who is he?"

"We don't know," Seth answered, throwing his hands up.

Without taking his eyes off Seth, Josiah asked, "Mo, please check his wrists. What do you see?"

Mo was too busy wrapping the injuries. Instead, Aiden picked one arm up and then the other. When he looked back to Josiah, mouth agape, he breathed, "He doesn't have the mark."

"Then we'll send him back," Josiah retorted, "before he comes to and realizes where he is." Josiah started moving toward the man to pick him up.

Aiden stood, stopping him in his tracks. "I don't think you

heard me right. He has *no* markings of any kind. He's not one of them."

"Wait, what?" Josiah tilted his head. "How's that possible?" Josiah knelt beside the man and looked him over. "That can't be. Everyone has a mark."

They were all perplexed. At this point in the war, everyone had one of two marks: the mark of Sabaoth or the mark of Teivel.

Three and a half years into the war Teivel, the new world leader, had come up with an implanted chip that would allow the world to go completely money-and paper-free. Leaders had signed off on it and soon everyone was being forced to get the chip and a barcode tattoo to visibly indicate someone had received the chip. Not only did this chip allow you to make transactions, identify yourself, and supply pertinent information to the government, it also was an identifier that someone had given full allegiance to the new world order.

A month before the law was put into effect, a different kind of mark started appearing on the Notrzim. The mark of Sabaoth. A small yet ornate and incandescent cross imprinted itself on the left forearm of everyone who professed true faith. Inside the cross were the Hebrew letters ךרדה דיסח, meaning Follower of the Way.

"Is it possible he's a Hebrew?" Seth interjected.

Amina looked at him. She had forgotten Seth and the others were even there. "Come again?"

"The Hebrews, Sabaoth's chosen tribe of people. There was talk at the beginning of the war of a mass exodus by the Hebrews. No one knows where they went, but according to the Sacred Book, they ran to the mountains to hide and be protected by Sabaoth until the end."

"Isn't that just speculation?" Tallulah asked softly. "There's no actual proof."

"Of course there's proof. It's in the Sacred Book."

Amina pondered this idea for a moment. "I suppose he could be, but why would he be near the city and not hiding in the mountains?"

Seth shrugged.

Mo stood. "Whoever he is, Josiah, he needs medical attention. You can't send him back or he'll die. You also *need* to report this. Until he wakes, we don't know his story. We don't know if he's dangerous."

Josiah didn't answer at first. Amina could see Josiah's inner debate. She stepped forward. "I agree with Aunt Mo, he needs medical attention." Of course, she didn't agree with everything Mo said. Knowing the man had no markings intrigued Amina and she wanted to learn his story. That could only happen if he stuck around and no one alerted the authorities right away.

Josiah crossed his arms. "But he's not our responsibility."

"Of course, he is," Aiden chimed in. "We found him which means we have a responsibility to show him love and help him. Don't you remember the good Samaritan story we learned in worship?

Josiah huffed. "Fine. Go ahead and take him."

"And you'll report him?" Mo gave Josiah a stern motherly stare.

"Yes," he answered curtly.

"Good. Aiden, come help me. I have a collapsible field gurney in my bag, we can use it to carry him to the secure medical ward."

No one spoke as they watched Mo and Aiden gingerly lift the

man onto the gurney and take off down the tunnel.

Once Aiden and Mo were far enough away, Josiah stepped closer to Amina and spoke in a hushed voice. "I think we need to question them." Josiah subtly nodded his head toward Seth and the others.

"What? Why? They're not criminals."

"They brought an unmarked man into the tunnels. I don't want to make a report until I'm certain they weren't working with anyone or—"

Overhearing the conversation, Seth jumped in. "Whoa there. How long have you known me, Josiah? And you suddenly think I'm what, the enemy?"

"I didn't say that. There's just . . . something seems strange about this whole situation and I want to make sure you and your team had nothing to do with it. That it truly was random."

"Then you can take my word for it. This wasn't planned. We're not working for the Myriad. We just wanted to help another injured human being."

Josiah stood taller to assert himself. "If that's the case, Seth, then you and your team won't mind giving statements. The more information we have the easier it'll be to defend you when I make the official report."

Seth walked up to Josiah, stiffening his back so they were eye to eye. "How about you say nothing to the coalition and let us leave."

"You know I can't do that. I have to make the report."

Seth raised his voice. "No, you don't. You can just walk away and let it go."

"I'm trying to look out for you and your team." Josiah was practically yelling.

"You're trying to look out for yourself."

The air grew thick as the two stared each other down like two alpha dogs ready to brawl. Amina was certain neither would back down. The situation was intense enough, it didn't need to be worse with two friends beating on one another, but if someone didn't say something soon, that's exactly what would happen.

Amina stepped between the two and firmly pushed them back. "How about we take their statements here, then Seth can go with you to make the report and answer any other questions." Seth started to protest but thought otherwise. He pressed his lips thin and crossed his arms. Amina stared at Josiah, waiting for an answer.

Josiah clenched his jaw. "Fine, but we're using etymtorp." Josiah pulled a small white vial out of his pocket.

Amina put her hand on Josiah's forearm. "Is that really necessary?"

Seth raised his eyebrows. "I didn't agree to that." He pointed at the white vial and stepped away as if it were poison.

"Maybe not, but we need to make sure you all tell us the truth."

"But don't you think that," she pointed to the vial, "is overreacting? They're our friends, we should just trust them."

"You can't have friends when you're in leadership."

"You're not there yet," Amina argued.

Ever since Josiah's father had approached him about taking a spot in the elders' circle, it had gone to his head and Amina was convinced it was affecting his judgment. It was as if he felt obligated to start behaving like an elder even before he was one, and it was frustrating to watch a close friend fall into the pressures of parental expectations.

Roger, stepped forward. He had broad shoulders and a

square face with a crooked nose from a past fight that he loved to brag about. "We'll tell you whatever you need to know. We are brothers and sisters; we shouldn't have to resort to such cruel tactics."

"I am sorry," Josiah breathed, looking anywhere but at Roger, "but there have been a lot of security breaches. The City of the Northern Underground has recently been infiltrated and massacred. We can't take any risks, and you brought in an unmarked man."

Amina quickly placed a hand over her mouth as she listened to Josiah's report. This was news to her. She knew the situation was growing more dangerous and sightings more common, but an actual attack and massacre? Amina took a deep breath to try and calm the anxiety. Her life was being flipped upside down once again and she didn't know how to stop it.

The younger of the two, Bart, stepped forward. His bushy brows scrunched together as he pointed an accusing finger at Josiah. "Screw protocol. That stuff you have will make us sick for days. We won't be able to scavenge."

"And that is why we have multiple teams, Bart." Josiah hardened his look, his decision made. "You're taking it or I'll report all of you to the coalition right now for subversion."

Amina was not on board with this. "Josiah, this is wrong. You don't have to do this. Your father will never know." She wanted to convince Josiah, but he was adamant.

"He will find out what's going on, it's only a matter of time. And when he does, I want my father to know I did what was called of me."

"Do you really care more about doing what your father wants than doing what's right?"

"This is not up for debate. I'm doing this."

"No way," Bart shouted as he lunged toward Josiah in an attempt to knock the vial out of his hand, but Josiah was too quick. He shoved the vial in his pocket and grabbed hold of Bart, wrestling him to the ground. Roger jumped into the mix as well. Amina rolled her eyes and reached in to pull Roger out of the fight as Seth grabbed Bart. Even Tallulah had to help when Amina was elbowed in the face. There was a moment of flailing arms and loud obscenities until finally Roger, Bart, and Josiah gave up.

Amina rubbed the now tender spot along her left jaw as it throbbed. She hoped a bruise wouldn't surface.

Josiah took the vial out again and opened the lid revealing a small dropper. "You're taking this, we're getting statements, and then you're free to go."

No one moved.

"I can go get someone from the coalition right now and you'll be locked up or we do it my way." Josiah threatened.

The men exchanged looks but still didn't move. Tallulah was the first to step forward. "We'll do what you say, Josiah. We don't want any more trouble." She gave the boys a sharp look. "Do we boys?"

Roger and Bart hunched their shoulders and drooped their heads as they gave in to their teammate and joined her.

All they needed was one tiny drop on their tongue for it to take effect. As the liquid hit their taste buds, they each had the same reaction. They scrunched their faces and shook their heads as if they'd eaten a lemon.

Josiah put the vial away and watched them.

Amina wondered if it was working. She had heard of etymtorp, the truth serum they were using, but she had never actually seen it used before.

CHAPTER 3

After another minute of waiting, Amina noticed the group's faint swaying and heavy eyelids.

"You should sit down," Amina suggested. They did as they were told and a good thing too. Almost as soon as they sat, they each slumped over unconscious.

Josiah regarded the comatose crew members and asked, "Tell me, where did you go today?"

Amina was perplexed. They were unconscious, how could they talk?

But then the group responded in unison as if under a spell, "Bryton Heights, for food."

Amina jumped, startled at their unified voices. It was like something out of a science fiction movie.

"And did you find food?"

"Yes."

Josiah and Amina both surveyed the area, noticing that there were no rucksacks.

"Then where is it?"

Amina noticed Tallulah's eyes moving rapidly beneath her eyelids. Tallulah spoke. Her voice was breathy and light. "We dropped it when we were attacked. Roger, our lookout, was on the roof, but by the time he warned us it was too late. We tried to carry what we could and run, but the attackers were so close, they seemed to be surrounding us. We ditched the food to allow ourselves to run faster."

"Roger, why didn't you warn them sooner?"

"The attackers were already there hiding. I gave warning the instant I saw them, but they were too close."

Amina leaned over to Josiah and whispered, "If they were in waiting then-"

"I know." Josiah drew in a sharp breath. "What about your

fifth member? Why didn't she buy you more time?"

Bart, spoke this time. "She did. That's the only reason we survived, but we still had to ditch the food."

"She was a good strong woman," Tallulah started sobbing. "Was she killed?"

"Most likely," Roger answered.

Josiah paused for a moment letting Tallulah's sobs echo around them. Amina shifted awkwardly. She wasn't sure if she should comfort Tallulah or leave her alone.

As Tallulah quieted down, Josiah continued. "Someone tell me about the man. Who decided to bring him in?"

"It was Seth," Roger spoke. "I was against it, but Seth insisted."

Seth continued. "We were running fast. It was pitch black and Tallulah was leading. We were quickly making our way to the alternate entrance when suddenly I tripped. When I fell to the ground it wasn't trash or rocks I felt."

"You alright?" Roger asked.

"What was that?" Bart placed his hands on the ground to help himself stand. Suddenly, he felt someone grab his shirt and a voice moaned. Bart screamed batting at the bloody hand holding on to him.

"There's a person down there," he yelled, struggling to get up.

"Leave him. We don't have time," Roger snapped.

"We can't just leave a man dying out here," Seth spoke.

Gunfire was still ringing in the distance as Xena, their scientist, fought to hold the attackers back with her protection shield ray.

"We don't know who he is. What if he's one of them?" Roger argued.

"We don't have time to argue boys," Tallulah shouted. "Let's go. At any moment Xena will have to rejoin us. She can't hold them

off for long."

Seth bent down and picked up the man, slinging him over his shoulder. "Then it's settled, we're taking him with us. Doesn't matter who he is, he's someone in need."

"He'll probably be dead by the time we get him back, why do we need to worry about it?" Roger argued.

"I'll take responsibility, but we're taking him."

"Good, now let's go." Tallulah turned and continued leading.

"Geez, Seth," Roger grumbled as he continued walking behind Tallulah at a brisk pace, being cautious not to trip over anything again. "What if he's one of them and you bring him down there and–"

"I'm not changing my mind, Roger, so drop it."

Once they got to the entrance Roger opened the manhole to let everyone in. When it was Seth's turn, Roger stopped him for a moment. "Last chance to change your mind. There's no going back from this." Seth stared at Roger defiantly as he lowered himself down into the tunnel. Roger shook his head irritated.

Roger gave one last look around for Xena hoping she was right on their heels. When he didn't see her coming, he quickly shut the lid and sealed it.

The team entered an alternate entrance, making their way several miles through the tunnels before resurfacing, running through the open field, and into the system of tunnels where they lived. Because of all the meteors destroying the earth, large sections of the tunnels were also destroyed.

Inside the final tunnel, Bart ran to the fuse box and turned on the lights.

"Holy–" Roger swore as he discovered the condition of the man.

Seth laid the man down. "Stay here and see if you can stop this guy's bleeding. I'm going to get help." Before waiting for a response, Seth darted down the tunnel toward the nearest dwelling.

Tallulah knelt beside the man, tearing pieces of her own tattered clothes to use as pressure bandages on the wounds. "Now don't you die on us." Tallulah looked up. "Someone grab my kit."

"He better be worth it," Roger spoke as he paced back and forth.

"It's always worth saving a life."

"Not if he's the enemy."

Tallulah threw the blood-soaked clothes onto the floor and took off her jacket and pressed it to the man's abdomen. "He's bleeding bad; I think I need a belt to make a tourniquet."

Bart took off his belt and gave it to Tallulah who proceeded to wrap it around the man's right forearm and tighten it as hard as she could. Bart turned away, his face growing whiter by the minute. That's when he noticed Xena missing.

"Roger, where's Xena?"

"I didn't see her coming."

"You don't think—"

"Let's not think about that yet. She may have just found somewhere to hide."

"A little help over here!" Tallulah shouted. "Where's my kit? I need water to clean these up and find out how deep it all is."

Grabbing Tallulah's medical bag, Bart pulled out a canteen and started pouring water onto the man's wounds, but no matter how much he poured the blood kept coming. At one point, Bart was able to flush the blood out just long enough for Tallulah to see bone."

"This is a lot worse than I thought," Tallulah whispered to herself.

"I think I'm gonna be sick." Bart stood and stumbled to the wall of the tunnel where he vomited.

"Good thing you're not a medic." Roger teased.

CHAPTER 3

"Shut up."

"That's when Seth came back with help," Seth finished.

Amina leaned over to Josiah and whispered, "That sounds pretty straightforward to me, Josiah. I don't think there's any secret motive for bringing this man below."

"I don't know, something seems off. Who do you know that's clean? Everyone still alive at this point has one of two marks or they're dead." Josiah addressed the group again. "Did the man say anything while you were with him?"

"Yes," Tallulah spoke. "As I was trying to stop the bleeding, he kept muttering to himself. It was quite difficult to hear, but it sounded like he was calling someone's name. I couldn't tell who. It almost sounded like Teivel."

Josiah's face didn't change, but his body tensed.

"Is it possible he was running away from the Myriad since he's not marked?" Amina questioned.

"But then why call out for Teivel?"

Tallulah spoke again. "He seemed to be begging for mercy as he said it." Tallulah suddenly burst into uncontrollable tears as she screamed, "Leave him alone; he's innocent! Please, stop hurting him! Stop it!" Tallulah screamed in horror.

Amina and Josiah took a step away as they watched Tallulah writhing on the ground.

"What's happening to her?" Amina watched Tallulah in horror. "That doesn't seem normal."

Josiah shook his head, fear in his eyes. "I don't know. This shouldn't happen."

Amina reluctantly moved to Tallulah's side and took her into her arms whispering in her ear. "Shhhh, it's okay Tallulah, you're safe. No one's going to harm you." Amina wasn't the comforting type, but she needed to calm Tallulah down before

43

something serious happened to her. Amina continued to rock back and forth as if lulling a child to sleep.

As Tallulah quieted down, Amina looked at Josiah. "I think they've had enough. We need to wake them so they don't have some sort of mental breakdown."

"Fine," Josiah answered reluctantly. "I don't think we'll get any more information out of them that would be crucial anyway."

Josiah pulled out a second vial filled with a green liquid. He poured the liquid onto a small cloth and held it over each of their noses.

Roger, Bart, and Seth soon began to stir. Bart rolled onto his hands and knees and vomited. When he sat again, he wiped his mouth and swore.

Roger, on the other hand, sat grabbing his head and squinting his eyes. He massaged his head and mumbled to himself.

"Did you get what you wanted? Because I feel horrible," Seth asked irritated as he rubbed his temples.

"Yes, we did," Josiah said still refusing to show any emotion. "I am sorry we had to do that."

"No you're not," Roger snapped. "I've got a headache the size of Neptune that probably won't go away for days." Roger tried to stand, but his knees went weak and he collapsed back onto the floor.

"We'll help you to the medical ward if you like."

"No, I just want to go home."

Josiah went to Roger's side to help, but Roger shoved him away. Amina still sat with Tallulah in her arms. She wasn't awake yet.

"What's wrong with her?" Bart asked when he saw Tallulah not moving.

CHAPTER 3

Amina answered calmly. "She's had a bit of an episode while under."

"She what? What did you do to her? If you've hurt her, I swear I'll kill you all myself." Bart tried to rush to Tallulah's side but collapsed onto his hands and knees.

"She'll be fine," Amina reassured Bart, but in fact, she wasn't sure if that was true. Messing with someone's frontal lobe can do things that aren't reversible.

Suddenly, Tallulah sat rigid and screamed at the top of her lungs, her eyes bloodshot. Amina wrapped her arms around Tallulah to calm her down again, but Tallulah fought to get loose as she screamed and cried. Amina refused to let go until finally, Tallulah gave in and relaxed into the embrace. Amina stroked her hair and whispered soothing words into her ear.

"That does not look okay," Bart scoffed.

"I know, but she will be," Amina reassured him. "It just takes longer for some people than others." She prayed that was true. Amina stood and helped Tallulah do the same. She was like a beaten child, fidgety and withdrawn. It was painful to watch.

Josiah kept his eyes to the ground, seeming almost guilty for what he'd done. Who could blame him? Etymtorp was a nasty drug.

"Let's get you guys back home," he spoke quietly and then walked down the tunnel, helping Bart along the way.

Chapter 4

Aiden's triceps burned with fatigue and his pace slowed as they made their final turn. It was a long trek from the southeast entrance to the secure medical ward, but he could finally see the entrance. He really needed to work out more. Mo didn't even sound winded from the walk.

At the circular door, Aiden stopped. They put the gurney on the ground and Aiden wiped the sweat from his forehead, thankful for the reprieve.

Mo walked to the door and used her key to unlock it. As soon as it opened, they were met by a guard. Further down the hall, Aiden saw two nurses rushing toward them. Mo and Aiden carried the gurney through the door and the guard locked it behind them as the nurses rapidly rattled off questions. Aiden couldn't keep up, but Mo, so calm and collected, explained everything.

The medical ward was one long tunnel with several doors leading into tiny closet-like rooms. This part of the underground seemed pre-constructed, as if it were a secret bunker used in years past. For what, Aiden had no clue, but it was convenient.

They carried the man into one of the tiny rooms and with the help of the other nurses, they transferred him to a cot.

Immediately one of the nurses on call went to work cutting off the bandages and barking commands to the other woman. Mo pulled off her bloodied latex gloves and crossed to a small water basin to rinse her hands.

Aiden stood, staring at nothing, too shocked to do anything else. What was happening to his home? First, they were seen, then this man appears out of nowhere with no markings of any kind. Who was he?

"Aiden." Mo waved her hand in Aiden's face to pull him out of his daze. "Let's step out, they can handle it from here."

Aiden opened his mouth and closed it again as Mo gently guided him out of the room and shut the door.

"I think you should get home and get rest. It's been quite a night."

"Yeah I guess. . ."

"I'm going to stay here and help."

"What will you tell Uncle Paul?"

"That I was called in. That's not unusual, and he'll learn soon enough once Josiah makes the report." Mo put a hand on Aiden's shoulder. "I need you to make sure he does that."

"Of course." Aiden was starting to realize what this stranger could mean for their home. "Do you really think this man is dangerous? Are we not safe here?"

Mo crossed her arms and shifted her weight. "I don't want to jump to any conclusions just yet, but. . ." She took a breath, choosing her words carefully, "there was an attack in the Northern Underground, and I fear we may be next if we aren't careful."

Aiden let out a high-pitched laugh. This was beyond belief. He always assumed that Mashiakh would return and save them from their demise before the Myriad found them. "What do we do?"

"We can pray, and let the elders make the big decisions. Your uncle has already been wracking his brain on this. You need to pray they find a solution before word gets out and fear spreads in the tunnels."

Aiden nodded. Fear was already clawing at his chest and he struggled to breathe. He closed his eyes and let out a slow breath. "You're right. I'll go, but you be careful."

Mo smiled and hugged her nephew.

A nurse poked her head out the door. "Mo, go get Dr. Sterling, quick."

"On it." Mo gave Aiden one last look. "I'll keep you posted," she said and then took off jogging down the hall.

Aiden wound his way through the maze of tunnels, returning to Dwelling Three. His mind felt just as twisted, and while he was able to navigate the tunnels without problem, his own thoughts were another issue.

The one thought that scratched at him most was what if the tunnels were compromised, that it was only a matter of time before they were found?

As he passed an intersection, he heard shouting and profanities echo down the tunnel. It sounded like Seth.

Aiden slowed his gait and cautiously slinked toward the noise. He stopped just short of the opening so as not to be seen.

It was Seth. He was pacing back and forth near the southeast corner. Bart and Roger sat by watching.

Aiden crouched down, staying in the shadows. Seth had a temper, and Aiden didn't want to be found spying.

"Seth will you sit down already?" Bart snapped. "You're making me sick."

CHAPTER 4

"Yeah this etymtorp serum hasn't quite worn off yet." Bart closed his eyes and rubbed his temples. "How are you not this woozy?"

"Guess it doesn't affect everyone the same," Roger presumed.

Seth pressed his palm to his forehead and closed his eyes. "I'm still a little dizzy, but I'm even more pissed. We have to do something! We can't just sit around and let them strip away all our dignity. Josiah thinks he's king of this place and can do whatever he wants!" Seth kicked a can and it flew toward Aiden, clanging on the wall a foot below him. Seth sat down and put his head in his hands trying to think.

"Look, we'll have our day in court," Bart tried to reason, "and then we can share the injustice done to us. They'll have to listen and judge fairly."

"You think I'm going to let Josiah actually make that report? It'll be completely skewed if he does. I'm not going to be punished for *his* wrongdoing."

"No one's going to be punished."

Roger looked at Bart, still holding his head. "I don't know about you, but I feel like I'm being punished right now. And Tallulah's still out cold in her tent."

The men fell silent, the only sound was the crackling of the fire and a few kids playing kickball.

Roger was the first to break the silence. "What are we going to do then? I'm tired of living in the shadows. Of always being strong armed. I've been stuck down here for five years, some of us longer, and for what?"

This time Bart was the one to speak outraged. "You know exactly why, Roger. If it hadn't been for Mashiakh you'd be up top like the rest. Lost, hopeless, and destined for the wrath that is coming. We're waiting for Mashiakh to come, clothed in white, riding victorious so we can fight in the final battle of victory with him. We can't forget that."

Roger frowned. "I want to believe you. I once had that zeal and passion for Mashiakh, but it has been so long."

Bart crossed to Roger and knelt in front of him. He slowly turned his arm upward revealing the mark they each bore, sealing them for the day of victory. "He hasn't forgotten about us, Roger. He will return."

"And until then, what?" Seth snapped. The anger had subsided a little, but his voice was still tense. "We go on living petty lives ruled by power hungry men? No thank you."

"Then what do you propose we do? Fight the Myriad?" Bart asked, almost laughing.

"That's not a bad idea."

Bart looked at Seth incredulously. "Come on Seth, that's crazy talk."

"Maybe not. Other guys have been talking about another underground where they're actually doing something to prepare for the war instead of waiting around like sitting ducks. They have military-grade weapons, combat training, the whole shebang. They've even gone above and wreaked a little havoc in hopes of weakening the Myriad bit by bit so when the real war begins, it's an easier win. And there are those who want to do the same thing here."

Bart raised his eyebrows. "Now Seth, let's think about this before we do anything rash. Right now you're upset, understandable, but soon this'll all blow over and things'll be back to normal, then–"

"That's the problem. I don't want *their* normal, I want something more." Seth stood and took off down the nearest

CHAPTER 4

tunnel, which happened to be the same one Aiden was standing in. Quickly, Aiden searched for somewhere to hide. When he didn't see anything, he jumped up grabbing on to a metal grate above and pulled himself up. From there he was able to hook his legs around a pipe. His arms shook, still weary from carrying the man on the gurney, and he prayed that his arms would last long enough for Seth to pass.

He held his breath as Seth finished climbing the ladder and stomped his way down the tunnel. Aiden could hear Roger and Bart's voices calling for Seth to come back, but they didn't go after him.

When Seth turned the corner, Aiden lowered himself, practically falling. His arms were like rubber. Rubbing his arms tenderly, he followed, curious where Seth was heading.

Seth hadn't bothered to turn on the lights as he walked, so it made it easy for Aiden to follow undetected. Thankfully he had a keen sense of hearing, and over the years his eyes had adjusted well to dim lighting. He could see like a prowling lion in the night.

It helped too that Seth seemed too consumed with his own thoughts to give any notice, but either way, Aiden used stealth. After multiple turns, Seth entered Dwelling Five where Aiden noticed a large gathering near the far east end. Seth descended the ladder and joined the group.

It was hard for Aiden to make out any of the people who were there, but then, he heard a familiar voice speak.

"Thank you, my brothers and sisters, for joining me today," Terrance's voice bounced off the cement walls, but Aiden still had to strain to hear. "As we all know, over the past month there have been more and more sightings, and through our networks we have learned that the City of the North has been destroyed."

Gasps and murmurs spread through the crowd. Terrance held his hand up to get their attention again. When it was quiet, he continued. "This is the third city in two months. We cannot sit here like chickens in a coop. We're not chickens, we're warriors. I won't pace around hot porridge like a cat. We must prepare, we must stand and fight." The crowd let out a resounding holler of agreement.

Aiden stood and slowly backed away. His palms were sweating and his head swirled. He wasn't sure if he agreed with Terrance or was terrified. Could this be the answer he was looking for; a way to protect everyone he loved? But at the same time, it seemed clandestine. Aiden was not the type of person to break the law. He believed rules were made for everyone's protection and they should be followed. In any case, there was nothing wrong with listening to more, and he wanted to hear more. Aiden moved toward the ladder but stopped when someone called his name.

Aiden spun around and saw Uncle Paul and Emily staring at him.

"Oh hey." Aiden cracked a nervous smile and walked to them.

"We're heading to Mitchum's to see what sort of junk he has. I want some new art pieces for market day. I know how much you like going through Mitchum's things as well. Want to join us?"

Mitchum was the local scrap metal trader and engineer. His place had everything imaginable for building anything from pieces of art to toy robots. He was also the one people went to if anything broke or if people wanted to simply off load items scavenged in years past. He could build, invent, or take apart

CHAPTER 4

just about anything. The man was brilliant.

Emily smiled big. "Please."

Aiden felt out of sorts, his head still trying to process what Paul said. When he didn't respond right away, Paul put a hand on Aiden's forehead. "Are you feeling okay? You look a little pale."

"Yeah, I'm fine." His voice was forced. "I'd love to go with you." Aiden took Emily's hand and walked with them, trying to forget what he had just heard.

Amina pounded on the secure medical hall's large metal door. She was anxious to get inside and find out what was going on with the man. *Is he okay? Is he coherent enough to talk? And who is he?*

The security guard opened the door looking peeved. "What is it Amina? You're not supposed to be here."

Down the hall, Amina could hear shouting and metal clanging.

"What's going on in there, Mike? Is he okay?" Amina tried to walk past Mike, but he stopped her.

"I need you to leave."

"But we're the ones who had him brought here. We need to make sure he's okay."

"I think you'd better let the coalition and the elders take care of it. You did your part, now let it go."

"Do they know already?" Amina looked at Mike frantically. They can't know yet, she still had questions.

The guard shook his head. "The doctor hasn't been able to report anything yet, but I'm sure it's only a matter of time."

"Can you ask the doctors not to report it just yet?" Josiah

stepped in. "I would like to be the one to make the report, but I need to talk to that man first and assess the situation. You understand right?"

Mike mulled it over, his jaw moved around like he was chewing on gum. "Fine. But I can't promise anything."

"Thank you." Josiah shook the man's hand. "Can we come in and wait?"

"Yeah but don't bug the nurses, they're irritable right now." Mike stepped out of the way, letting Amina and Josiah in before closing the door again.

Josiah wandered down the hall and stopped a few doors away from the action. Amina followed. Sometimes Josiah's obnoxious need to feel superior paid off.

Amina leaned against the wall, tilting her head back. The cool cement felt good against her bare shoulders. She closed her eyes so as to avoid Josiah's earnest stare. She was afraid he'd be able to tell how scared she really was despite her façade.

"Everything's going to be okay." Josiah tried to reassure her, but she wasn't so sure. There were so many unknowns.

"I don't like this," she admitted.

"I don't either, but when he's awake we'll talk to him and then take whatever precautions or actions we need."

Amina's eyes met his. "Josiah, things are falling apart down here." Amina could feel her throat tightening as she ran a hand over her head and down the back of her neck where it rested.

"It's not falling apart."

"How can you say that? First, we're almost caught, then Seth's team is spotted, and now this man with absolutely no markings, no identification, just appears. We need to get out of here, find somewhere safer or we'll be the next Northern Underground."

CHAPTER 4

Josiah squatted across from her and clasped his hands. Amina wanted him to say something, to have some sort of plan, but he was silent. If she was being truthful with herself, she didn't blame him for not having a plan. She didn't have one either and she hated that.

"Let's just take it one step at a time," he concluded. "And right now, that means waiting."

Amina pushed away from the wall. He made it sound so easy. Amina's head was swirling with a million questions and he wanted her to wait. Pushing back her chair, Amina stood. "I'm going for a walk." Josiah stood, but she stopped him. "I want to be alone." When Josiah didn't object, she walked away.

Amina had paced around the halls for an hour before she felt the anxiety physically subside..

The hallway was quiet and deserted. The nurses and doctor were most likely taking naps or hiding in some far-off room hoping not to be disturbed.

The secure medical ward in the hospital was the least occupied. Earlier in the war, when there were still uncertainties about whose side people were on, the ward was packed with around the clock security, constant escape attempts and two fatal fights.

When the marks started appearing on people, that's when it got easier. Suddenly it shifted from a war zone to a mission field. Those with the mark started to desperately plead with the unmarked, believing that if they did not receive Mashiakh's mark they'd be doomed.

It turned from utter chaos to a beautiful time of redemption and healing; people found new hope and peace in the midst of devastating loss. It was also a time when Amina's zeal for Mashiakh was still at an all-time high. Although Amina wasn't in the tunnels yet, she passionately ministered to the spiritual needs of those unmarked above ground, desperate for them to accept the good news as she had twelve years before. If only she could go back to that time when she felt important and useful.

Amina sat and leaned her head back on the wall and closed her eyes, succumbing to her fatigue.

When she awoke, Amina was no longer in the hospital, but in a thick forest, filled with vibrant green trees and moss, like it had been before the land was burned and the water poisoned with wormwood. She saw rabbits hopping, lizards running, and birds moving from branch to branch as they sang their joyful tunes. All around her, she felt a thick mist that clung like a blanket.

In front of her was a mossy path lined with fireflies. Curious, Amina followed the fireflies that seemed to be guiding her. Without warning, the path opened to a large waterfall and behind it was a cave.

Again, Amina followed the fireflies along the rocks leading into the cave. Deeper she went, losing light with every step. The fireflies were soon the only thing she could see. She took another step, but there was nothing below her. She fell like Alice down the rabbit hole until she landed on a giant pillow of feathers.

Crawling her way out of the feathers she found herself staring into an entirely new scene, a cave filled with iridescent lights that glowed and reflected off a stream of water. Stalactites and stalagmites covered the cave creating a maze of pathways leading into dark unknown places. It was both breathtaking and chilling.

The stream that ran through the middle of the cave was as

CHAPTER 4

smooth as glass and emerald-colored. In the stream floated a small boat. Drawn to it, Amina crawled inside.

Without hesitation, the boat began to travel down the river as if being pulled by some invisible string. As she floated further down the stream she started to hear music, like that of a Celtic flute. Then a man appeared. His face was so familiar yet she couldn't place it.

As the boat came to a stop, the man stopped playing and smiled. Without a word, he turned and ran.

Perplexed by his strange behavior, Amina ran after him, trying to keep up, calling for him to slow down, but he kept running.

Amina ran faster until she came to a jarring halt at the edge of a massive cliff. With no time to think, Amina was thrust down the cliff by an invisible hand, forcing her to fly again, faster and faster, until at the last minute, she slowed and floated to the bottom.

Once again in a new place, Amina took in her surroundings. She was no longer in the cave, but rather a valley like that of Eden. Amina audibly gasped, taking it all in. The colors of the trees and flowers were more vibrant than anything she had ever seen and there was a sweet decadent smell that filled her nostrils. Amina closed her eyes and breathed in deeply, enjoying the calming floral scent.

As her eyes fluttered open, off in the distance she saw movement. It wasn't until she moved closer that she started to realize the movement was not that of animals, but of people, including the man she saw in the cave. He too noticed her and smiled. He opened his mouth to speak but no words came out of his mouth, and Amina's vision went black as she started falling again.

Amina jolted awake with such force that she lost her balance and fell. Rubbing her face she found Josiah standing over her, laughing at her.

"You alright there?"

Amina's face burned. "I'm fine," she snapped. "What do you want?"

"I came to get you. He's awake."

Amina pulled herself up quickly and smoothed out her long chestnut ponytail. "Really? Let's go then."

Amina led the way, speed walking down the hallway, but when they arrived a nurse had just come out of the room nearly toppling over Amina.

"Whoa there," she said. "Where do you think you're going?"

"We need to talk to the patient."

The nurse looked at Mike who was now guarding the door. He nodded silently to her before replying. "Well he's eating right now. You'll need to wait."

"We've been waiting. We need to talk to him now," Amina insisted.

Josiah took Amina's arms and gently pulled her back. "Let him eat. He's been through a lot and if we want to learn anything he needs to be in a good state."

"You should listen to him," the nurse said before taking off down the hall.

"Josiah, we don't have all day. I need to know who he is." The dream was still fresh in her mind and she had an inkling that the man was connected to the dream, though she didn't know why.

"I get that, but if we act too quickly we may shut him out completely."

"It's a risk we have to take." Amina pushed the door open and entered the room.

Inside the man was sitting in bed with a small pouch of food in one hand and a metal fork in the other. He had electric blue

CHAPTER 4

eyes that stared at her expectantly. Just above those awaiting eyes was a large bandage that went up to his buzzed, dirty blond hair.

The bandages around his forearm and abdomen had been replaced and the blood was cleaned up to reveal numerous scratches and developing bruises. Amina tried not to stare, but he had a striking appearance, and he was clearly in good shape because everything about him was chiseled.

After getting a good look at him, Amina made the connection and her mouth dropped open slightly. He was the face in her dream, and while she wanted to believe that meant something, she wasn't ready to trust that thought yet.

Amina stepped closer to the bed but stopped short, not wanting to get too close.

The man took another bite from his MRE and lifted his chin curiously.

"Who are you?" he asked. When he spoke, his voice was confident and unexpectedly friendly. It didn't seem to fit his hardened appearance.

"I'm Amina, this is Josiah. We have a few questions for you, if that's okay."

There was a long pause of silence as the man stared curiously at Amina. He wouldn't take his eyes off her, and she found herself taking a slight step back. She couldn't figure out what he was thinking, but she didn't trust him.

He smiled at the game they seemed to be playing. It was his move. "Are you the ones who saved me?"

"Well um-" Josiah's voice croaked. He cleared his throat before speaking again. "It was some others who found you, but we helped get you here."

The man never looked at Josiah when he spoke, but kept his

eyes locked on Amina. "Thank you," he said. Amina didn't speak, but nodded. What was going on with her? She wasn't easily intimidated, and yet something about him beguiled her. "So where am I?" He browsed the barren room. "This doesn't look like Holy Family."

"It's not," Josiah answered, keeping the details short.

The man waited for more information that never came. "That's all you're going to tell me?" The man eyed Josiah, challenging him. "Look, I appreciate the help, but if you don't mind, I'd like to go home."

Finding her voice again, Amina asked, "And where is that?"

"Far from here."

"Where exactly?" Amina insisted. The discomfort of his stare and the lack of direct answers was turning her cautious intrigue into annoyance.

The man set his food pouch and fork next to him and pushed himself up so he was sitting taller in the bed. He eyed Amina. "That mark on your arm," he nodded at Amina's dangling left arm, "that means you're Notzrim right?"

Instinctively Amina folded her arms. She wasn't ready to let him in on any sensitive information, not until she was certain he was safe. The man shook his head, baffled. "I thought all of you were dead."

"You didn't answer my question." Amina pursed her lips.

The man was about to speak again but didn't have the chance. The door swung open and in walked Mike and two others. One wore a long black robe while the other wore a black shirt, black cargo pants, and a bullet proof vest.

"Dad," Josiah gasped. Amina was just as startled as Josiah looked.

The man leading the way was Matthias, the head elder, and

CHAPTER 4

he stood six foot two with wide square shoulders that made him tower over people. He had the same square jawline and wide nose as Josiah. "What in the world are you two doing in here? You know better than to be questioning a prisoner."

"Prisoner?" Amina stepped forward. "This man was a victim of the Myriad and we saved him." She surprised herself, coming to the defense of someone she didn't know or trust.

"We'll see about that." Matthias motioned to the coalition officers. "Get them out of here."

The two men stepped forward and took hold of Amina and Josiah's arms to forcibly remove them from the room. "I'll deal with you two later." Josiah's father walked to the bed as Josiah and Amina were escorted out.

Mike stayed outside the door while the other officer went back.

"I suggest you go home, Josiah," Mike ordered.

"You told him, didn't you?" Mike didn't reply. "Will you at least let me know what my dad finds out?"

Uneasy, he glanced at the closed door and then back to Josiah. It took him a while to respond before he nodded.

Aiden sat on a small stool in front of his makeshift table created from wooden crates. After spending some time at Mitchum's metal dump, Aiden discovered some pieces he could use to possibly recreate a wind-up music box.

He loved to create. It didn't matter whether it was building something out of metal or drawing with charcoal, being creative always helped calm and re-center him when he was feeling overwhelmed, and right now, with all this uncertainty about the above-ground attacks, the mysterious man in the hospital, and the possible uprising, he could feel himself getting wildly overwhelmed.

Aiden was so focused on filing down his makeshift comb to just the right length so it was in the right octave that he didn't notice his sister walk into his tent.

"What's gotcha lookin' so down, brother?"

Aiden jumped and threw the metal file up into the air unexpectedly. Amina quickly caught it, letting out a small laugh. "Geez Amina, ever thought of knocking first?"

"I'm not sure that would've made a difference, except then I wouldn't have seen you jump out of your skin." Amina laughed.

Aiden thought about making a snide comment but stopped. He looked around for the metal file but stopped when he saw Amina holding it out to him. He grabbed it from her and went back to his work.

Amina sat across from Aiden. "No, seriously, what's up?"

Amina knew him well and knew that he only got like this when he was stressed. He stopped and looked at her. "You know . . . this situation with the visitor." Aiden wasn't about to tell his sister what was really happening. She had enough on her mind.

"And?" Amina sat beside him.

"And it just doesn't make sense. Why is this getting so much harder?"

"Because we were told it would and we can only do so much." Amina started and slowly ramped up as she spoke. "Because there have been two close calls back-to-back. Because the City of the North was attacked and everyone as far as we know is dead."

"It was?" Aiden stopped his work and stared at Amina,

feigning shock.

"Yes, and now I'm afraid we're going to be next."

"So, what do we do? Do we leave like Aunt Mo suggested, or stay and fight?" He was fishing for an answer—or was it approval he wanted?

Amina gave him a bewildered look. "Fight? We don't stand a chance against them."

"Right, of course." Aiden lowered his gaze to the floor. Who was he kidding? Amina was right. He didn't have the skills-let alone the guts-to fight. And yet, he was drawn to Terrance's group. He hungered to know more and even—this sounded crazy- join the group.

Amina and Aiden's eyes met. She held his gaze with all seriousness. "Look, I don't know the answer. I feel like this guy might be a sign, but I don't know. I don't know if he's good or bad. I don't know if he would be willing to help. But I do know that if he's the enemy, and we find out Seth's crew was lying to us and they purposely brought him in . . ." She trailed off and Aiden could see the dread in her eyes.

He placed a comforting hand over hers. "Aren't we all family? One body? One mind?"

"Yes, but—"

"But nothing. We trust each other. Did Seth say he just wanted to help a hurt man?" Amina nodded. "Then trust him." He needed to hear those words just as much as she did. "Why is that so hard for everyone?"

Amina stood, still jittery. "Because Teivel is up there, out to get us! Because the Myriad seem to be getting closer by the day! And because families stab each other in the back!" Her eyes were ferocious. Full of hurt, vengeance, and betrayal.

Aiden knew what she was talking about, and it had nothing

to do with Seth or the underground or Teivel, but it had everything to do with their father's death and how she blamed their mother for it.

Aiden stared deeply into her glassy eyes. "Not everyone will betray you. It's okay to trust."

"How can you say that after all that's happened?"

"Because . . . I have faith. It's the only thing that keeps me going."

Amina leaned her forehead on the table. Aiden came around the table to her side and grabbed her into a hug. They held each other tightly.

"Sometimes I think my faith is fading away," Amina whispered. Aiden didn't respond; there were no words. And if he did speak, he'd have to admit that his was wavering too.

"Is the visitor awake yet?"

Amina lifted her head, pushing loose strands of hair away. "Yes, but we didn't really get to talk to him."

"What happened?"

Amina rolled her eyes. "Matthias came barging in with two coalition officers and kicked us out to do his own questioning."

"How did he find out?" Aiden asked.

Amina shook her head. "Who knows, it could've been the doctor or Mike, who was standing guard. Either way, Mike did say he'd fill us in later. Maybe if we're lucky he'll let us sneak in there to talk, but I really don't know." Amina sniffled a bit. "Anyway, I'm going to go. I'll see you later."

Aiden cleared his throat. He knew his sister could only take so much emotion before shoving it back down in order to keep focused on her self-made mission.

"Okay, sounds good. I'm going to keep working on my music box."

Amina inspected the pile of gears, screws, and other random pieces of metal. "Is that what that's supposed to be? I thought it was some weird abstract art thing," she teased.

Aiden made a face. "What? No way. This is going to be the greatest musical box since the Marble Machine."

"I don't know what that is, but okay Einstein."

"Just call me, Mr. Antoine Favre."

Amina shook her head as she rolled her eyes.

"What?" he asked innocently with a goofy grin on his face.

Chapter 5

Amina paced back and forth in her tiny tent, squeezing a homemade stress ball. Now that the elders knew about this new visitor it was going to be harder to talk with him. Despite knowing it wasn't her responsibility anymore, she wanted to finish the conversation she started. Her curiosity was growing and after realizing that he was the same face in her dream, she wondered if Sabaoth was trying to tell her something.

Amina made a cup of weak tea from the ground ginger she found during a raid months back and sat at her table with her journal of the Sacred Book. All she wanted was to know why this man had come into their lives and why he was in her dream. There had to be some connection.

Amina wasn't much of a prayer anymore. She struggled with her relationship with Sabaoth, but in that moment, she didn't know where else to turn. Sabaoth had given her a dream for a reason and she needed to know what that reason was. *Sabaoth*, she prayed, *I don't understand right now what it is you are doing or why this man is here or why you showed me that dream. Please give me insight. Please reveal to me the meaning of my dream. Tell me if this man is good or evil. I need to know.*

Letting out a sigh Amina opened the sacred writings and read:

CHAPTER 5

Now a great sign appeared in heaven: a woman clothed with the sun, with the moon under her feet, and on her head a garland of twelve stars.

Then being with child, she cried out in labor and in pain to give birth. And another sign appeared in heaven: behold, great, fiery red dragon having seven heads and ten horns, and seven diadems on his heads. His tail drew a third of the stars of heaven and threw them to the earth. And the dragon stood before the woman who was ready to give birth, to devour her Child as soon as it was born. She bore a male Child who was to rule all nations with a rod of iron. And her Child was caught up to Sabaoth and His throne. Then the woman fled into the wilderness, where she has a place prepared by Sabaoth, that they should feed her there one thousand two hundred and sixty days.

At the end of the passage Amina stopped to ponder what she had read. Sometimes the imagery in the sacred writings completely alluded her. She knew that much of the imagery used was to help describe the indescribable. Amina reread the passage, attempting to translate the imagery into something concrete. As she did, Seth's comment about the visitor possibly being a Hebrew came to mind and something clicked. Could the woman's child represent Sabaoth's race, the Hebrews? And if so, according to this passage, they were clearly taken to the wilderness. *They did flee to a protected land. It's not a myth.*

Amina smiled as a plan formed. If Sabaoth took the Hebrews and hid them safely away during the Great Desolation, then why couldn't the adopted holy people, the Notzrim, who believe in Sabaoth and Mashiakh, do the same? Why couldn't they find this safe haven and join them? Surely fellow brothers and sisters of the faith would allow them to stay.

Amina felt the excitement bubble inside as her conviction strengthened. There were a lot of rumors and theories out there about where the Hebrews had gone. It was a safe haven for a reason. It was supposed to be undetectable. So how would they get there?

Amina then thought of her dream. The trail she followed led her to a secret hidden valley in the middle of who knows where shrouded with the invisible protection of Sabaoth. The only way she found it was by following the man. Could it be that Sabaoth has brought a Hebrew into their tunnels in order to lead them back to his home?

Amina jumped, ready to speak with the man again, but then remembered she couldn't. She slunk back on her stool. She yawned, feeling the lack of sleep catching up to her, but her excitement kept her mind racing. Amina took another sip of tea hoping it would relax her.

"Amina, you in there?" A voice called from outside the tent.

"Yes."

"May I come in?" It was Josiah.

Amina stood and poked her head out the tent flap. "What's going on?"

"Mike wants to meet with us."

Amina perked up. "Already? That's great news, let's go." Amina stepped out of the tent. This was it. Things were going to move forward. Butterflies bounced around Amina's stomach. "Where are we meeting him?"

"Just outside the secure medical ward. There's a blocked off utility closet there where we can meet privately."

"And is he going to let us talk with the guy too?"

"I don't know, maybe, although I'm not so sure we should anymore."

CHAPTER 5

Amina couldn't help but roll her eyes as she started toward the ladder. Once again Josiah was more interested in what his father thought about him.

Amina grabbed the ladder and started climbing. "Whatever, you don't have to, but I need to know who he is and assess if he can help. I've been thinking about what Seth said about him being a Hebrew. I think he might be right."

"Really? Why's that?"

"Just . . . a hunch." She didn't want to let Josiah know about her dream. He was skeptical about visions and dreams. "Anyway, if he is, then we can go to the elders with a plan." When she reached the top she kept walking, but there weren't any footsteps following. Amina stopped and found Josiah frowning. Amina threw up her hands, palms facing upward, quizzically. "What?"

"Look I'm just as concerned about this whole thing as you are, but it's not our job anymore to figure out what to do about this."

Amina glared at Josiah. "But it was your job when you chose to use etymtorp on the others, right? So, you get to pick and choose when to assert your supposed authority and when not to? Is that it?" Amina shook her head as she continued walking. Her pace quickened as her irritation grew.

"C'mon Amina, that's not fair."

Amina stopped, whirling around so she was face-to-face with Josiah. "You only jump in to act like a leader when it suits you and your reputation, but you never make decisions on your own, Josiah. Right now, we need to focus on helping our community. We are under threat and there is a good possibility that we could be attacked soon. We need to let the elders know what's going on and I don't want to do that without giving them a suggested solution. C'mon, I mean, we know the threat up there is bigger than anything else. And you've seen firsthand how close it's getting to our home. Where's the humanitarian Josiah I once knew? The one who cared more about helping others than helping himself? That's who I need right now." Amina's eyes softened, pleading with him to understand.

Amina continued walking, leaving Josiah behind. As she rounded the last turn toward the secure medical ward, Josiah's father, Matthias, appeared nearly running face-first into Amina.

"Amina." There was a hint of suspicion in his voice as he lifted an eyebrow.

Amina heard footsteps behind her. Matthias' gaze fixed on his son. "Josiah, what are you two doing over here?"

Josiah was about to speak, but Amina quickly jumped in. "Coming to see you, sir, and the other elders. We were hoping to request an audience in order to discuss some concerns we have about the Myriad sightings and attacks."

Matthias' expression softened and turned to concern as he looked from his son back to Amina. "There have been actual attacks? On you?"

Josiah nodded. "Yes sir. I filed a report on it, but then it occurred again during Dwelling Seven's last raid with Seth and his crew. That's why we wanted to speak with you."

Matthias' expression changed yet again at the mention of Seth. He was a fickle man. "Was this attack also the same night our visitor was brought in?"

"Yes sir."

Matthias took a step closer to Josiah, getting in his face. He kept his voice low and stern. "And the same incident you tried to take charge of and keep hidden from me?"

Josiah seemed to cower under the scrutiny of his father. Quietly he answered. "No sir, not hidden. We were going to inform you as soon as I could make a solid report about the situation. The man was also in no condition for questioning when he was first brought in."

There was a pause before Matthias spoke again. Amina could feel the tension burning.

"You might think because you're next in line that you're in charge now, but you're not. And I don't need you deciding what I need and don't need to know. Understood?"

"Yes sir." His voice barely audible.

"Now get out of here, both of you. You will have a hearing before the council tomorrow to determine the consequences of your actions." Not waiting for a response, Matthias turned and headed toward the secure medical ward.

Amina watched him go until she heard a click, saw a light from inside the hospital ward flood the tunnel, and then it was dark again as the door rattled shut.

Amina walked the same direction as Matthias.

"What are you doing? Didn't you hear what my father said?"

"And your point?" Amina stopped in front of the closet door and opened it. "Mike is supposed to meet us here, right? So, I'm going to meet with him. Stay or don't stay, doesn't matter to me, but I need answers. I'm not giving up just because your father is upset."

Josiah huffed but followed Amina into the closet and closed the door behind them. She could tell he was just as curious as she was about the man.

Years seemed to pass and still no Mike.

If he wasn't going to show, then Amina was going to find

her own way to sneak back into the man's room.

Amina groaned. "I don't think he's coming. I think he lied to you."

"Or something came up when my father went in there. I'm sure he wasn't expecting that to happen."

"That was hours ago."

Josiah tilted his head to the side and lifted his eyebrows. "We haven't been in here that long. You just have no patience."

Amina wasn't going to deny that. "So how long should we wait?"

Just then the door creaked open making both Amina and Josiah jump. Amina couldn't see who was behind the door, but she could feel her stomach flutter. As the door opened further and someone stepped inside, Amina saw the bald head and scrawny build of Mike. She let out the breath she had been holding. He quickly closed the door behind him and turned to face the others.

"Sorry that took so long. Your father showed up and . . . I don't want to get into it. Let's just say, things aren't looking good for our visitor."

"What do you mean? Who is he?" Amina pressed.

Mike stood at ease with his hands crossed in front of him. "His name is Paxton. He claims to be a Hebrew and that he got lost. Supposedly, the Myriad found him and started questioning him. When he wouldn't tell them anything, they beat him and left him for dead."

Questions were whirling around Amina's mind. "How did he get lost? Where did he come from? Why was he near the city?"

"I don't know. He wouldn't tell them much beyond that. And even then, the elders don't seem to believe. They're holding a meeting right now to decide what to do. I was ordered to stay and keep guard."

"So we can go talk to Paxton ourselves?" Amina stepped forward, hopeful.

Mike hesitated. He looked to Josiah, to the floor, and then back to Amina. "I don't want to get in trouble. Things are pretty tense right now and one slip up could mean the boot for me, you know."

Amina stepped forward and put a hand on Mike's shoulder, hoping that would somehow ease his concerns. "I get it, Mike, but the elders never have to find out. If you haven't heard, the Myriad are getting closer. I have a plan, but I need to talk to Paxton first."

She could see the wheels turning in Mike's head as he weighed his options. "Okay." He nodded. "But you'll have to be quick about it."

Mike led the way out of the closet and back into the secure medical ward, checking each spot to make sure the coast was clear before allowing Amina and Josiah to move forward.

When they reached Paxton's room Mike opened the door, allowing Amina and Josiah to slip through. "I'll be on guard. If someone is coming, I'll knock three times. When you're done, knock twice and I'll open the door if I think it's safe."

"Thanks, Mike. I really appreciate this."

Mike gritted his teeth. "They better not find out about this." Mike let the door close.

Amina turned toward the bed and saw Paxton staring at them. He had such an intense stare, but at the recognition of Amina and Josiah his eyes softened and his lip curled into what might have been a smile. "You're back," he said. "It's nice to see you again, Amina."

Amina grabbed a chair and placed it at the end of Paxton's bed. Sitting in the chair she leaned her elbows on her knees and examined him. Even though she was excited just thinking about the prospect of having a way to escape, she didn't want to seem too eager. What if everything was all in her head? "Are you willing to answer some questions now?"

"That depends."

"On what?"

"On whether I can trust you or not."

"We're not Myriad if that's what you're thinking," Josiah snapped.

"I know that. I've dealt with Myriad, you're not savage enough to be them, but you are Notzrim, aren't you?"

Josiah squared his shoulders as if to appear more threatening. "Yes, we are."

Paxton nodded his head as the muscles in his body relaxed. "Good. I'm Paxton." He held out his hand but Amina ignored it. She wasn't ready to relax. Josiah shook his hand before Paxton continued. "I'll tell you whatever you want to know, but I'm not sure what else I can tell you beyond what I told Matthias."

"And what did you tell Matthias?" Amina inquired.

"Let me first say I was attacked by the Myriad for no good reason." Paxton described what he had been through in the past seventy-two hours and it was brutal.

He claimed he had been hiding in the mountains with the Hebrews, completely oblivious to anything happening with the outside world. He left with his parents nine years ago. The only thing he had been told was Sabaoth was calling them to a new land of protection because the end of the world was coming. "I was skeptical at first, but when your elderly parents say

CHAPTER 5

they received a message from Sabaoth and they were insistent on going out to live in the mountains, you go with them. I wasn't about to let my parents travel alone, but after nine years of waiting in a tiny village and seeing life still progressing, I started to wonder. My parents were content, but I was restless. So, I left."

"Despite all the warnings?"

"Look, I was told the world was ending, but we were protected. There was no evidence of anything going on. I started to doubt what I was told. I thought maybe my parents had gotten sucked into some crazy cult, but when I left." Paxton stopped and shook his head as he lowered his eyes. "I was devastated to see what had happened. There's so much that's just dead and hard to believe. I mean, the water is red, it looks like blood. Not to mention there're craters the size of houses, burnt trees, and so many abandoned and bombed buildings. To think, people still live here. Why has no one left?"

Josiah interjected. "It's like this everywhere, the entire world has been destroyed. There's nowhere to go."

"That's unfortunate." Paxton let out a sigh. Amina shifted uncomfortably in her chair, waiting for someone to speak again. Just as she opened her mouth, Paxton continued. "So, as I kept walking, I began looking around to see if there was any sign of life. No one was around. It wasn't until I arrived at what I think was a perimeter fence that I ran into the Myriad. I tried to approach them and ask for a local hostel. They started shouting at me and pointing their guns. I immediately threw my hands up and lowered onto my knees. I didn't want any trouble. They rushed me and pinned me to the ground while pulling my sleeve to check my arms. They seemed to be looking for something that I clearly didn't have. That's when another soldier, who looked to be in charge, walked up to me. He asked me who I was and where I was from. He wanted to know why I didn't have the mark. I tried to explain that I didn't know what he was talking about, that I was from out of town, but he didn't seem to believe me. He asked over and over again who I belonged to and what was my allegiance. I insisted I was a nomad living in the mountains alone. I couldn't tell them the truth and risk my people being found. Eventually, the man gave orders to the others. That's when they beat me and I blacked out."

Amina liked to believe she was a good judge of character, and Paxton's story seemed plausible. A glimmer of hope flickered inside her.

Josiah on the other hand was staring at Paxton, examining him. Josiah cleared his throat. "Why didn't you just turn around as soon as you saw how depleted everything was? Why go toward the city?"

"I was kinda hoping to find out what had happened. I thought that if I kept going things would be better. I don't know. I guess my curiosity got the best of me."

"It does get better the further in you go, but it also gets harder to get there. You have to have the right papers to live in certain areas of the city," Josiah explained. "A lot has changed in nine years."

"No kidding."

Paxton certainly seemed friendly enough and was willing to answer each question without hesitation. Amina's muscles relaxed. This was good.

"Paxton, we're in a bit of a situation here and I wondered if you'd be willing-" Amina started to ask.

Josiah quickly cut her off. "To show us proof?"

CHAPTER 5

"Proof?"

"That you are in fact a Hebrew."

"I have Sabaoth's mark of the Hebrew, it's just kind of bandaged right now."

"No, you don't," Josiah responded.

Paxton's expression shifted. "Um, yeah, I do."

"When you were being bandaged, we saw no mark."

Paxton shook his head. "I don't know what to tell you. I have the mark." He pointed to his forehead.

Amina was perplexed. Did she miss something? "You mean it's on your forehead?" Paxton nodded. "That's an odd place." Amina sat back in the chair.

Paxton shrugged nonchalant. "I didn't pick it."

Josiah moved a little closer to the bedside. "If we're going to plead your case, we have to be certain–"

Paxton leaned forward. "Wait, I'm not a prisoner, am I? Have I done something wrong? Matthias said nothing about me having to stay once I'm healed."

"No, you haven't done anything wrong, however, there are a lot of security risks in allowing you to leave."

"What does he mean security? Where am I? I still don't even know."

"You're in the Notzrim underground." Amina so desperately wanted to tell him more, to explain their situation, but Josiah stopped her before she could say anything else.

"You now know where we are hiding, and if we let you go you could easily lead the Myriad to us."

"Why would I do that? *And I don't know where we are.* The last place I remember being is near the city."

"The Myriad have their ways of making people talk."

Paxton rubbed his face. He was clearly frustrated. "I get that

77

you don't trust me, but I swear to you I have no interest in running into those guys again. I just want to get back home where I know it's safe."

Josiah stood and motioned for Amina to follow. "Give us a minute." Josiah knocked twice on the door. As soon as Mike opened it they stepped through.

"You done?" Mike asked.

"Not yet." Josiah walked down the hall, far enough away that Mike couldn't listen to their conversation.

Amina stared at Josiah expectantly.

Josiah's big brown eyes were filled with uncertainty. "Do you trust this guy?"

"I think I do. Earlier today I had a dream, a vision." Amina paused, still uncertain if she wanted to tell Josiah what she thought. It wasn't likely he'd believe her. At the same time, if this truly was a vision from Sabaoth, Josiah needed to know. "Paxton was in it, leading me to the Hebrews. I think that's why he was brought to us, albeit with odd circumstances surrounding his arrival, but Sabaoth works in mysterious ways, right?"

Josiah crossed his arms, his square jaw was tight from clenching his teeth. "I don't know. Something still isn't settling with me. I think it's time to let it go." Josiah approached Amina and gently rested his hands on her shoulders. "You've had your chance to talk to him, now just leave it alone."

He made it sound like that was an easy thing to do, that after the dream she had, she was supposed to just walk away and do nothing.

Amina pulled away from his grip. "I can't do that, Josiah. If I don't share what I know, it could lead the elders to make a horrible decision that most likely entails us staying here and the Myriad finding us, but if I can go to the elders, I think I can convince them that we need to leave and Paxton can help."

"What makes you think Paxton will be willing to help us? What if he leads us into a trap?"

"We have no reason to believe he will."

"We have no reason to believe he won't." Josiah spat back.

Amina clenched her fists tightly. "Look, I'm not saying this is a solid plan right now. This is our chance, Josiah. Our chance to save our people and go to a better place before we are all found and killed."

Josiah looked at the ceiling and let out a sigh. "Look I've played along with this delusion of yours long enough. The elders know what they're doing and have measures in place to protect us. You need to trust their judgment."

Amina put her hands on her head, agitated. Why was he being so adamant? "The elders are no match for the Myriad and their technology. We are sitting ducks down here, and I don't want to watch my people, *my family*, be massacred, do you? Because that's what will happen if we don't do something about it. They're reasonable men, don't you think they'll listen to someone who comes to them with a solution to this problem?"

Josiah didn't flinch at Amina's rising voice. If he was good at anything it was keeping calm in the midst of intense conversations. "The elders along with the coalition will protect us. We need to let them handle it."

Amina threw her hands up and took a few steps away from Josiah. "Of course you'd say that. You want the elders to make a decision? Fine. But I'm going to make sure they make the *right* decision." Amina stormed off. It was time she let the elders know what she thought about this whole situation.

Amina made her last turn and arrived at the elders' chambers. As she made her way toward the door into their office, a young woman with frizzy auburn hair and a pair of scratched glasses stopped her. "I'm sorry, but you can't go in there right now. They're in session."

Amina tried to step past the woman. "Don't worry, Jade, they'll want to hear what I have to say."

The woman squeezed between Amina and the door. "They don't like to be interrupted. You need to wait."

"Well how long will they be?"

The woman shrugged. "They've been in there for forty-five minutes, but the meetings differ all the time."

Amina rolled her eyes. "I can't just wait indefinitely. This is important."

Jade put a hand up and firmly planted her feet. "Not as important as their prayer time. If you want them to listen to you, I suggest you sit down and wait your turn."

"Fine, I'll wait," Amina huffed as she spun around and sat on the bench across the way.

"Thank you." Jade took her seat again at the desk in front of the door.

Amina leaned her head back on the wall and stared at the ceiling. There was a small crack where water was accumulating and slowly dripping. If she listened carefully she could hear the water droplets splashing onto the cement floor. It reminded her of the leaky faucet in her bathroom that her father tried to fix on his own when she was young. He was not much of a handyman but he insisted on trying to do it on his own to save money. Amina was so excited to be his "big helper."

As she sat next to him on her tiny step stool beside the tool box she watched her father crawl underneath the sink. He took his first tool from Amina and started to unhinge the pipe from the rest of the sink, the only problem was, he forgot to turn the water off. As soon as he loosened the pipe, water started spraying everywhere. Her father quickly re-tightened the pipe, but not before the water had soaked them both.

Amina laughed until her stomach ached, especially when her dad finally got the water to stop and came out from under the sink looking like a wet dog.

Amina blinked back tears; those were the days.

Just then the door opened and a group of men and women in their fifties or older started filing out. They were quietly chatting with one another and not paying any attention to the fact that there was someone else in the room.

Amina jumped and stood in their path.

"Excuse me please, but could I borrow a moment of your time? I have some urgent news."

One of the men stepped forward, he was much taller than the rest and also much younger with a red goatee and green eyes. He was also Amina's Uncle Paul. "Amina, is everything alright? This is quite unusual of you."

Another man, with a head of gray patchy hair and thick black glasses spoke. "I'm sure whatever she has to say is not so important that she can't wait until open session tomorrow." His demeanor was most unwelcoming. The man tried to walk past Amina but she stood her ground pleading with them.

"Please, this is not something that can wait, and I don't want to bring it up in front of too many people. I don't want to cause more alarm than there needs to be."

Paul came to Amina's side, examining her to make sure what she said was genuine. "Go ahead Amina, you may share." Paul looked at the group expectantly. There were several wandering eyes along with grumbling, as if they had something better to do. Paul pushed. "I'm sure we can spare a few extra minutes for one of our hard-working scavengers."

The man with the glasses furrowed his brow making him look like an angry raccoon. "Fine. What is it?"

Amina was about to start talking, but Matthias had come out of the room and saw her. He immediately cut her off. "Amina, didn't I tell you to not bother us? If you're here about the security issue then I've already made the others aware. We prayed, and have decided that we can give the scavengers some extra surveillance from our end if you feel that would better protect the crews. Otherwise I think—"

Amina stopped him before he could say more. "Thank you, but that's not why I'm here. Well it is, but it isn't. I . . . I um, want to talk specifically about Paxton, the Hebrew we found."

Amina took a deep breath before she explained the events that happened over the past day. She could tell Matthias was angry with her, but she kept going. As she rattled off all the details the elders listened more intently that she expected. Some expressed shock and concern while others seemed unaffected by this new danger. When she finished explaining the details of her vision and plan, she saw them collectively lose interest. "So you see, if my vision is right about Paxton, and I am able to convince him that we are in need of refuge, I'm sure he would take us. Then we would be safe from the Myriad for good."

One rather skinny and almost sickly-looking woman threw her head back and scoffed. "That's ridiculous! What makes you think the Myriad could ever find us down here?" Amina heard a few others mumble in agreement.

A man, much fatter than the rest with a bright red face, spoke.

CHAPTER 5

"We must remain here ready for when Mashiakh comes for us. He is the one who will deliver us out of this place and into His kingdom. It's going to happen any day now."

Amina clenched her fists and took a deep breath. "But what if He doesn't?" The elders sneered at her comment, but she kept talking. "Our people are being attacked right now. If this keeps happening, the Myriad are going to find us, and then we'll be the next Northern Underground."

"We will get you more surveillance and protection. I already told you this," Matthias argued.

"Yes, but eventually, someone is going to slip up and an entrance is going to be found. Wouldn't it be better if we were in a place free of fear so that we can be strengthened and ready for Mashiakh? Right now, no one is ready to fight a war."

Matthias stepped forward, towering over Amina. "We have protocols for that and systems in place to protect us of any such thing." Matthias rubbed his forehead. "I'm done listening. If you choose to leave, we can't stop you, but we are not leading some mass exodus because you're afraid." Matthias pushed past Amina and stormed off, the man with the glasses quickly followed, mumbling to himself about Amina's so-called ridiculous plan.

But it wasn't ridiculous, was it? She wasn't wrong about the danger growing, she was certain of that, but maybe they did have enough protection that if something should ever happen, they'd be okay.

Paul regarded Amina with fatherly eyes. He put his hand to Amina's cheek lovingly. "I know that you are scared, we all are in some way, but we have to trust Sabaoth and the elders. We're seeking His plan for us."

"But what if this is His plan for us? What if wants us to leave here and go prepare for Him elsewhere?"

"Don't you think He would've told us?"

"Maybe *this* is His way of telling us. By sending a Hebrew to us. I don't want another massacre." Amina's eyes stung as she blinked back tears of frustration. Why was she so emotional about this? She needed to stay composed.

"Neither do I." He sighed deeply. "I will pray about it and convince Matthias and the others to do the same." He eyed the other elders as they stood waiting, like puppies needing to be told where to go and when. "Will you agree that we can at least pray about this?" They nodded hesitantly; some shrugged their shoulders. "Good." He turned and placed both hands on Amina's shoulders. "Until then, sit tight, pray, and trust Sabaoth."

"What about Paxton? What are you going to do with him?"

He pursed his lips and looked up to nowhere in particular. "For now," he paused still trying to decide, "he must stay in the tunnels under close watch, but I don't believe he needs to be in containment. Can you be his watchman?"

"Me? Why not someone in the coalition?"

"Because I trust you, and you've clearly established a relationship with him." Paul gave her a knowing look. Amina couldn't fool her uncle; he knew her stubborn curiosity always put her where she didn't belong.

Amina nodded. "I think I can handle that."

"Good. Now excuse me because I have a date with two very beautiful ladies." Paul winked and smiled.

"Tell Mo and Emily I said hello."

"You're welcome to join us for dinner this evening."

"Thanks, but I have my own things to attend to. You did just put me on guard duty, didn't you?"

CHAPTER 5

Paul wagged his finger. "That I did. Very well, another time."

"Sure."

Paul hugged Amina before setting off down the tunnel. The others followed suit. Soon it was just Amina and Jade, who was busy reading through some papers and making marks all over them. Not once had she looked up during their conversation, but Amina was certain she had heard every word.

Amina took off down a different tunnel from the others, a short cut back to the hospital. She wanted to give Paxton the good news and get him out of there. The sooner he got out of the medical ward and saw how the Notzrim lived, the sooner she could convince him to help.

Despite the elders' hesitancy, Amina wanted to move forward with her plan and get Paxton on her side. She was feeling confident that if Paul was on her side, the other elders would agree to leave for the mountains.

Arriving at the hospital, Amina walked over to Paxton's room and waltzed through the door, ignoring the startled look on Mike's face.

When Paxton saw her, he sat forward and stretched. "You're back. Where'd you go? I got worried when you left looking so pissed off."

"Yeah, sorry about that. There was a difference of opinion, but that doesn't matter anymore. What does matter is that I went to speak with the elders. The good news is, you can leave the medical ward and you don't have to be put into confinement. You'll be free to move about."

"Great. As soon as I get the all clear from the doc I want to start heading home. You'll help me find supplies for my journey, right?"

Amina gave a halfhearted smile. "That's the bad news: you can't leave the underground." Amina pressed her lips together and offered an I'm sorry look, but the disappointment on his face stabbed her.

"So I'm a prisoner."

"No of course not. You're allowed to move about and live here freely, with a guard, just until the elders have come to a decision." Amina tried to make it sound like a good deal, but who was she kidding? "And at least you'll get to move around and see things. Though there's not much to see. After you've seen one dwelling, you've pretty much seen them all."

Paxton gave a puzzled look. "Dwellings?"

"Yeah, the sewer is made of hundreds of tunnels that all connect in one way or another to these big openings, we call them dwellings here. We've occupied eight of them, and then five others are used as our common areas, like the medical ward and the coalition station. The rest are scattered about but we can't get to them without going above ground."

"Coalition?"

"Law enforcement."

Paxton stifled a laugh. "You have laws down here?"

"Well yeah, we can't just let everyone run around doing whatever they want. That would be chaos."

Paxton observed the drab walls stained with rust. "So back up, we're in the sewer tunnels right now? As in where human waste and water go?"

"Yes, but these tunnels are no longer in use. We're on the outskirts of the city. When the Great Desolation hit, so many people died, Tievel forced everyone to relocate. No one's allowed to live outside of the designated cities around the world. Not to mention, when we first came to inhabit this

CHAPTER 5

place, several people went and sealed off a few tunnels to help keep it dry."

Paxton's eyes were big. "When was the last time you went above ground?"

"Me? Just a few days ago." Amina sat in the chair that was still beside the bed, making herself comfortable. It was nice getting to talk to someone new. "That's because I'm part of our food scavenging team, but there are some people here who haven't been above in more than nine years."

"Huh." Paxton chewed on the side of his cheek as he thought. "I feel bad for you guys."

Amina shrugged. "You get used to it after a while, but you do start to miss fresh air and a real sky. But it's not like being up there is all that great either."

"No, it's definitely not."

"What about your home in the mountains? I bet it's amazing there, untouched and thriving, since it's protected by Sabaoth and all."

"Right." Paxton leaned against his pillow imagining. "It's amazing there. Untouched, green, full of life. I'm looking forward to going back."

"Is it east to get to?"

"I guess." Paxton shrugged. "It's a bit of a hike but not terrible."

"And is there a lot of land or are you all crammed together?"

"Oh, there's a ton of land. We could fit twice the amount of people there."

Amina smiled. She was tempted to tell Paxton everything about her plan, but she didn't want to put that kind of pressure on him before she knew he'd be willing to help. "Let me go find the doctor so you can be checked out of here and settled into your new place."

Paxton laughed. "I don't think they're going to let me out of here that quickly. They said I still have swelling in my abdomen, and they want to watch me until the swelling goes down to make sure I don't have any new injuries."

Amina rolled her eyes and grabbed his chart by the door, as if she knew how to read it. "It's probably more of them wanting something to do. We don't get very many patients in here anymore."

"And you used to?"

"Oh yeah, tons. But when we stopped accepting people into the underground, we weren't getting a lot of people with injuries. Now it's just your typical issues. You don't see a whole lot of people coming in and out of here anymore." Amina put the clipboard back. "But if they want you to wait . . . I guess you'll just have to wait." Amina shrugged. "It's probably for the best anyway. This place is nicer than anywhere else in the underground." Amina looked at Paxton's concerned face. "Have you tried going for a walk at all today?" she asked, quickly changing the subject. She didn't want to scare him too much about the rest of the underground.

"I walked to the latrine and back, does that count?"

Amina glanced behind her at the curtain hanging in the corner, hiding the makeshift toilet and laughed. "Not quite. That's only like what, five steps away?"

"Eight to be exact," Paxton playfully corrected her.

"We should go for a real walk."

Just then a nurse walked in with a tray. On it was a syringe and a container of blue liquid. "Time for your medicine, Paxton." When she saw Amina, she smiled sweetly. "Oh, I see you have company. Hello Amina, nice to see you again."

"Hi Theresa. I was just telling Paxton he needs to go for a walk and get the blood flowing in his legs."

Theresa's shoulders sank as she frowned. "I don't think that's such a good idea. With his swelling it might prove to be very painful. This medicine should help. We're hoping he'll be better in the next couple of days. Come back then, won't you?"

"Alright." Amina shrugged. "See you later Paxton." Amina waved and left. She knew fighting with Theresa was a moot point, she was more stubborn than Amina, especially when it came to the well-being of her patients, which was a good thing Amina supposed but inconvenient for her.

Chapter 6

Amina tried to be patient, she tried to not worry about the previous day's events and the impending future, but every quiet moment she had, her mind drifted back to everything that had happened, which filled her with frustration and a little anxiety. She wasn't good at waiting.

When her mind flooded with overwhelming thoughts about how to convince Paxton to reveal the Hebrew's location and convince the elders that they should go there, Paul's voice would come back to her: *Sit tight, pray, and trust Sabaoth.*

Amina sat on the small wooden stool in her tent with her journal of sacred writing open on her makeshift table. *I want to trust you, Sabaoth, I just don't know how.* She pressed her face into her hands.

"Amina?" A voice called from outside.

Aiden's head was popping through the tent, looking at her hesitantly.

"Hey brother, what's up?" Amina asked as she closed her journal.

"The elders are summoning us."

Amina rolled her eyes, disinterested. She knew this was coming, she just wasn't ready for it. "Sounds great," she replied sarcastically.

CHAPTER 6

"Maybe it won't be so bad. Maybe they'll be understanding."

Amina got up and walked out of the tent. "After the last conversation I had with Matthias, I highly doubt it."

The walk to the elders' chamber felt long and the wait even longer. Amina stood in the cold concrete chambers with her arms crossed and eyebrows furrowed. She was not happy with having to be there, practically on trial, as if she had done something wrong.

Beside her stood the rest of her group plus Seth and his crew. No one looked happy or comfortable. They all stood, shifting and fidgeting like little children waiting in line.

The rectangular room was small and unwelcoming. There was a large conference table in the middle and a few short bookshelves lining one of the walls. On the wall opposite hung a few paintings of nature scenes. Probably something to help them keep their hopes up, but to Amina it was depressing; a constant reminder of what they had lost.

After waiting in the chambers for what seemed like hours, the elders filed ominously into the room and took their seats at the table ready to condemn. The air in the room shifted.

Matthias took his time shuffling papers and writing on his notepad, which just caused the tension to thicken. Amina let out a slow breath as her dark brown eyes tried to catch those of her brother. He was busy picking at a scab on his pale arm, making Amina wince at the thought.

Finally, Matthias looked up from his notepad and spoke. "I hereby call this hearing to order." He examined the room and then landed his gaze upon Josiah. Their eyes locked for one long second before Matthias continued. "Now, you are all here today to discuss your actions whereby you broke security protocols, brought in an unknown man into our tunnels, and then declined to inform the proper authorities in a timely manner.

"Now, you all know as well as I do that these are unsafe times and we can never be too careful. This is why we have certain measures in order, and because of your blatant disregard for this community's safety, there could be detrimental consequences that we're still unaware."

There was a long pause, letting the words settle. Like a father scolding his child, Matthias made sure the group felt his disapproval. Amina stared at the floor, not because she felt guilty, but because she was trying to hold her tongue. They were all being treated like insolent little children, when in reality they should be thanked for the way they handled the situation and for the godsend Paxton really is.

"Therefore," Matthias continued, "the elders and I have discussed reasonable discipline to be carried out immediately."

There was a quiet mumble of complaints that rose in the crowd.

Seth stepped forward. "We were only trying to help a person in need. What's so wrong with that?" Seth asked sharply.

"In most cases, nothing. We are called to love and care for all, but we are in a war where our lives are at stake. We cannot afford to reveal our location to anyone."

"So you think we should have let him die?" Seth sneered at Matthias, jabbing him with his words.

Matthias ignored the question and continued to explain the details of their discipline. "For breaching security and risking our safety, Seth, you and your crew will be grounded for the next two months. During that time, you will not be allowed above ground for scavenging or any other activity. Instead, you will be required to volunteer in the dumps. You will also be required to report all whereabouts to your dwelling deacon."

"What!" Roger stepped forward ready for a fight. Tallulah put a hand on his chest and shook her head.

Tallulah spoke for the group. Her voice was quiet and gentle, as she tried to sooth the tension. "With all due respect, sir, don't you think that's a little harsh? We were doing what we thought was right. We were under duress and we-"

"Even more reason for you not to pick up strangers." Matthias snapped back, making Tallulah jump a little. "There is no debating here. You will follow orders, or you will be confined. Do you understand?"

Tallulah lowered her head as Roger walked to the back of the group putting his hands on his head and letting out a frustrated grunt. Amina could practically see the steam blowing out his ears.

Matthias continued without flinching. "As for Josiah and your crew, you each failed to report the situation and further jeopardized the security of our home. Therefore, you are required to report your whereabouts for the next two months to your dwelling deacon. You will be allowed to scavenge, but during your off days you will be required to help with the cleaning crew."

Amina hoped Josiah would say something to defend them, but he kept silent, his eyes lowered to the ground. It figured.

"If I might say something," Amina spoke, trying to keep her voice even. If Josiah wasn't going to say anything, she would. "We brought Paxton to the secure medical ward, we ensured that we took precautions when transporting him so no one would see him and cause panic, and we made sure that everything was secure. By the time Seth and his crew brought in Paxton, there was nothing we could do but respond by helping a man in need, so he didn't die."

Matthias shifted in his chair. "And while I appreciate that, why weren't we informed? I had to be told by a nurse hours later. That is unacceptable."

As much as she tried to keep her emotions at bay, she heard her voice rise in pitch as she continued. "Considering Paxton's condition at the time, we knew he was incapable of endangering anyone here and therefore knew we had time to come to you. We wanted to ensure-"

"There is no excuse for waiting. Your job is not to make such decisions. Your job is to tell the authorities immediately and let them make the decisions."

Amina felt someone's hand on her arm. She kept going, ignoring the warning. "Yes, but we feared that the instant you heard about the situation, you wouldn't even consider Paxton to be friendly. You'd assume the worst." Amina winced at her own words, immediately regretting them, but it was too late.

Matthias slammed his fist on the table and stood. "How dare you be so disrespectful. We are men and women of Sabaoth and we take everything into careful consideration. We are not so closed minded as you think, but rather we use wisdom and discretion, which I cannot say the same for you. We are concerned about the safety of our community and want to do what's best. Amina, I want you to stay." Matthias addressed the rest of the group. "The rest of you may leave, but I expect you all at the town meeting in three days where we will be informing everyone about the situation at hand and our course of action. Until then, no one is to speak of this visitor's origins or the Myriad sightings above."

Without hesitation, the "troublemakers" did as they were told, wanting to flee the uncomfortable room as quickly as possible.

Aiden was the only one who lingered a moment, giving Amina a pitied look as he squeezed her hand.

Amina sighed as her face softened.

Matthias walked around the table and stood in front of Amina. "I was informed that you believe you've had a vision from Sabaoth in regards to our Hebrew visitor and his home."

"Yes sir. I believe this is the answer to our predicament."

Matthias crossed his arms. "And what predicament would that be?"

"I told you sir. The Myriad are closing in, we're not safe here. I believe our best option is to leave."

Matthias nodded. "I was afraid of that. We have given it some thought and we cannot approve such a risky plan."

"What? No, please sir you can't. I know it's a risky plan but it's the right plan."

"Our mind is made up."

"But sir-"

"One more outburst, Amina, and you will spend two days in confinement on top of your other consequence." Amina closed her mouth.

Although she believed in her heart that she was right, she wondered if she'd ever get anyone else on her side or if her aggressive speech would continue to turn people against her.

Amina eyed her uncle, hoping he'd come to her aid; instead he avoided her gaze. Amina's turned to leave. As disappointed as she was, she wasn't done fighting. She would find another way to change their mind. What was it that father Stephen had said in his story? There is wisdom in being persistent, especially when you persist in asking for good things.

Amina wasn't far down the tunnel when a young man,

another scavenger, bolted past her nearly knocking Amina over. Just as he entered the chambers and before the door closed, Amina swore she heard him say *there's been another attack.*

Later that day, Aiden made his way to Dwelling Six. He was hoping he could scavenge through Mitchum's junk pile. He was still working on the music box and had to stop when he realized the crank he originally found didn't fit.

As Aiden made his way across the open space to Mitchum's shop, he noticed Terrance standing by his aunt's shop, deep in conversation with a couple others. They looked to be discussing something serious, and by the sober looks on their faces, Aiden was certain it had something to do with Terrance's plans.

This was his chance to learn if this was a group he could affix to. Aiden meandered over to the group but stopped a few feet away in front of a pile of clothes. He was trying to look nonchalant about it, as if he were there to look at the junk piles sitting around and not to eavesdrop. It didn't work.

"Hey, Aiden, what's up? You look like a dog in church." Terrance stated, walking to him.

"Oh, hey Terrance. I didn't see you there." He laughed and it came out forced. "I was just coming to see what sort of items Mitchum has, but thought I'd swing by here first for a new jacket."

Terrance eyed Aiden for a moment, then glanced at the others and nodded his head. They took that as a sign to leave. Terrance took a step toward Aiden. "What's really going on?"

Aiden took a deep breath, trying to stay calm. "I should

CHAPTER 6

be asking you the same thing." Aiden waited for a reply, but Terrance stood silent as a rock. "What are you planning, Terrance? I know there's something transpiring, and whatever it is . . ." Aiden debated with himself, unsure how he wanted to proceed.

After a painful moment, Terrance spoke. "I don't know what you think you know, but I don't have anything planned other than keeping myself and the others here as safe as a porcupine in summer."

"And what does that entail exactly?"

"Never you mind that." Terrance patted Aiden on the head like a puppy. "You don't need to concern yourself with it." Terrance started to walk away.

"But what if I want to concern myself with it?" Aiden blurted out.

Terrance stopped for a moment but didn't turn around. He seemed to be waiting for Aiden to say more. When he didn't, Terrance kept walking.

Aiden followed as if an invisible hand were pushing him forward. "I want in! I want to be more prepared for the final battle," he practically yelled.

Terrance spun around and placed a large hand over Aiden's mouth. "Shhhh! You trying to get us in trouble?"

Aiden pulled Terrance's hand away and lowered his voice to just above a whisper. "As the days pass, I'm feeling more and more unprepared and unable to protect myself. I don't like feeling that way." *Where did that come from?* Aiden closed his eyes regretting his own words. It's not that the words he spoke were untrue. Aiden just wasn't ready to join some illegal militia or whatever this might be.

Terrance stopped again. "I thought you were all about

peace?"

"I am, but I'm not a fool either. I know how important it is to be prepared."

Terrance stepped forward pressing his finger into Aiden's chest. "You better not be hanging noodles on my ear."

Aiden tilted his head. Terrance's idioms made no sense. "I'm not," Aiden responded hesitantly.

Terrance looked around to make sure no one was close enough to hear. "Dwelling Three in an hour," he whispered, and then started climbing the ladder to leave.

Aiden squeezed his eyes closed. Was this really what he wanted to get himself into? Terrance was known for being a bit of a troublemaker at times and Aiden preferred to avoid people like that. But then again, what would it hurt to go hear him out?

Aiden headed to Mitchum's hoping to find a crank handle for his music box while he waited. The hour passed like sludge. The whole time Aiden aimlessly wandered the piles of scrap, more focused on the meeting than combing through hundreds of tiny pieces of metal.

Searching through the scraps was proving fruitless. So, Aiden walked back to his tent to find something that could help calm his nerves.

Inside his tent Aiden boiled a small pot of water, and then added three drops of peppermint oil. He grabbed his sketchpad and headed to the dwelling's firepit. Paper was not easy to find, but Amina had come across a pad of plain white drawing paper during one of their raids a couple years ago and gave it to Aiden as a gift. He had been able to make the paper last for this long, but it was about to run out.

Before the sketchpad, Aiden would draw in the dirt with

sticks or graffiti the walls with charcoal. The walls were in desperate need of some artistic enhancements. Aiden was convinced his drawings made the dwellings feel cozier, and since no one complained, he and other artists in the community tag-teamed the dwellings in order to give people more beauty and a sense of home. Now the walls in all eight dwellings were covered with murals full of life.

He flipped back through the filled pages, looking for some tiny spot of white he could fill.

The only space he found was on a page where he had drawn several self-portraits with his family. He stared at the page, running his fingers along the drawings. They took him back to a simpler time, when life wasn't so dangerous. Aiden yearned for that but knew that things could never be as they once were.

Aiden grabbed a long stick and shoved it into the firepit to drag out smaller charred pieces of wood. Once he moved several to the edge, he took a smaller stick that he had carved into a pencil and dug it into the char, covering his pencil in soot. Putting pencil to paper, Aiden drew a new portrait. He started with the outline of the face. He wasn't sure who he was going to draw yet. Every time his pencil ran out of soot, he'd stick it into the char. In between segments of drawing, Aiden drank his tea, feeling the cooling sensation of the peppermint run down his throat.

By the time he downed the last sip of tea, his drawing had really started to take shape. He decided to draw his niece Emily. Children were simple and right now Aiden needed simple.

Aiden could've worked on that drawing for another hour, but he knew he needed to leave. He quickly dropped his things back into his tent and headed toward Dwelling Three.

Aiden's stomach was in knots and he thought he was going

to throw up. He took a slow deep breath and let it out again. *Sabaoth give me wisdom.* He needed to keep reminding himself that he wasn't fully committed yet. He was just going to see what it was all about. If it seemed too dangerous, he'd walk away, and he'd inform the elders. It was as easy as that, right?

Inside Dwelling Three, Aiden saw a group of people heading toward one of the largest tents on the east wall. Considering there was no one else to be seen, Aiden assumed that was where he needed to be.

Aiden looked around anxiously before scurrying over to the tent.

Inside the group was formed of men and women from all over and of all different ages. Some were seated, some standing, and the tent kept growing, packing them all in like sardines. Aiden slid against the wall of the tent, trying to stay close to the opening. As more and more people crowded in, however, Aiden found himself getting pushed deeper and deeper into the tent.

The overcrowding made the tent stuffy with body odor and incense, which caused Aiden's stomach to twist even more. He closed his eyes and fanned his face, trying to allow the wave of nausea to subside. All around him he could hear bits and pieces of conversations. Each of them was shrouded in bitterness and discontent.

Soon Terrance stood from out of nowhere and held a large stick that had several carvings up and down it as well as several strips of leather tied around one end. At the end of each dangling leather strip were decorative shells. It was hard to make out much detail due to how far back Aiden was in the tent, but as soon as Terrance raised the stick above his head, the room quieted.

CHAPTER 6

"Thank you for being here." Terrance lowered the stick. "We have all come together tonight for one reason. We each believe that our current way of living needs to be changed. That the status quo is no longer acceptable." There were a few shouts of agreement. Terrance nodded, bolstered by their affirmations. "Now I myself have spoken with the elders and it is clear to me that they are not interested in doing anything but sit like bumps on a log. They don't believe that we need to do anything to help prepare us for the end, but I say that's bull." His voice grew louder and more passionate. "We can't pluck feathers off a bald chicken." There were a lot of awkward and confused looks in the crowd, but several still cheered. "We are never told to sit back and be passive. We are warriors for Sabaoth and warriors fight." This time the group erupted in one unified cheer.

As Terrance continued to talk, Aiden looked around the room. Everyone seemed to be nodding in agreement. And while Aiden liked what he was hearing, he wanted to be cautious not to get pulled in too quickly. He still wasn't sure the group was legitimate.

Then when Jared, a coalition officer, walked forward, rigid and militant, Aiden's face lit up. If a coalition officer was a part of this group, then it must be sanctioned. Jared stood with his feet apart and his hands folded in front of him. His black buzzed-cut hair and hard lined jaw made him even more intimidating. "The elders and coalition have been stock piling all the guns and ammunition from the early days. They are currently locked in a hidden safe they created just west of the coalition office. With my knowledge, and a small tactical team, we could easily get what we need." There were several murmurs through the crowd.

Jared calmly held up the stick and waited for everyone to quiet before continuing.

Aiden listened intently to Jared speak for the rest of the meeting. He liked what he was hearing. They were structured, they had a plan, and they knew how to execute it. Aiden liked that reassurance, but at the same time, he didn't know if he would be successful in such a physically demanding group. *Just one training. I can go to one training and see if I'm cut out for this, if not, I can back out. No problem.*

Since Amina had to find a new way to convince the elders that her plan was the right plan, Amina decided she'd start by visiting Paxton every day and build his trust. If she could get him on her side along with a few other select people, maybe they could ban together and change Matthias' mind. And since Paul had put Amina in charge of guarding Paxton, she had an excuse to be in the medical ward when she wasn't helping with the cleaning crew or scavenging so no one would question her whereabouts.

So, Amina spent time with Paxton, learning everything she could about him and telling him stories about her life in the tunnels. He in turn shared about his life before leaving and what it was like living in such a secluded village. He told her how he wanted to join the police force after college, but never had the chance. Instead, he became the village's local carpenter with his father.

It was going on the fourth day of visiting and Amina was getting anxious. Even though she hadn't heard of any new attacks above ground, or experienced any herself, she was certain another was inevitable.

CHAPTER 6

Amina walked into the hospital corridor. It was empty and quiet, as usual. She felt her heart beating faster than usual; she wasn't nervous exactly, but there was some anticipation to Amina's visits with Paxton that she didn't have before. There was a kind of comfort that Amina felt being around Paxton and talking. With him, she could be herself and let her guard down. She liked that feeling. She had almost forgotten what it was like to trust someone other than her brother.

Amina walked into Paxton's room. He was already dressed and putting on his boots. The hospital had acquired some new clothes for him. He wore a plain black t-shirt and jeans and a beanie that covered his forehead.

Amina's eyes lit up. "They're letting you go?"

"I got the all clear. They say I still need to take it easy, but the swelling from my bruises has gone down enough to release me."

"Great, now I can show you around the rest of this place. And, great news, today is flea market day."

"Flea market day?"

Amina nodded and smiled, but didn't say anything. She wanted it to be a surprise.

Paxton slowly stood but quickly grabbed his head. "I still get a bit dizzy if I move too fast."

"Well we don't have all day, but there's time to take it a bit slow."

Paxton walked over to Amina. He was taller than she realized, and under all his cuts and bruises she could see his full lips and prominent jawline. Amina wasn't used to being this close to him and her body tingled.

"Amina?"

Snapping herself out of it she blurted, "Um . . . what, yeah, you ready? Good. Let's go." Amina quickly spun around shoving her feelings aside.

As Amina walked her usual pace down the hall toward the tunnels, Paxton tried to keep her pace, but he was slowly lagging further and further. "Hey, I need you to slow down."

Amina stopped and let Paxton catch up. "Sorry." Amina turned back around and continued out of the medical corridor and into the tunnels at a much slower pace.

As soon as the door shut behind them, it grew dark. The string of lights was on and it was enough for Amina to see, but she noticed Paxton squinting and blinking.

"Is it always this dark?"

"Pretty much, sometimes darker." Amina started walking, her footsteps echoing all around. "Come on, your eyes will adjust soon enough."

"Give me a sec." Amina watched as Paxton put his hands out and shuffled his feet forward like a zombie. Amina rolled her eyes. "Would you like me to buddy carry you or can you walk like a normal human being?"

Paxton put his arms down and scowled. "I can walk, but I might puke." He scrunched his nose in sheer disgust. "This is the worst smell ever."

It had been so many years, Amina had become nose blind to the smell of rotting sewage, mold, and musk. "You get used to it, but if it helps, here's a handkerchief." Amina pulled one out of her pocket and held it out to Paxton. He gladly took it and tied the blue cloth around his nose and mouth. Once he was ready, Amina continued, and this time she could hear Paxton's feet echoing behind her.

Amina twisted her way through the tunnels with Paxton only slightly lagging behind. She only had to stop twice to let him

CHAPTER 6

fully catch up and not get lost as she took a couple turns close together.

"Geez, this place is a maze. Where are you taking me?" Paxton asked as they rounded yet another corner.

"The Main Hall Dwelling." Amina looked past Paxton, on the side of the tunnel was a small scratching – T2S4. "We're almost there, just one more tunnel." Amina turned to her right. As they walked, she could see a light at the end of the tunnel and started hearing a crowd of booming voices.

They had reached the Main Hall dwelling where all the action and community meetings took place. It was much larger than any of the other dwellings, three stories high with numerous tunnels leading in and out at all levels. Looking down at the floor there was a reservoir of water running through the middle and catwalks going in all directions. The water was their drinking source. The engineers were able to bring it in from a nearby spring and then the scientists used their chemicals to clean the water.

Amina and Paxton were on the second level. Down below everyone milled about like ants.

Since today was flea market day that meant everyone was there. While there was certainly bartering and trading happening on a daily basis, the flea market was special. It only occurred every forty days and it was a chance for people from all the dwellings to come together and enjoy a bit of entertainment, crafts, performances, and games. The flea market had been established in order to help life feel a little more normal.

People from all over the community would prepare a variety of items and bring them to the flea market. There were always crafts and art made from the junk and trash, carnival type games for kids and a performance of some sort. Today was a sock puppet show.

Living in the maze of tunnels had always seemed small and suffocating. Amina never felt there were a lot of people living in them, but when they all got together it reminded her that they were a mighty group of seven hundred strong.

Sure, compared to the rest of the world that was tiny, but compared to the death toll and the overwhelming amount of people flocking to join Teivel, seven hundred felt large. And she knew they were not the only Notzrim underground out there. Hundreds of communities hid around the world, waiting and preparing for the day Mashiakh would return and establish His kingdom.

Paxton raised his eyebrows in awe at the scene. It was a sight to see, especially for someone who had never seen something like this before. He slowly lowered his handkerchief, revealing a gaping mouth. "I had no idea there was so much life down here."

"Yeah, there's quite a few of us, and we like to try to make things seem normal as much as we can. Hence the flea market." Amina extended her arm like she was making a presentation. "It's one of the best events we have."

Amina swung herself onto the ladder and headed down to the floor. Once Paxton made it down Amina took off, walking up and down rows fill with people and blankets spread out containing novelties and games.

Being in with the crowds made it feel much more crowded than it appeared from above, so much so that Amina kept looking back to make sure Paxton wasn't falling behind or getting lost.

She noticed as people walked by him they gave him curious

CHAPTER 6

looks. A small community meant everyone knew everyone else, so any outsiders stuck out like a sore thumb. Amina circled back to Paxton and nudged him to keep moving. He had stopped to look at a collection of wood carvings.

"You gotta tell me when you stop. I can't lose you."

"Right, because you're my *guard*. We wouldn't want the cripple to run off and cause a riot, now would we?"

Amina rolled her eyes. "That's not what I'm worried about. I'm more worried about what everyone else will do to you."

They spent the next hour walking up and down the rows, looking at everything, playing all the games and even watching the third performance of the puppet show.

Whenever Amina looked at Paxton he was smiling and seemed to be enjoying himself. She was glad. The last things she wanted was him being so miserable that he tried to leave.

When the sock puppet show ended, Amina clapped along with everyone else. As she turned to leave, she heard Aiden shout her name. She turned as Aiden, Josiah, and Maya approached.

"There you are, I've been wondering if you were going to spend the whole day in the medical ward again." Aiden smirked. When he laid eyes on Paxton he stopped talking and stuck out his hand. "I'm Aiden, Amina's big brother, nice to meet you." Amina scowled and wanted to say something but held her tongue. She knew he was just trying to get a rise out of her.

Paxton stepped forward, standing a good five inches taller than Aiden, and shook his hand. "I'm Paxton."

"Yeah, I know. It's good to see they've let you out of your jail cell. Those nurses can be quite strict."

"Merciless," Paxton responded, playing along.

Maya stepped forward and also introduced herself. "I'm glad you are feeling better. Are you all healed now?"

"Mostly. Still a bit sore in places and I'll have scabs and bruises on me for a while."

"Are the elders going to let you go?" Josiah asked. His arms were crossed and he wasn't smiling. Amina couldn't quite figure out why Josiah seemed so threatened by Paxton.

Paxton eyed Josiah seriously. "Not right now. They want me to stay here for a bit, but I pose no threat. I'm only interested in getting back home. No offense, but the mountains are a million times better than here."

"None taken, this place isn't exactly paradise." Josiah responded, still sounding cold. "But hasn't Amina told-"

"So," Amina cut in quickly and much too loudly. "We were just going to head back to the dwelling. He hasn't gotten the grand tour yet or been set up with a place to sleep. Want to join us?" Amina looked sharply at Josiah to keep him quiet. Josiah stared hard back, but closed him mouth.

"Yeah sure," Aiden said. "There wasn't anything here that caught my attention this time anyway."

"Did any of you pick out your special gift yet?" Maya asked before anyone got too far.

"No not yet." Aiden turned back around. "We should do that before all the good stuff is gone."

The group agreed and headed over to the gift booth. Paxton followed but was puzzled. "Special gift?"

"Yeah. It's the best part about the flea market," Aiden explained with childish excitement. "The elders have a collection of high value items that they keep locked away, but on flea market day everyone is allowed to pick out one item. I guess they want to give us things to look forward to."

CHAPTER 6

At the booth Amina walked over to the food items first. As a scavenger, her food choices were always leftovers, which tended to be the most unappealing items. But on flea market day, there was an assortment of small food baskets filled with delicious goodies.

Amina looked them over carefully until she found a basket that had dried fruit, nuts, and a small chocolate bar. Her mouth watered just thinking about the smooth rich taste of the chocolate mixed with the salty crunch of the nuts. She picked up the basket and turned to find the others grabbing their gifts.

Josiah grabbed a dodge ball, Maya grabbed some loose-leaf teas, and Aiden grabbed a pair of boxing gloves.

"What are you going to do with those?" Amina asked taking them out of Aiden's hands to look them over. They were pretty worn in and one of the gloves was starting to split.

Aiden grabbed the gloves back indignantly. "I signed up for the self-defense class. I thought these could come in handy."

Amina looked at her brother curiously. He wasn't the fighting type, but she had noticed over the last several months that he was becoming more unpredictable with the things he was willing to try.

Aiden peered into Amina's basket and his eyes lit up. "Y'know sis, sharing is a very important virtue."

"You're not getting my chocolate, Aiden."

"Who said I wanted your chocolate?" Amina looked unconvinced.

That's when Paxton walked up beside her holding three odd-looking tools. They appeared to be knives, but not with a typical shaped blade. One had a hook at the end, while two others looked like skinny spoons.

"What are those?" Amina asked.

"Whittling tools. I like to carve wood." Amina nodded her head, impressed. She knew Paxton worked as a carpenter for his job, but didn't expect him to do it as a hobby too.

When they arrived to Dwelling Three, Paxton once again gaped at the sight of tents scattered all around, the giant firepit in the center of the room, and piles of junk strewn about.

"So this is one of the living quarters you have here?"

"Yep. Dwelling Three. Home sweet home." Aiden smiled.

"How many of these dwellings do you have again?"

"Eight. And each holds around eighty to ninety people. It makes for a very tight-knit group."

The group made their way to the firepit, where they received their ration of food from the scavengers on duty that evening. They then proceeded to find an open space to sit and eat. Amina plopped down, feeling the ache of her muscles from all the walking she had done. Before heading to the medical ward, Amina had to join everyone else for cleaning crew duty as part of their punishment.

Cleaning had never been one of her favorite chores. Her mother used to put her in charge of the bathrooms and mopping. Being on cleaning crew brought back flashbacks of dirty toilet bowls and muddy floors that just never seemed to get clean enough.

As everyone else settled into their spots, and before anyone opened their food, they each bowed their heads to pray. Amina peeked at Paxton who looked around and then awkwardly followed suit.

Josiah prayed. "Our great and mighty Sabaoth, giver and sustainer of life, thank you for this food we have to eat today. Despite our circumstances, you care for us and you provide

CHAPTER 6

for us. Might we always be grateful to you for all you provide each and every day until Mashiakh's return. Mashiakh, come quickly. Amen."

As tradition in their group, each person opened their item, took some, and then passed it around to share, giving more variety to their meal. Tonight's dinner consisted of canned corn, canned yams, dried apple chips, potato chips, and beef jerky.

"We have a nice spread tonight," Josiah pointed out as he took a couple potato chips and passed the rest to Paxton.

Maya smiled. "I for one, am very thankful for this food." Maya addressed Paxton. "Usually our food consists of Spam, tuna, or prunes. All the things people don't like to eat very much."

"Thanks for sharing with me." Paxton passed the potato chips to Amina. His hand seemed to linger on the chips and his fingers slightly brushed hers as she took the bag away. Amina tried to ignore him, but she had a hard time looking away.

"This is probably junk to you after coming from the medical ward. There they actually have good food," Aiden commented.

"I'm not sure you can call an MRE good food, but I'm thankful for anything I can get. I hadn't taken much food with me when I left, so I resorted to only eating once a day. I haven't had this much food in weeks."

The group continued to eat, pass food around, and chat about their days. It was one of the best ways to end the day, among friends. Amina, Aiden, and Josiah had been a team for the past year, and Maya joined only two months ago, but she quickly fit in despite the age gap. Amina appreciated Maya's gentleness and wisdom. As a scientist, Maya had knowledge of all sorts of unique serums, medicines, and plants that baffled Amina.

She never knew one person could have so much knowledge. And when she listened to Aiden and Maya get into discussions about technology or biophysics, Amina would often tune them out because it was all over her head.

"Pillow or mattress?" Maya asked out of nowhere.

"Pillow!" They all replied in unison except Paxton who looked around with utter confusion.

Josiah went next. "Pineapple or grapes?" Amina and Maya responded with pineapple, but Aiden chose grapes.

"That way I can make some wine." Aiden smiled dreamily before continuing. "Books or movies?"

"Books, they take more time," Maya answered first. Amina and Josiah agreed.

"Man you guys are nerds." Aiden joked.

Amina thought for a moment and then asked, "Pool or lake?"

"Is there a diving board?" Josiah asked.

"Sure."

"Then pool."

"Lake for me," Maya said. "I like the nature that comes along with it.

Aiden shook his head. "I say pool. There's more hot chicks in bikinis." He raised his eyebrows up and down knowingly at Paxton.

"Seriously Aiden?" Amina tried to smack him upside the head but he moved out of the way.

"What, I'm a guy. I can't help it." Aiden looked expectantly at Paxton who had been quietly listening the whole time. "Your turn."

"Oh, I didn't know I was playing."

"Of course you are. Name two things to pick from. They have to be something we can never get again or are rare."

CHAPTER 6

"Okay." Paxton put his hand to his chin as he thought of what to ask. "Ummm . . . beach or mountains?"

There was a moment of silence. Of all the things to bring up, he had to bring up places to live?

Finally Maya spoke, "Beach. I love the waves." Josiah and Aiden agreed, but Amina still didn't answer.

"Amina? What do you choose?" Paxton looked at her as if he already knew the answer.

What game was he playing? He knew her answer would be mountains. During their time visiting in the hospital, Amina had let it slip a few times about how she wished she could live with the Hebrews and about how she used to go camping all the time.

She could feel his gaze, as if he were trying to tell her something. Did he already know her plan?

Amina opened her mouth but then thought twice about saying anything. Her mind was once again frazzled and anxious. She knew time was running out and still she hadn't changed the elders' minds. Amina stood and walked off.

"Aw come on Amina." She could hear Aiden call after her. "He didn't mean anything by it."

"I'm tired Aiden, I'm going to bed." She called back but didn't look at the group.

"Every party has a pooper and the-"

"Shut up Aiden!" She was tempted to go back and slug him, but she knew if she went back, Paxton would probably try to apologize or explain himself and Amina wasn't in the mood anymore.

"Did I say something wrong?" Paxton asked as he continued

to watch Amina walk away.

"Naw, she just gets emotional sometimes." Aiden brushed off his sister's sudden shift in mood.

"It could have something to do with her idea," Josiah remarked.

Aiden looked at Josiah with uncertainty. "What idea?"

"About us no longer being safe here because the Myriad are moving in. She wants us to leave."

Aiden looked at Maya and Paxton, hoping they knew what Josiah was talking about.

"Where would we go?" Maya inquired.

"To the mountains," Josiah spoke nonchalantly.

Aiden slowly nodded his head as realization hit him.

Maya was now the one to look perplexed. "Why would we go there? It can't be any safer than where we are now. And how would we live? The land is barren."

"I know how," Paxton spoke. He looked wary, hearing this for the first time. "She wants me to lead you to the Hebrews, doesn't she?" Josiah nodded. "Both the land and the people are protected by Sabaoth. It is its own oasis there. Untouched by the desolation."

"Is that something you're willing to do?" Maya leaned forward, a new-found excitement flashed across her pale face.

Paxton was quiet. He opened his mouth as if to speak and then closed it again.

Aiden could see Paxton's discomfort. "Let's not put so much pressure on him just yet." Aiden jumped to his defense. "We don't even know if the elders will go for it."

Josiah crossed his arms. "Considering your sister's outburst last week, I don't believe the elders are too keen on listening to her ideas anymore." Josiah stood. "Either way, the town meeting is tomorrow and we'll know more. They have been assessing all the past Myriad attacks and forming a plan to strengthen security. I'll see you all then, I'm heading to bed."

Aiden motioned for Paxton to follow him to his tent. "You'll be rooming with me until we can find you more permanent living quarters."

"I hope not too permanent. I don't plan on staying here forever."

"Of course not." Aiden waved at Maya. "Night Maya."

"Goodnight boys." She waved before standing and leaving.

Aiden and Paxton walked to the far west end of Dwelling Three where rows of tents were assembled. Aiden stopped in front of one small army green tent and held back the flap to let Paxton in first.

There was a table to eat and next to that was a rolled up sleeping mat, a pillow, and a note from Amina: *Found this for Paxton.*

Aiden pulled the rope off the sleeping mat and it immediately sprung open. Aiden had to turn his mat horizontal in the tent so that Paxton's mat could fit beside it. It was a tight fit, but they'd make due.

"Hey, thanks for letting me stay with you," Paxton said as he grabbed the pillow and fluffed it.

"Sure thing. I haven't had a roommate since I was a teen at summer camp. It'll be nice to have the extra company."

Aiden pulled an extra blanket out of a crate. It was a small and thin green blanket. He felt bad giving it to Paxton, but it was all he had.

"We'll find you something better tomorrow."

"That's fine."

The two settled into their beds and were quiet the rest of the night.

The next day Aiden made his way to Dwelling Two where they were holding sanctioned self-defense classes for all interested citizens. From the first day Aiden had heard about this class he wanted to join, but now, having joined Terrance's group, he wanted to get a head start with his training. He still hadn't heard from Terrance or anyone in the group about the next meeting and he was getting antsy.

Aiden glanced around the room. It was his first day joining and he wanted to scope out the crowd. He saw Terrance and Jared at the sparring mat warming up with some light wrestling. Several scavengers clustered together talking, including Seth, and then he saw his Uncle Paul.

Aiden waved. "Hey Uncle Paul, over here."

Paul smiled at Aiden and greeted him with a hug. "I'm glad you decided to come. This is a good class. You'll learn a lot."

"I hope so."

Aiden watched as Jared flipped Terrance on his back and pinned him. Sweat dripped off the hair that hung in Jared's face as he refused to let Terrance out of his firm pin, despite Terrance's efforts.

Terrance shouted at Jared to let him up and when he still wouldn't, Terrance jabbed Jared hard under the ribs with his fingers. Jared flinched and loosened his grip enough for Terrance to wriggle his way out. When he stood, he gave Jared a swift kick in the butt. Jared snapped his head in Terrance's direction and scowled.

Aiden didn't know what was going on between the two of them and he didn't want to find out.

CHAPTER 6

Once Terrance walked away, Jared stood and walked to a bench where his water bottle set. He took a swig of the water and then poured the rest on his head, allowing the water to stream down his face and neck.

"Alright everyone, it's time to get started." Jared's voice boomed. He toweled himself off, surveying the room. He seemed distracted by something.

Those who were there for the class meandered closer and either stood or squatted, awaiting Jared's instructions.

Jared clasped his hands behind his back and began his lesson. "Welcome to self-defense 101. If you came to my last session, thanks for coming back. I'm glad I didn't scare you off. For those of you who are new, I'm going to start by telling you what I told the others. Life is a gift, but it's also unpredictable. In the world we live in, there might come a day where you are attacked without warning. This can be alarming, but not if you are prepared. Self-defense helps to prepare you for those unexpected situations and could save your life."

A guy, probably a few years younger than Aiden, raised his hand. "So, when do we get to kick someone's ass?" The others beside him quietly chuckled.

"You think you're ready for that, tough guy?"

"Yeah, punching and fighting aren't all that difficult."

Jared tilted his head. With a cocked eyebrow, he smirked. "Alright. What's your name?"

"Huxley."

"Alright, Huxley, come up here. Let's fight."

Huxley's confidence faltered for just a second, but he stepped forward and faced Jared on the sparring mat. He planted his feet firmly and held his fists up in front of his face. There was a slight sway to his movement as he seemed to be hyping himself up for a good fight.

Jared stood tall and confident with his hands at his sides. He nodded at Huxley, indicating he was ready to begin.

Again Huxley glanced at the others, uncertain for just a moment. Then he faced Jared and moved forward to take his first swing.

Huxley let out a loud grunt as he swung his right fist hard and fast, but he didn't make contact. Jared was faster and dodged out of the way with ease. This continued several times. Huxley would charge and swing and Jared would dart and dodge. Huxley's face grew red with rage and the veins in his neck bulged.

"Are you ready to give up?" Jared asked calmly.

"No way, you haven't even tried to fight me."

"If I did, you'd be down in one hit. You're too heavy and too predictable. You can't fight with brute force and anger. Sure, you might get in a few good punches, but in the end, you'll lose to any professionally trained fighter." Jared gave up on Huxley and turned his attention toward the group. "Now, to be a good fighter you must start with a solid foundation."

Huxley, fuming with rage, lowered his head and charged Jared from behind. Aiden was certain Jared had no idea, but as Huxley drew closer, Jared spun to his right grabbing Huxley by the neck and arm. Using Huxley's momentum, Jared was able to bring Huxley down to the ground and dig his knee into Huxley's back while still holding his neck and twisting his arm in a way that looked unnatural. Huxley let out a yelp that echoed through the room. Several people stopped what they were doing to look at the commotion.

"I think you've had enough, Huxley." Jared stood, leaving Huxley breathing heavily from getting the wind knocked out of him. "Now, where was I? Right, self-defense." Jared peered down at Huxley. "Thank you for being our first example." He looked at the group and went on to explain how to use the momentum of the attacker for your own benefit.

Huxley slowly got up and hobbled over to the group, holding his arm and scowling at Jared, his pride more injured than his body.

For the next two hours Aiden spent his time listening and practicing self-defense tactics with his uncle. He learned that he was a lot better at self-defense than he expected, and he liked the strength and confidence it gave him.

By the end of the session Aiden was worn out. He and Paul sat on the ground and leaned against the concrete dome.

Aiden rested his hands on his knees and fumbled with the hole in his pants. He wanted to ask his uncle about the militia group and get his opinion about it, but he wasn't sure how to bring it up. "Hey Uncle," he started, "what made you join the self-defense class?"

"Honestly, I just felt it was time to use more than just my mind to protect my family. I don't think we'll be able to stay safe down here for much longer."

Aiden bit the side of his cheek. "So if you had the chance to do something more to help protect our community, would you do it?"

Paul tilted his head. "More than this class? It depends, what are you thinking?"

This was his chance. "What do you think about building a militia where we actually prepare to fight against the Myriad and defend our home?" When Paul didn't say anything to oppose him, Aiden continued. "They're only getting more aggressive and I'm not sure staying on the defense is such a great idea anymore. Maybe it's time we fight back." Aiden looked at Paul expectantly as Paul sat rubbing his goatee. There was such a pregnant pause that Aiden second guessed himself. *Maybe telling Uncle Paul wasn't such a good idea after all.* "Hypothetically of course," Aiden added.

"You pose a striking notion. We elders have always held to the ideal that we ought to be pacifists. I've often questioned it myself, and I've searched the Sacred Book and there are arguments for both sides. To fight or not to fight." Paul chuckled to himself. "If you have the conviction and the drive to do more, I support that, but make sure it's done the right way."

"What do you mean?"

"I mean it needs to be under the oversight of the coalition and approved by the elders."

"Right, of course." Inside Aiden was doing a little dance. It was encouraging to hear his uncle approve of such a thing and confirmed that joining the militia was the right path.

Chapter 7

The bridges were covered with people packed together like sardines all looking to the third level where the elders stood on a large platform.

It was their monthly town meeting, so everyone was there to hear any new updates or changes to life in the tunnels and what was happening above ground.

Amina still hadn't talked to Paxton about her plan, nor had she found anyone to side with her idea, but she wasn't going to give up. Seeing everyone coming together reminded her that each of them was her brother and sister and she ached with the thought of something bad happening to them.

Amina jumped onto a ladder and climbed to the next level just as the crowd erupted in a unified, "AMEN!"

Amina climbed onto the catwalk and pushed her way through the crowd until she found herself against the railing toward the middle edge of the dome. She tried to listen as Matthias droned on about food rationing and needing new ideas for where to find food.

"If anyone has ideas as to where we can hunt down new food, or would like to do reconnaissance, come see us in our chambers after the meeting is over.

"Now on to some alarming news. Over the last several weeks

several of our scavengers have had some close calls with the Myriad. We fear that they may be getting closer to finding us."

Alarm rose through the crowd. People looked at one another and murmured. Amina heard the worried comments all around her.

Matthias held up a hand to settle the crowd. "Now I know that this is alarming, but the elders ask that you stay calm. We have a plan and we want to reassure you that nothing bad will happen to us." Matthias motioned for an elder to step forward. A stout woman with gray streaked hair pulled back into a bun and almond shaped eyes stepped forward. "Josephine will explain everything to you." The two switched spots and Josephine proceeded to lay out the new protocols and projects that were meant to bolster security.

Amina listened to Josephine, waiting for the right moment to speak. All the new protocols and projects sounded good in theory, but would they work? They seemed more like temporary fixes. You can't put a band-aid on a gash that needs stitches.

When it was time to open the floor to questions, Amina didn't hesitate. "You talked about an escape route you want to build, but how and where do you plan on re-establishing community life if we are forced to escape?" Amina spoke with a booming voice that echoed loudly. She knew the dome's acoustics well and where she was standing was the perfect place for her voice to be heard by everyone. People looked around, trying to match a face with the voice. She had their attention. Before Josephine could answer, Amina continued. "Because I know of a place where we can go right now and not have to wait until the last minute to flee. A place where we can be safe and have an abundance of food. Fresh food. Enough

CHAPTER 7

food that no one will ever go hungry again until the end of our days."

Excitement filled Amina as she saw the crowd nodding and smiling. They were curious, they were anxious, and they were yearning for a better option. "Tell us!" "How can this be?" "What must we do?" Amina heard them shouting and it gave her confidence. Amina thought she heard Matthias say something, but she ignored it.

"There is a place in the mountains where we would be safe from the deadly hunt of the Myriad. A place protected by Sabaoth himself."

"She speaks of the village of the Hebrews!" Someone called out. Amina searched for the disembodied voice. Shockingly, it was her aunt. Mo came to her side and placed a reassuring hand on her shoulder.

"That's nonsense!" "They don't exist!" The crowd shouted.

Bolstered by Mo's support, Amina fought against the doubts. "It's not nonsense. If you would just believe, we can leave these dingy tunnels and find our way to a land where we can grow more crops and live life in the light again."

The crowd laughed and jeered at her idea. She was losing them.

Matthias jumped in, trying to put a stop to Amina's words. "Enough with all this nonsense. We all know the Hebrews are a myth. If we left here, we'd all be dead within a day or wander the mountains until we died of starvation."

"We'll succumb to the same fate if we stay."

"I assure you that will *not* happen. We are doing everything we can to keep everyone safe, as Josephine explained. We have more coalition officers posted at entrances, more security cameras have been placed, and we've expanded our perimeter.

If anyone gets within 500 yards of an entrance, we'll be notified."

"What if that's not enough?" Mo queried.

"I assure you, we will do everything we can to find new ways to keep you safe and if the time comes to find a new home, then we will. But for now, we are safe. Trust Sabaoth."

"Instead of waiting, we should take action!" A male voice from below yelled and several others agreed.

Amina was strengthened by the other voices and continued talking. "I have proof that the Hebrews are real. There is one among us right now who can lead us to his village, to safety."

At those words the crowd erupted into conversation. Some had excitement and hope in their voices while others were laughing and crying out for proof. Soon the talk turned to arguing and they were shouting more vehemently. Amina's eyes widened, concerned that she had incited a mob.

"Where is this so-called Hebrew of yours?" "We need proof!" "Show us!" "How can we trust you?"

Amina scanned the crowd below, hoping to find Paxton in the midst of them. That's when she felt a hand on her shoulder. Instinctively she grabbed the wrist, and as she spun around, she twisted the person's arm and put them in a tight wrist lock. She saw the pain in their eyes but didn't relent. It took her a moment to realize it was not an attacker but Paxton. Her eyes softened as she let go and backed away.

"Sorry, instinct."

Paxton straightened rubbing his wrist. "What are you doing? We can't take all these people to my village. They'll never allow it."

"I have to do something. If I get enough people on my side, the elders will have to say yes."

CHAPTER 7

Amina hoped Mo would side take her side and encourage her to keep going. Mo nodded at Amina and then turned to the crowd. "My family, please, there is no need for arguing." The arguing slowly died down. "We have been through incomprehensible times the past nine years, and I know it's terrifying, but we must unite together to overcome this. And we must have faith in our great Sabaoth who cares for us."

Amina grabbed Paxton by the arm and pulled him to the rail shouting, "This is Paxton, the Hebrew." Amina avoided Paxton's glare burning into her.

The crowd grew even louder and more divided.

Matthias snarled. "We don't know this man. He could be lying to you. He is merely a prisoner we found lurking in our field. How can-"

"That's not true and you know it! This man can lead us to a better place. A safer home." Amina yelled back, her entire body now shaking with rage. How dare he lie like that.

"That is quite enough from you." Matthias turned to calm the crowd with his soothing words.

Amina had to think fast. She needed to convince them. If Paxton wasn't enough, what would make them believe? "What if I got proof?" Amina yelled, her voice high pitched and strained. "Would that convince you that the Hebrews are real?"

"Not possible!" The crowd broke into loud shouts of denial. She had lost. She couldn't persuade them. This was the most crucial debate of her entire life. One that really was a matter of life and death and she failed. Amina let out an exasperated sigh.

Mo squeezed her shoulder. "We'll figure out another way. I believe in you."

Amina was thrown by the support, but was too infuriated by Matthias to acknowledge Mo at that moment. Instead she stormed off, heading to nowhere in particular.

She should have known that one person could not convince an entire crowd, especially one so inadequate as herself. It was high school debate class all over again. She felt herself shrinking inside, quivering even. Her face flushed, her throat constricted, and her eyes welled. She tried to shove the tears of anger down, to tell herself that she couldn't give up. She had to persevere, but at that moment, it felt hopeless. And while she was thankful for Aunt Mo's support, she felt the fight was too big for the two of them to take on alone.

Amina let out a cry of frustration as she kicked a small rock lying on the ground. It flew down the tunnel into the darkness and clanged as it bounced to a stop. Amina leaned against the wall and slid down till she was crouching. She rested her head on her knees and let the tears come. They were silent tears. Tears of frustration, fear, and maybe a little sadness.

Maybe she should just give up. If trying to take the entire community was too much and people didn't want to go, she could just take her family and Paxton.

"Amina." A quiet voice above her spoke. It was Paxton, he had finally caught up to her.

Amina kept her head down, hiding her tear-stained face. "What?"

"Look, I'm sorry I couldn't be of more help, but-"

"No, you're not." Amina wiped her face with both hands as she looked at Paxton. "Why would you care about a bunch of strangers? You just want to leave here and go home, back to what's familiar, right?"

Paxton sat beside her. "It's not that I don't care. We're

still one in the same, aren't we? We're waiting for the same Sabaoth to come take us away. I should think that makes us family."

"If you feel that way then why didn't you help?"

"For starters, you kinda took me off guard. I wasn't expecting it. And, well," he paused for a moment with his mouth open, trying to find his next words, "I don't know if I can return home because . . . I don't remember how to get there."

Amina stood. "Then you're of no help to me. Apology not accepted. I'll just find another way." She started down the tunnel again.

Paxton stood and followed. "Amina don't be that way."

Amina didn't stop but eventually, Paxton's footsteps did.

Back in Dwelling Three, Amina felt a little calmer but no less defeated. She saw Aiden and the others standing by the fire talking, but she ignored them and headed toward her tent. Inside she laid on her mat. It wasn't long before she heard a quiet voice calling her name.

"Amina, can we talk?" Aiden asked with concern.

She didn't move. "Why?"

"Because . . . after what you pulled at the meeting . . . well, I think you need to tell me what's going on in that head of yours."

Amina rolled her eyes. She was in no mood to talk, but it was her brother. Her blood. She couldn't say no. Amina got up and came out of the tent. "Fine, but just us. I'm not interested in spewing my guts to anyone else." She crossed her arms as she walked back into her tent.

Aiden followed her inside. "Fine by me." He stopped just inside the tent and shook his head. "It's crazy. All this time I flip flopped as to whether to believe that the Hebrews really existed. And now . . ."

"So, you believe me?"

"Of course, I believe you. You are many things Amina, but a liar is not one of them." Aiden paused and gave Amina a thoughtful look. It was one of those looks of deep love and concern, the kind that said, *I'm worried about you and your choices.* And said, *if you don't wise up, you're going to get yourself hurt.* Finally, Aiden spoke. "So . . . you thought you could take on the entire village?"

"Not take on, I just thought I could convince them. The elders certainly aren't listening. I thought maybe the rest of the village would be convinced of the truth." That's when Amina spewed everything that had happened and everything she was thinking. Why she felt they were in such danger. How she knew, based on what Paxton told her and what she'd read in the Sacred Book that they would be safe in the mountains. Then she shared about her vision and that she was convinced this was what Sabaoth wanted.

As she shared everything on her heart Aiden quietly listened, taking it all in. He had always been a good listener. Amina came to the end of her rant and looked at Aiden expectantly.

He took his time to respond. He was cautious with his words, never wanting to come off the wrong way when he shared. "So, I hear what you're saying sis, and it's a noble cause, but it's a bad idea. It's too dangerous out there and honestly pointless. How do you know that by the time you get there and back that we won't already be gone?"

"I don't, but I still have to try."

"No, you don't. You have to trust."

Amina laughed. "Trust who? The elders? No thank you."

Aiden let his arms fall by his side and his eyes softened. "No,

CHAPTER 7

trust Sabaoth."

Amina was quiet. Aiden was always good at going for the heart of the issue. He could see right through Amina's fear. She looked away. Aiden's eyes were too empathetic and made her feel guilty. He didn't mean to do it. He just had a way of seeing into her soul. It must be a twin thing because he was the only one who could do that to her. Sometimes, they could have an entire conversation without even speaking.

She sat down on her small stool and put her head in her hands. "But isn't that what I'm doing? I believe the dream I had is from Sabaoth. I have faith that this is what he wants us to do. So why don't you trust me?" A lump formed in her throat.

Aiden knelt down and put a hand on his sister's shoulder. "Not all dreams are signs from Sabaoth. Sometimes they're just coincidental, our subconscious revealing our deepest desires."

Amina stood again and brushed past Aiden's touch. "I have to do this. I can't sit around and hope Mashiakh comes before the Myriad do. It's been nine years; he's still not here."

"I understand, but I also think you need to have a little more faith that Mashiakh will come for us. He doesn't break promises, ever. I will pray that he restores faith in you." Aiden stood and smiled broadly. "Now, who's ready for some Evoeball?"

Amina raised her eyebrows. "Really? Now?"

"Yeah, we were just talking about it before you came over, and *you* need some cheering. Let's take a minute and just not think about anything of importance, except for how we're going to crush Josiah and Maya again."

"I don't know, Aiden."

Aiden slung his arm around his sister and pulled her close. "Aw come on little sis, you need more fun in your life."

Amina pointed her finger into Aiden's chest. "Don't call me that. We're the same-"

Aiden slowly backed away and gave her a smile. "What's wrong, *little sis?*"

"Oh, I'm going to get you." Before Amina could move, Aiden took off toward the center of the dome. Amina sprinted after him shouting for him to come back, daring him to call her little sis one more time.

Aiden slowed as he reached the firepit and picked up a ball that he tossed at Amina as hard as he could. She was quick though and caught the ball before it smacked her in the face.

Amina flinched to make Aiden think she was going to chase him again and when he turned to run, she launched the ball at him, hitting him square in the back. He let out a pained grunt as he arched his back from the impact. His speed slowed down allowing Amina to catch up to him. She quickly pressed against the backs of his knees with her foot, causing his legs to buckle, and he fell to his hands and knees. Amina jumped on him and pinned him down smiling with victory. "Now what did you want to call me?"

Aiden forced a smile. "The best twin sister ever."

"That's what I thought." Amina laughed and helped Aiden to his feet. Aiden dusted the dirt off his slightly too small shirt and ratty jeans while Amina looked at the others. They were staring at her warily. It wasn't as if chasing down and fighting Aiden was anything unusual, but perhaps, given the events of the town meeting, everyone was a little wary of Amina and her emotions.

"What are you guys staring at? Let's play some Evoeball."

CHAPTER 7

"But we have an odd number now, we'll need one more person," Maya stated.

"I can sit out," Paxton suggested. He must've joined the group after Amina left him. "I don't know how to play."

Amina shrugged. "Suit yourself." Grabbing the ball, she tossed it to Josiah, you two can start, you need the extra advantage."

Josiah crouched into position. "Oh, is that right?"

Amina did the same getting ready to face off. "You know it is. How many have we won compared to you?"

With that said, Josiah faked left and took off right, down the imaginary field and toward the empty barrel they used as a goal. Amina quickly recovered from the fake and charged after him, but before she could get to him, he bounced the ball to Maya who took a shot. It landed with a loud clang inside the trash can. Josiah ran over and high-fived Maya, then he looked at Amina and laughed. "I'm sorry, who needs the advantage?"

"I see you've been practicing. Not bad, but it'll be your only goal."

"We'll see about that." Josiah passed Amina the ball for her to start the next round. They each made their way back to their original positions. Josiah and Amina squared off, glaring at one another, seeing if they could read what the other was about to do.

Without ever taking her eyes off Josiah or really moving at all, Amina rolled the ball to her left. Confused Josiah looked behind him and saw Aiden now with the ball and was dribbling it with his feet down the field. Maya quickly caught up with Aiden and blocked him from continuing, but before she could get the ball away, Aiden kicked the ball high in the air toward Amina. She jumped and caught it. As she landed, she quickly took off toward the goal and took a shot. It went in. Amina held her hands up in victory. "Goal!!!!" She ran around the trash can and back toward Josiah so she could shout in his face. Josiah playfully pushed her away.

"Hey, we're just getting started," Josiah insisted.

"So am I." Amina crouched into her defensive position like a leopard ready to pounce.

The game went on for about an hour. Sprinting, leaping, dribbling, and throwing. It was an unusual sport that mixed basketball and soccer. It was something they had made up years ago to help pass the time. Aiden was a big basketball fan and Josiah loved soccer, but when the two couldn't decide which to play, they compromised by playing both at the same time. The first game of evoeball was more of a free for all, but over time they developed a few rules. Word spread and now the game is played throughout the entire underground, with some variances.

Even now, that game constantly changes. Some days they played with four players, other times a big group played teams up to seven each. Once they had so many people, they tried playing with three teams and three goals. Another time they had multiple balls and they decided to mix in some dodge ball with the regular rules. It was an ever-evolving game, hence the name, and all that really mattered was that it kept them active and kept their mind off reality for a while.

The game ended with Amina and Aiden once again winning, although it was the closest score they'd ever had, 30-28. The group sat down next to Paxton exhausted and breathing heavily.

Aiden flopped onto his back and let out a loud breath. "That was a good game."

CHAPTER 7

"The best we've ever played I'd say." Maya sat down beside Aiden and pulled out a handkerchief to wipe the sweat off her forehead.

Josiah grabbed his canteen next to the pit and opened the lid. He took a large gulp, then passed it along.

Amina took a swig of the water and then poured some on her hand to smear over her face. "I still like kick boxing better, but this is a close second." Amina handed Aiden the water and then leaned back on her elbows.

"Yeah and we almost had you beat this time," Josiah remarked.

"Almost, but not quite," Aiden chimed in.

Maya was the last to take a sip of water.

The five of them talked a while longer before Maya finally called it a night. They all said their goodbyes before taking off to their own tents to rest. Tonight was their night to scavenge and they wanted to make sure they were well rested.

Just as Amina was making her way back to her tent, she saw Mo and Paul climbing down the ladder into the dome. Amina slowed her gate and watched as they made their way toward her. When they stopped Amina looked at them confused.

"Amina," Paul spoke first. "Can we speak with you privately?"

"That depends, are you here to scold me for going off the rails?" she asked, hiding her worry with annoyance.

"Of course not, Amina." Paul looked at Mo and then back to her. "What you did today was very brave, speaking out for what you believe."

"And very stupid," Mo chimed in, "but brave."

"Okay, thanks?" Amina was taken off guard by their complimentary attitudes, but still wary. She was waiting for the other shoe to drop.

"So, can we talk?"

Amina nodded and led them to her tent. Once inside Amina and Mo sat on the two stools while Paul stood.

Amina was still uncertain about the purpose of their visit and waited impatiently for one of them to speak.

Mo was first. "Were you serious about wanting to go and bring back real proof of the Hebrews' existence?"

Amina's eyes lit up. "Of course, I was."

"Good," Mo nodded her head. "I spoke with your uncle and convinced him that you should go."

Amina stared at them. Her eyes grew wide and the corners of her mouth turned up just barely. "I'm sorry, you *want* me to go find proof. But I thought Matthias-"

Paul held up a hand to stop her. "Never you mind about Matthias. For now, I think it would be best for you and Paxton to go to the Hebrews, tell them of our situation, and when you come back, you must bring us proof."

"What kind of proof?"

"I'm not sure, but I trust you will figure that out when you're there."

"How long will it take you?" Mo inquired.

Amina was still shocked that she was actually being given permission, orders actually, to go find the Hebrews. She was so certain that her window of opportunity had shut, but then to hear her Aunt Mo on her side. Amina opened her mouth and then closed it again remembering what Paxton said earlier about not remembering how to get there. "I'm guessing a couple of weeks," she lied.

"Good," Paul spoke. "While the two of you go there, we will continue to fortify our security here in case of any attacks.

Sabaoth willing, we will be safe and protected long enough for you to get back and get us out of here. We're counting on you, Amina."

"I won't fail."

With that Mo and Paul turned to leave but before they left the tent, Amina stopped them. "Wait, Aunt Mo, what convinced you to take my side?"

Mo smiled sweetly. "I too have been feeling unsettled about our time down in the tunnels. And after hearing your plea, I was certain that this was an answer to my prayers. I knew I had to convince your uncle to do something about it."

This time Amina didn't hide her smile. She had people on her side, people who believed in her. Amina crossed to Mo and hugged her. It was the first hug Amina initiated with her aunt in more than nine years. At first Amina felt Mo stiffen, but she soon settled into the hug and wrapped her arms around Amina.

"Sabaoth be with you, Amina."

Amina hugged her uncle as well before they left the tiny tent. Finally, everything was falling into place. But as soon as Amina's heart soared, it came crashing back down again. How was she going to find this place? If Paxton couldn't remember, she was going to need another plan and quickly. Her people were counting on her.

Chapter 8

Rrinnnngggg.

Amina's wind up timer went off, pulling her out of a deep sleep. She felt groggy and wanted to roll over and fall back asleep, but she knew that wasn't an option.

Amina pulled herself out of bed and threw on her boots, black leather jacket, and then tied a black handkerchief around her neck. She pulled some mouthwash off her tiny bookshelf and took a swig. She had found it one night on a raid and decided to keep it for herself. She swished the minty liquid around in her mouth and it burned. When she couldn't stand it anymore, she spit the mouthwash into her chamber pot, grabbed her rucksack, and headed to the firepit. The fire was much smaller than last night but still glowing.

Josiah and Aiden were already at the pit, and as she approached, Paxton walked up.

Amina looked at him questioning, but it was Josiah who spoke first. "What are you doing here?"

"I want to help."

"I'm not sure it's safe for you."

"I have skills, and I can be another set of eyes."

Amina considered his proposal. It would be nice to have an extra set of hands to carry back even more food. While she was still slightly annoyed at his lack of support yesterday, she could tell he was trying to make amends.

"He should come with us." Amina decided.

Josiah and Aiden stared at her baffled.

"Isn't he supposed to be under house arrest?" Aiden queried.

Amina crossed her arms. "I was put in charge of watching him. I'll take responsibility."

"I won't get in the way. I just want to help," Paxton insisted.

After a moment of what seemed to be Josiah agonizing with himself, he finally agreed.

The group took off toward the west tunnel just as Maya was running to catch up. When she saw Paxton she paused a moment. "Is he coming too?"

Josiah furrowed his brow. "Yes." Before she could respond he jumped onto the ladder and started climbing.

Above ground Amina breathed in the air. It wasn't the cleanest, it wreaked of sulfur and smoke, but it was cleaner than the stagnant smell of sewage. She was certain everyone below ground was dying a slow death from mold toxins.

Once everyone was out of the manhole, Maya closed it. Without a sound the group made their way through the field and toward the highway. The night was dead. No cars, no crickets, nothing. Even their footsteps seemed muted, as if Amina had cotton stuffed in her ears. The lighting wasn't any better. Amina looked into the sky. It was so much darker than it had once been. The moon was a dim reddish color and there were half the stars as usual. When the Great Desolation began, astronomers noticed an unusual amount of stars burning out for no scientific reason. The phenomena baffled them, along with every other cursed disaster that had happened since. It came to a point that astronomers and other scientists stopped trying to give explanations to what was happening and chalked it up to the universe disintegrating.

As they approached the highway, they came across a graveyard of cars, chunks of old highway, and occasionally animal and human skeletons.

When Tievel required everyone to relocate, certain decimated highways were patched and used only for delivery trucks and Myriad patrol units.

The group followed along the edge of the highway, using the cars as cover, keeping their eyes peeled for patrolling Myriad units.

Eventually they all made it inside an old restaurant. Aiden stayed outside as the lookout while the others walked through the broken door as stealthily as a SWAT unit invading a criminal's home. Once they checked and cleared all the rooms, Amina felt her body relax as she went to the kitchen and started opening cabinets.

Paxton was still standing at the kitchen door looking lost. Amina gave him a signal that meant, start looking. Paxton moved toward what seemed to be the refrigerator and tried to open it. It didn't budge. He kept trying and when it still wouldn't move Josiah and Amina went to help him. It took a moment but they finally got the old metal door to pull open and when they did the most hideous smell leaked out.

Amina's stomach wrenched and she had to walk away. Paxton ran to a sink and threw up in it while Josiah quickly pulled his handkerchief over his face.

Amina pulled her own handkerchief over her nose and held it tightly. Once composed, Amina stepped into the fridge. Using a flashlight she started looking around the shelves for anything that might be canned. It was unlikely, but it never hurt to look.

CHAPTER 8

Most of what they found were jugs of curdled milk, boxes of meat that were covered in green and blue mold, and green slimy produce riddled with maggots.

Josiah joined her in the search but didn't dare touch anything. As the two of them poked around Amina came across cans of coconut milk, olives, and a few different varieties of vegetables. It was peculiar to find them in a fridge but at that moment, Amina didn't care about the lack of logic. There was probably more food there than what the five of them could carry, which meant they had food for days. Amina motioned for Josiah to come over. She could see the smile spread across his face under his handkerchief and his eyes lit up. Amina smiled back and then started filling her large rucksack with as much as it could hold, while Josiah went to get Maya and Paxton.

Once Amina's bag was full, she helped Josiah and Maya fill theirs. Amina slung her giant load over her shoulders and headed out to grab Paxton's bag. She assumed he couldn't stomach the smell. Amina scanned the kitchen but didn't see Paxton anywhere.

She walked into the dining area search for Paxton, and heard Aiden's high-pitched whistle warning them that someone was coming. Amina ducked behind a booth and waited. Chills spread across her body as tiny hairs prickled the back of her neck. She hated these encounters. A Humvee rolled by with its large search light swiveling around in all directions. Amina prayed they didn't have a drone with them tonight.

Even after the light disappeared and she could no longer her the Humvee's engine, Amina stayed crouched in position in case there was a second Humvee or footmen. After waiting another long five minutes, Aiden gave a short whistle for the all-clear.

Amina let out a breath of relief. After one failed look around for Paxton, Amina headed to Aiden's hiding spot inside the dumpster. She tapped on it three times, paused, and then tapped two more times before she jumped inside.

"Hey," she whispered, squatting inside the empty dumpster. "We found a ton of cans. Good stuff too. Go fill up."

"Okay." Before Aiden left, Amina felt him press a small device against her arm. She took it and held it to her face. They were night vision infrared binoculars. She scanned the area all around and then whispered, "All clear."

Aiden opened the lid and jumped out, leaving her alone.

Amina continued to scan slowly back and forth, looking for any sign of movement. The patrol units seemed to have no set pattern or schedule, so they could appear at any moment and in any capacity, including drones with infrared. Those were the worst. It happened only once before, to another team, but Amina knew it was a possibility.

As Amina scanned the perimeter, slowly moving in a counter-clockwise direction, she froze at the sight of movement behind the building. She zoomed in to make sure it wasn't a stray cat, and when she did, she noticed it was Paxton heading into the building. Amina fumed. Could he really be that ignorant to the danger above ground? He was putting everyone at risk by being out in the open.

Amina continued scanning but she was livid. She saw a head moving inside the restaurant and then a hand raise with two fingers. They were finished inside and ready to leave.

Amina finished her scan, going slowly; if she missed anything, anything at all, they could be dead.

Once she was certain the coast was clear she let out a spurt of three short, quick whistles. Amina jumped out of the dumpster and met them behind an old school bus.

The most dangerous time to be above ground was when they were heading to and from the tunnels. They had to be on high alert and keep their eyes open. Especially coming back with so much food, they couldn't move as fast, and they didn't want to risk being spotted and have to abandon everything. If they had to drop food, it was likely they'd never find it again.

One at a time they moved from the bus to a suburban, then climbed over the center divider toward a sports car. Unfortunately, Amina caught sight of two clothed skeletons inside who appeared to be holding hands. She quickly looked away, feeling her chest tighten.

When the coast was clear, they sprinted across the highway and into the ditch before any new patrol units came. They continued to use the cars on the opposite side of the highway as cover until they were able to reach the crater-filled field.

The rest of the way, Maya lingered behind to ensure they weren't being followed.

The journey back always felt longer, but finally, Josiah knelt down and opened the hidden manhole for everyone to climb down.

Safely inside, Amina walked over to Paxton infuriated. "What were you doing outside? Don't you realize how much of a risk that was?"

Paxton was taken off guard and stuttered a response, "I-it was disgusting inside. I just thought- I needed fresh air. Look it turned out fine, didn't it?"

"No thanks to you."

"We're all okay Amina, nothing happened," Aiden remarked. "Let's just get this food to the others.

"Whatever." Amina charged past everyone and took off

down the tunnel. Sure they were lucky that time, but what if he'd been seen? Paxton put the entire group in jeopardy and he didn't seem to care.

Aiden and Paxton sat in the tent, waiting for the water to boil for his peppermint tea. It had become a tradition that after raids, Aiden would have a cup of tea and then take a nap. Of course, today he'd have to skip the nap because he had to report to the cleaning crew, but he had some time to still fit in his cup of tea.

Aiden poured the hot water, added a couple drops of peppermint oil, and handed Paxton a cup. "Here, it'll soothe your stomach."

Paxton took the cup and blew on it. "Thanks. I don't usually drink tea, but I could use something to calm my nerves. I never realized how stressful it is to go scavenging."

"Tell me about it. And that was an easy raid. Sometimes they go much longer or we see more Myriad patrolling. Every time we go out there, we never know what to expect."

"Do you go every day?"

Aiden shook his head. "We don't, but there are multiple crews and we all rotate. I don't think I would last if I had to do that every night. I'd never sleep."

"What about places? How do you find resources and know where to go?"

"It's hit or miss. Sometimes we go to the same place if we know it has a lot of food, but once it's out, we have to find somewhere new, but we always try to stay as far on the outskirts as possible. Although, as food runs out, we'll have to venture closer to the border." Aiden took another sip of his tea. He breathed in deeply, feeling the cooling after effects of the peppermint run down his throat.

Paxton leaned forward onto his elbows. "Have you ever considered hitting a delivery truck?"

Aiden laughed, not because it was funny, but because he was so startled by the suggestion. "We couldn't possibly. It's way too dangerous."

"But what happens when the food runs out?"

Aiden shrugged. He hoped it would never come to that—that Mashiakh would come for them before their food supply ran out.

Aiden took one last swig of his tea and then stood. "I gotta get going. It's time for my punishment job."

"Can I come along?"

"You want to come clean sludge?"

Paxton shrugged. "What else am I going to do?"

"Anything."

"I don't really know anyone here, and there's only so much napping and whittling I can do while the rest of you are out working. I need something new to do."

"Suit yourself." Why anyone would choose to clean over having free time was a puzzle to him, but he wasn't about to argue.

As Paxton and Aiden headed out the door, they spotted Josiah and Amina.

"Hey wait up!" Aiden shouted after them. They stopped and waited. "Ready for some good old-fashioned fun?" Aiden asked sarcastically, as if what they were about to do could be considered fun.

"Right, my favorite. Trying to make a dump clean." Amina answered with little enthusiasm. Even as a kid both he and Amina hated cleaning, and now, being a part of the cleaning crew in the tunnels meant attempting to make a sewer presentable. It was an impossible task and yet, the elders insisted it needed to happen. Aiden actually felt bad for those whose full-time job it was.

"And what are you up to this afternoon?" Josiah inquired.

"I thought I'd join you."

Josiah stared, unblinking. "I'm sorry, you want to come with us?"

"Like I told Aiden, I need something new to do. I'm getting tired of the same old things while you all are off working."

"Suit yourself."

When they arrived in Dwelling One, they found the cleaning crew debriefing. Quietly they joined the back of the crowd and listened as assignments were given. Today they would be cleaning the tunnels of any new sludge that had formed. There had been a leak recently that the maintenance crew fixed, but it caused a lot of leaking into the tunnels and there was a large build-up of new sludge and water. It was their job to clean it.

"Masks are here in this bag," a woman standing at the front of the group spoke. She had bright blond hair pulled back into a tight bun and she wore a nurse's mask around her neck and a black rubber smock. She was holding a trash bag that she then dropped to the ground. "We also have rubber boots and smocks to protect your clothes. Some of you will be going to the outer perimeter and the water there is at least ankle deep."

The group moved forward to suit up, grab their tools, and head out.

Aiden groaned like a little child as he put on his smock and mask.

As they were suiting up, Maya, who had quietly joined them

soon after they arrived, pulled out a small vial of clear oil. She uncapped it and dabbed the oil under her nose and then passed it around to the rest of the group. "It's a mixture I created to help block out bad smells. It works quite well."

Aiden took the vial and sniffed it. A strong citrus smell invaded his nose and blocked out all other odors present. Tilting the vial on his index finger he dabbed the oil under his nose and breathed deeply. "Thanks Maya, this stuff is amazing."

"The next four hours might suck, but at least it won't stink." Aiden laughed at his joke and caught Amina smiling as she too dabbed her upper lip.

The next four hours did suck. Aiden had never shoveled so much muck before. It was slimy and thick. If it hadn't been for Maya's oil, he would've gotten sick. Especially when Amina's shovel flung into the air a little too high and caused sludge to land in Aiden's hair. Everyone else seemed to find it funny, but Aiden did not.

At the end of the four hours Aiden wasn't convinced that their efforts had made a difference. He was heavy with fatigue, and his entire smock was covered in filth.

The group made their way back to Dwelling One where they were able to de-robe and throw all their cover ups into a giant bin for the laundry crew.

Once they returned the outerwear, they headed to the showers. This was the only dwelling that had showers, and while anyone could use them, the cleaning crew had first priority. The strong odors they worked around seemed to seep into their skin and so the showers were necessary.

Aiden gladly undressed and hopped in. It felt good to have the water wash off all the dirt and oils that clung to him, even if the water was only lukewarm.

It wasn't long before the woman in charged yelled, "Time's up, switch!" forcing everyone in the showers to quickly rinse and get out.

When Aiden made it back to his tent he noticed a small piece of paper lying on his table. Curious, he opened it. *T-D4-MID*. Aiden flipped the paper over to see if there was anything else written. Nothing. That was curious.

Aiden sat still staring at the paper. He repeated the code over and over again, wracking his brain. *What could it mean?*

It dawned on him that the only person who would send him a cryptic message was Terrance's group. Why they felt the need to be so cryptic was uncertain. Wouldn't it just be easier to post an announcement? Then again, maybe this was a select group and they didn't want just anyone showing up. They only wanted those who were serious about the fight.

In any case, the note must have something to do with the next meeting. Dwelling Four at midday? Or was it midnight? And could it be duct four? Not sure why you'd meet in a tunnel duct but maybe they had some hidden location nearby for training. And what was the T for? Terrance?

It was a shot in the dark, but Aiden was certain it had to be Dwelling Four and midnight. But he still wasn't sure what the T stood for. Although, did it really matter? As long as he knew the time and place, he'd discover the rest once he got there.

Aiden lay on his mat staring at the ceiling, waiting for the perfect time to sneak out. He was still sharing a tent with Paxton so he had to make sure Paxton was fast asleep before he could leave. Over the last couple of days, he learned that

CHAPTER 8

Paxton was a pretty heavy sleeper, but he took forever to get to that state.

Eventually he heard Paxton's breathing become slow and steady. Aiden found Paxton on his back with one arm thrown across his eyes to block out the extra light caused from the never-ending fire.

Aiden lightly nudged Paxton. He didn't budge. He nudged again, a little harder. Still Paxton didn't move. He slept like the dead.

When Aiden was positive Paxton was asleep, he got up, threw on his boots, and headed out.

It didn't take long to make it to Dwelling Four. Once he was there he looked to see if there was anyone standing around. There was no one. Aiden crawled down into the pit and started to wander around, looking and listening for anyone who might be awake. The place was fast asleep. Maybe the T did stand for something. An important detail he had somehow missed.

Aiden kept looking around searching for things that could represent T. Tent. There were dozens of tents, that wasn't very descriptive. Terrance. Except, Terrance didn't live in this dwelling so it couldn't be his place.

Aiden made it to the opposite wall. Still nothing. Maybe he got the time wrong. Aiden looked along the wall as he walked the perimeter, still listening for footsteps or voices. He was growing frustrated, but he kept waiting. Someone had to come eventually, right?

Aiden was about to give up and go home when he heard footsteps echoing. Above him he saw two figures climbing a ladder that led to the top of the dome-shaped walls.

Any thought of leaving washed away and Aiden quickly followed the two figures. He had never climbed so high before and the ladder felt rickety. His palms sweat as adrenaline pulsed through his body.

Don't look down. Don't look down. Aiden wasn't usually afraid of heights, but tonight, on this rickety ladder, he was terrified. At the top he noticed the opening was still a good foot above him with nothing to grab to hoist himself. How was he going to get up there?

His hands grew sweatier. Suddenly his left hand slipped. Aiden quickly grabbed the ladder and hugged it as sharp pangs of fear shot through his body.

"Here grab my hand," a voice whispered from above.

Aiden saw Seth standing above him holding out a welcoming hand. "Thanks." Aiden reached and took Seth's forearm, and Seth helped lift Aiden the rest of the way.

With his feet planted on solid ground a sigh of relief flooded him. He was hot and felt beads of sweat forming on his forehead.

"That last bit can be nerve-wracking, huh? It's a good thing I was here to help you."

Aiden wiped his palms on his pants. "Yeah. Thanks again. So, where do we go from here?"

"Just straight ahead. The training has already started so you should hurry."

Aiden nodded and hurried down the pitch-black tunnel. This area had no lights. No one ever went into the upper tunnels. There was no need, so it made the perfect location for a secret training room.

Aiden kept walking until he slammed face first into a metal wall. He let out a loud cry as he rubbed his forehead. It felt hot and sticky.

Aiden wiped his hand again on his pants and started feeling

CHAPTER 8

around for some sort of lever or knob. This had to be a door of some sort, but when he couldn't find anything, he knocked. At first there was no answer. Aiden was about to knock again when he heard metal sliding and then a jolt from the door as it opened just wide enough for Aiden to slip inside. The door quickly closed behind him and he heard someone whisper, "keep going straight. It opens up ten feet from here."

This tunnel seemed to have some light trailing in from the other end like a beacon leading the way. Aiden's eyes adjusted, just enough for him to tell where he was going. It was a good thing too because when he reached the opening there was a short three-foot drop.

Aiden stopped when he reached the end of the tunnel and took in the surrounding training ground. There were at least eighty people spread around in small groups either watching or practicing. A couple of groups were learning hand-to-hand combat, another was learning small weapons combat, while two other groups were holding guns. Aiden stared, unblinking as his heart raced at the sight of everything. This really did look like a well-organized training session.

Aiden was apprehensive, though he wasn't sure why. He knew Terrance and the others had no interest in hurting anyone in the tunnels, but the things they had planned could completely upset the current way of living and the peace they had built, which unnerved Aiden. And still he stayed, feeling an inexplicable desire to be a part of their mission.

Aiden jumped down into the room and looked around, hoping someone would tell him where to go. It wasn't long before Terrance saw him from across the room. He was training someone with a gun, but when he spotted Aiden, he handed the gun over and made his was to him.

"You made it. I was afraid you wouldn't be able to figure out the code. Sorry it's so cryptic, but we can't take any chances."

"No worries. I'm a smart cookie." Aiden couldn't believe the amount of people. It was at least double that of the previous meeting. "So, where do you want me?"

"You're with me over at guns." Terrance started walking back as he continued to talk. Aiden took that as a hint to follow. "You ever held a gun before?"

"No and honestly–"

"Well don't you worry. I'll teach you everything you need to know."

Aiden was feeling highly uncomfortable with the prospect of having to use a gun. "Thanks, but I think I'd be better suited somewhere else."

"Nonsense. You're a scavenger, you're already familiar with the terrain above ground. We need you up there and that means you need to know how to protect yourself."

Terrance grabbed a gun off the table and shoved it into Aiden's chest. Aiden held it, the cold metal burned under his fingers, and he could feel his hands start to shake.

Terrance didn't seem to notice the deer-in-the-headlights look that Aiden was giving him. He just continued to address the whole group about gun safety, handling, and loading. After drilling into their heads the rules of safety, they spent the time practicing how to hold, load and even unload the gun properly with rubber bullets. They practiced over and over until Aiden's mind went numb and his eyelids drooped from the lack of sleep. He was used to late nights and not getting much sleep, but this was a lot of learning that overloaded his brain. Yet, by the end of the night, Aiden felt confident and reading for target practice–which incidentally did not happen that night.

CHAPTER 8

"We'll see everyone again in a week. Be sure to keep up on your personal training lessons and participate in Jared's self-defense class." Terrance announced to everyone at the end of their training.

"Hey Terrance." Aiden approached. "Just a quick question. Why all the secrecy?"

Terrance looked at him quizzically. "Why do you think? If the coalition found out what was happening, they'd shut us down. The elders don't want us fighting."

"Oh, right, of course." Aiden nodded as a sinking feeling settled in the pit of his stomach. *So it's not legal. Great. Now what do I do?*

Amina stepped out of her tent feeling more rested. After a long grueling day of raiding and then cleaning she had needed a nap, but while she felt rested, she also felt guilty. She knew she had overreacted with Paxton and needed to apologize.

Near the south wall of the dwelling, Amina noticed Paxton sitting alone whittling a piece of wood that he had picked up while out on their raid. He was deeply concentrating on his artwork, making a small cut here and a thin shave there. He spun the wood around and around gently cradling it in his hand like a delicate flower.

Amina sat beside Paxton and leaned against the dome wall. She watched Paxton work. It was fascinating to see his random nicks and shavings turn into intricate designs.

Eventually, Amina spoke. "What're you making?"

Paxton didn't look up from his work. "A handle for a knife."

Amina nodded. "Who taught you to do that?"

"My grandpa."

Another long pause. "You're really good at it."

Paxton grunted.

Amina was trying to make conversation, trying to be friendly, but he was being short with her. She couldn't blame him, really. She had gotten upset over something that didn't happen.

Paxton spoke first this time. "Did you really think I would purposely put the people who saved my life in danger?" He stopped whittling and looked at her with deep hurt.

"No, I suppose not. But when we're above ground you've got to use your head."

"I was being cautious. I'm not brainless."

"I know that."

"So then trust me, don't control me."

Amina let that sink in a moment. *Don't control me.* Is that what she was trying to do, because that was never her intension?

"Anyway," Paxton broke into her thoughts, "let's just move past this. If I'm going to be stuck down here for the rest of my life, I would like to know I have a few friends."

"I can do that." Amina smiled, glad to have things smoothed over so easily. She needed him on her side, especially for what she was going to request next.

Amina still hadn't told Paxton about Paul and Mo approaching her. Now was the time because if Paxton wasn't on board, she wasn't sure she could find the Hebrews on her own.

Amina breathed in deeply. It was now or never. "Hey, so, my uncle-he's an elder-he came to me yesterday asking if we would go to your village. They want proof of existence and assurance that they'd be welcomed there before they decide to move everyone out of the tunnels."

Paxton sighed and shook his head. "Amina, I already told

CHAPTER 8

you. I don't remember how to get there. And those mountains are dangerous, especially if you don't know where you're going."

"I know, but we can find a way for you to remember." Amina stared at the dirt. Surely there had to be some way to get him to remember. Weren't there people who could do hypnosis or some sort of deep memory recall? She vaguely remembered in the fifth grade having an assembly where a guy came to their school and hypnotized several students. He was able to get them to do all sorts of crazy things. Some even shared their most embarrassing moments with the whole school.

Shaking the memory off Amina had an idea. Of course, why hadn't she thought of this sooner? She could talk to Maya. Maya used to work for the government as a scientist. When persecution of the Notzrim began, Maya had to flee, but not before taking several vials of elements. She had all sorts of elixirs for various situations. Amina jumped up.

"Where are you going?" Paxton asked.

"I have an idea on how we may be able to get your memories back."

"What? Really?" Paxton stood seeming a bit nervous. "Will it be safe?"

Amina nodded. "Of course, Maya has all sorts of elixirs. Surely one is a memory extractor. You stay here and I'll go talk with her."

Amina took off across the dwelling for a tunnel that lead to Maya's place. This was it. This was surely the answer. Now she just had to convince Maya to go along with it. A twinge of doubt crept into Amina's mind. Maya was always hesitant to use her elixirs. She took her gift of science seriously and was cautious how she used it.

Amina pushed her doubts aside. Surely Maya would see that pulling out Paxton's memories so they could find the Hebrews was for the good of the entire village.

Amina quickly arrived at Maya's tent and called for her.

"Come in," Maya called back.

Amina pulled back the tent door and ducked inside. Maya was sitting on some pillows sipping tea with another woman about the same age. She had long golden hair that spun down in ringlets around her face and bony shoulders. She smiled at Amina kindly, revealing a large gap between her two front teeth.

"Hello Amina. To what do I owe this pleasure?"

"Oh, sorry to interrupt. I have a request."

Maya motioned for Amina to sit. When Amina did, Maya poured her a small cup of tea into one of her tiny bowl-like cups. "This is my friend Sasha. She's also a scientist. We like to have tea together often."

Amina smiled at Sasha to be courteous. Maya never felt there was so much urgency that one couldn't be polite.

"Nice to meet you." Amina returned her attention to Maya. "So, I wanted to know if you had an elixir that could help extract memories."

Maya looked at Amina warily. "That's a curious question. Is this to force out memories and draw out memories locked away?"

"Draw them out. Allow someone to unlock that part of their mind so they can remember."

Sasha leaned closer to Amina and placed a long hand on her arm. "Is this for you? Is there something you want to remember? Because I always say if something is forgotten, then your mind must have a good reason for it."

CHAPTER 8

Amina shook her head. "No, it's for the Hebrew, Paxton. He doesn't remember the details of how to get home, and I need him to lead me there."

Maya pursed her lips with uncertainty. "I was under the impression that after the village meeting you were supposed to leave that alone."

"Not anymore. Can you help or not?"

"How do I know-"

"My uncle asked me. He wants me to go and get more evidence." Amina snapped. She had no time to explain herself to Maya nor did she feel she owed her any explanations, but she did need her help. Softening her tone so as not to completely shut down Maya, she asked, "Now please, can you help? Or if you can't maybe Sasha can."

Maya stood. "No, no. I can help." Maya crossed to a large hutch worn with age. She carefully opened the doors and started looking through hundreds of tiny bottles lined on the shelves inside. She came upon one small bottle with a red liquid inside. She grabbed it, closed the doors again, and handed Amina the bottle.

"He only needs a drop of it. After that he should be able to recall anything you ask him, however, if he still can't remember, give him another drop." Maya started to hand Amina the vial but then pulled it away. "Do *not* give him more than three drops, understand?" she warned.

"Yeah, yeah, no more than three. Thanks." Amina took the vial and rushed out of the tent as she could hear Maya telling her to bring back the extra. "I will!" Amina shouted back.

Amina arrived back to where Paxton was sitting. He was still whittling, but had moved on to a new piece of wood.

Amina approached and smiled. "That was quick." Paxton

put down his wood and picked up the finished handle that was now attached to a small blade. He held it out to Amina. "This is for you."

Amina stared for a moment, unsure how to respond. She couldn't remember the last time she had received a gift from someone other than her family. Whenever she gained anything nice it was always to barter for more food or as a thank you for giving extra food.

"What's it for," was all she could manage.

Paxton was staring back and shifted his weight. "It's a knife. You know, a sharp pointy object you use to cut things." Paxton took Amina's hand and placed the knife in it. Amina felt lightheaded as her stomach fluttered. She quickly pulled her hand away. She tried to push her feelings aside, but at the same time she didn't want to. Holding the knife, Amina looked at the delicate engravings Paxton had made into the wood. There was a large cross the length of the handle on one side. And all around was swirling filigree. She was impressed at the craftsmanship.

"Thank you." Amina continued to look at it, lost in its beauty and yet completely baffled at the gesture.

"So, did you get what you wanted from Maya?" Paxton asked, breaking her out of her trance.

Amina looked up, startled. "Right, sorry, yes. I have something that's going to help us."

"What'd she give you?"

Amina held out the tiny bottle.

Paxton's face scrunched in revolt. "It looks like blood."

"Well you get to drink it, so get over it."

"I'm not drinking that. I don't know what it'll do to me."

Amina rolled her eyes. "Really it's just a drop or two and it's supposed to help jog your memories that's all."

"Really?" Paxton wasn't buying it. "How can you tell me that a little drop of that liquid is going to jog a memory that is clearly lost?"

"I can because Maya is good at what she does and I've seen her mixtures work before. Just try it. What does it hurt to try?"

Paxton looked to be struggling with how to answer, but he was out of excuses. "Fine, I'll do it."

"Good." Amina and Paxton sat facing one another as Amina unscrewed the top of the vial. The top was a tiny dropper so it made it easy for Amina to give Paxton one tiny drop on his tongue.

Paxton made a disgusted face and shook his head. "Oh, that was nasty. Like a rotten apple."

"How do you know what a rotten apple tastes like?"

"Trust me, I know. So how long does it take for this stuff to work?"

Amina shrugged. "Maya didn't say, but generally these things are pretty quick."

Suddenly Paxton grabbed his head and scrunched his eyes shut. He let out a small groan of pain. "Son of a . . . wow I think it may be working."

"What's happening?"

"All of a sudden I've got hundreds of memories flooding my brain all at once. Like a computer overload. It's giving me a headache."

"Okay." Amina straightened feeling the excitement pulsing through her. "I'll try to be quick. I don't know how long it lasts and I want to make sure we get what we need so you don't have to take any more of this. Tell me how to get to your village in the mountains."

Paxton was quiet for a while, still holding his head. He was now rocking back and forth and rubbing his temples to help ease the pain. Amina's stomach twisted in knots when he wouldn't respond. She was ready to give him another drop until finally he softly spoke.

"I see it. I see my village and me leaving. It's really dark. I'm heading . . . north." Paxton was quiet but Amina could see his eyes moving back and forth under his eyelids like a typewriter. He was visualizing and remembering everything. Amina's heart raced. This was it. She was getting somewhere again. Soon Paxton would have the exact direction to go and they could leave immediately.

Paxton spoke again, sharing a few more details. As he spoke his face started to relax and he stopped rocking. "I think it's fading."

"But did you remember everything? Can you take us there?"

Paxton opened his eyes and smiled. "Yes. I can."

Amina reached out and hugged Paxton. When she realized that may have been inappropriate, she quickly sat back looking apologetic. Her cheeks flushed and she looked away hoping he didn't notice.

Paxton smiled but didn't say anything until he covered his mouth and yawned. "Wow I feel like I ran a marathon."

"You did, in your mind, anyway." Amina stood. "We'll leave early tomorrow, before the sun rises."

Paxton looked around as if to try and figure out what time of day it was, but then he stopped. "When is that exactly?"

Amina thought a moment. "Probably in about ten hours."

"Great, I'm going to bed. I can barely keep my eyes open." Paxton gathered his things and stood. "Night."

Amina watched Paxton walk away, giddy with excitement.

CHAPTER 8

It was all coming together. She couldn't wait to get going. The sooner they could leave to get there the sooner they could make it back with the proof they needed.

She found it a bit laborsome to have to go on this first journey. It made more sense to her, and would be safer, to lead everyone out now and travel together, but Amina was willing to play by the rules despite her persistence and anxiety about everything. She ultimately knew that playing by the rules was the best and only option for ultimately getting what she wanted.

Amina took off toward Dwelling Three where they had a gym. She had too much adrenaline flowing through her that needed to be expelled before she could sleep.

Before Amina got too far, she saw her brother approaching. By the way Aiden was walking toward her, she had a feeling he was going to try and impart some brotherly wisdom about her upcoming journey. "What's up Aiden?"

He shifted his weight several times and crossed his arms. "Paxton told me what you two were up to tomorrow."

"Yeah, isn't it great? We're finally going to find the Hebrews and save our village."

"Look, I know Uncle Paul gave you the okay and all, but I don't think it's a good idea." He was so blunt it threw Amina.

"I don't want to have this conversation with you again. Uncle Paul and Aunt Mo came to me, asking me to go. It's happening whether you like it or not."

Aiden sighed. "I was afraid you were going to be stubborn about this." Aiden dug his hand into his cargo pocket and pulled out two small flip phones.

Amina gasped. "How did you?"

Aiden shrugged as if finding priceless working cell phones was no big deal. "I found them at Mitchum's place when I was looking for a new project. He helped me restore them and find a way to charge them and keep them powered. Not to mention getting them linked to a secret network. It took a while, but they work." Aiden handed her a phone. "They're solar powered. So when you're above ground you can charge it no problem. And mine, I can charge under a UV light when I'm getting my Vitamin D treatment.

Amina threw her arms around Aiden and squeezed him tightly. "Thank you," she whispered. "Not just for the phone, but for not pushing the issue."

"I couldn't push anything on you if I tried. You're too stubborn."

"Well either way, thank you." Amina put the phone in her pocket.

"Be careful and check in every once in a while."

Amina shrugged. "Maybe, we'll see." She smiled as Aiden playfully punched her arm.

Amina's throat tightened unexpectedly and she felt her emotions welling. She knew she wasn't going to be gone that long, but she was going to miss her brother. They had never been apart for more than a couple of days. And although she felt confident in the plan and knew she'd make it back, deep inside her a tiny flicker of doubt tried to creep in. Amina grabbed Aiden and hugged him hard. "I'll see you soon. I promise."

His arms wrapped around her tightly. "I know you will. One way or another."

Chapter 9

Amina lay on her mat staring at the knife from Paxton. She kept twirling it around, memorizing the beautiful design he created just for her.

Even after her workout, she still couldn't sleep. Too many thoughts were flooding her mind about the trip.

Amina got up and walked out of her tent. Maybe if she walked around a bit she could clear her mind.

As she quietly made her way to the firepit, she saw someone scurrying up the stairs. She watched them for a moment curiously until she realized it was Paxton. Where was he going at such an hour?

Amina followed as Paxton made his way down several different tunnels quickly, constantly looking around every corner and then behind. He kept to the edges and felt his way along; his eyes still weren't used to the darkness. When he made his way to the southeast entrance he stopped and climbed up and out.

Amina's heart raced. *Had he changed his mind about leading Amina to his people and he was going back on his own?*

The only weapon Amina had on her was the knife Paxton gave her, but at that moment she didn't care, she needed to find out what Paxton was up to. Amina ran to the ladder and climbed it. When she reached the top, she cautiously poked her head out of the manhole and scanned her surroundings. Tonight a low thick fog had settled and Amina couldn't see a thing. Closing her eyes, Amina listened for Paxton's footsteps. She could hear them, probably about one hundred yards ahead of her.

It was crazy to be going out alone, without anyone knowing, but Amina hoisted herself out of the hole and closed the lid, and then quickly followed after Paxton. He had turned on a small flashlight, which allowed Amina to follow more easily and quickly close the gap.

When she realized he was approaching the gate to the city Amina stopped. There were two guards standing at the entrance checking ID's. She hid behind a dumpster and watched as Paxton approached the gate, pulled out some papers from his pocket, and then proceeded through the gate. *Where did he got papers? And why would the guards let him through without question?*

This was all too strange and Amina's curiosity was growing. She had to know what was going on. Without papers, there was no way Amina could get through the guarded gate. She'd have to find another way.

Keeping her head down, Amina darted to an area of the gate that was unguarded. From there she searched around for an opening or weak point where she could slip through. Thankfully, the makeshift gate wasn't very well built, and she eventually found a tiny opening to squeeze through.

On the other side, Amina rushed back toward the street Paxton had entered. She was praying that he was still out in the open. Thankfully he was. Amina spotted Paxton just in time to see him walk into a tiny dive bar.

CHAPTER 9

Amina threw her hood over her head and held onto the sleeves of her jacket to ensure the glow of her mark wasn't noticed. There weren't a lot of people wandering the streets as she crossed it and made her way into the bar. Inside, however, was a different story. She wasn't expecting so many people to be crammed into such a tiny bar after curfew. Most people were sitting quietly by themselves, milking their drinks and staring into the unknown. The place was filled with exhaustion and disappointment.

There were two options for living, the outer or the inner city. The inner city was reserved only for those who expressed deep devotion to Tievel through their finances and in turn were well rewarded. Everyone else was forced to live low-class lives in the slums.

Amina hunched forward and kept her head down, trying to blend into the depressing crowd. She was thankful for the dark room and inattentive people. Amina found an empty booth just behind Paxton and slid into it.

She noticed he was sitting with another man. Amina wasn't sure who and it was hard to hear them talking. She closed her eyes and listened carefully, tuning out all other sounds until all she could hear was Paxton and the other man.

"Do you have a map?" There was silence. Amina assumed Paxton was showing him a map. "There's only eight?" The man seemed disappointed. "Most undergrounds are larger than that."

Amina's body trembled They were talking about the underground. Amina's underground.

Her heart sank as tears tried to blur her vision. She sniffled and pushed back the tears as she continued to listen.

"There might be more but they keep me on a tight leash

there. It was hard enough getting out to come see you again."

"Fine, how many entrances?"

"At least two."

"And security?" There was an edge of agitation in the man's voice.

"They have a small police force of about thirty-six people and they're well stocked with guns, knives, and some explosives."

"*About* thirty-six. *Some* explosives." The man paused and took a breath. His voice lowered. "You've been down there for two weeks. You should have more than this by now," he snarled.

"Well first, your guys did a number on me and I was stuck in the medical ward for a week. And two, I told you, they keep me on a tight leash. Some are not very trusting of me."

"Well then make them trust you. We need more accurate information. Do they have an evacuation plan? What security protocols are in place if there's a breech? Figure them out Paxton or do I need to re-motivate you. Don't forget what's at stake."

"I know." Paxton's voice was much quieter and he almost sounded scared.

"If anything, find a way to get that mark put on you so they think you're one of them."

"I can't now, they believe I'm a Hebrew. I've been keeping this bandanna on my head to hide that I don't have the right markings."

"Did you ask Sophie to put one on you?"

"I haven't had the opportunity. This is my first time above by myself."

"We're going to see Sophie." The men stood and walked to

CHAPTER 9

the door.

Amina put her head down and slumped in her seat. Once they passed, she got up and followed.

They walked deeper into the city. Amina was on edge with every step. Although she tried not to constantly look behind, she couldn't help but think someone was following. At any moment she could be stopped, they could demand ID, and that would be the end of her, but each time Amina looked back, no one was there. Amina kept moving forward. She needed to figure out how to get the map back and stop Paxton from telling them any other pertinent information.

Amina kept running through her head all the possibilities of how to handle this situation. Why hadn't she grabbed her go pack? Surely there would've been something in there to help her stop these two. All she had was a knife. A flippin' knife.

Amina followed them until she found an opportune time. The men turned down an alley; this was the perfect moment, there would be no witnesses.

Amina turned down the alley and boldly followed them. Amina shouted, "You traitor!" It was a dangerous move. The man could easily pull his gun out and shoot her, which he started to do, but Paxton stopped him.

"Amina?"

Amina stepped forward and pulled her hood down. Paxton let out a disappointed groan. "I'll handle it."

"If you don't. I will." He patted his concealed weapon. "Hurry up."

Paxton hurried to Amina. "What are you doing here? You shouldn't have followed me."

"How could you? After all we've done for you. After all *they've* done to you. Was any of it even true?"

"I need you to leave, now."

Amina shook her head. "I'm not going anywhere without that map. Where is it?" Amina started to walk past Paxton, but he grabbed her wrist. Amina quickly pulled out of his grip and went to throw a right hook, but Paxton was too quick. The two wrestled, forcing each other on the ground. Paxton was going to win, until Amina grabbed a nearby brick and hit Paxton hard across the head, knocking him out.

Without thinking, Amina jumped and sprinted toward the man who was now making his way toward her with his gun drawn. A gunshot went off, ricocheting off the brick wall. With all her might Amina tackled the man to the ground. He lost his grip and dropped the gun as they both went crashing to the ground. They rolled around throwing punches.

Being much larger, the man was able to overpower Amina. He threw a punch which landed on her right cheek. A sharp pain spread through her face that she ignored. As the man stood, he delivered several swift kicks to Amina's ribs and abdomen. Amina gasped for air and her vision blurred. She did her best not to move, praying he'd stop soon.

He did. When Amina regained her bearings, she saw the man looking around for his gun. It was dark and difficult for him to see anything, but Amina could see perfectly.

Adrenaline surged through her body giving her newfound strength. With the dagger drawn, Amina pulled herself up. *Who brings a knife to a gunfight?*

"Give me the map." Her voice was taut, but she tried to stay calm.

The man turned. When he saw her knife he laughed. "You're kidding, right? Go home rat."

"Not without that map."

CHAPTER 9

Ignoring her, the man shook his head and went back to looking for his gun. Amina charged the man, hoping to tackle him again and wrestle the map out of his pocket. The man heard her steps and turned. Amina's eyes grew wide as her drawn dagger thrust itself deep into the man's abdomen. The man drew in a sharp breath. Everything was in slow motion. Amina pulled the knife out as he staggered, clutching his bloodied stomach. Slowly he crumpled to the ground.

Amina froze. *What just happened?* Taking a few steps back Amina started to leave, but suddenly remembered the map. She quickly dug through the man's jacket pockets until she came across the map. He tried to bat her away as she searched, but he was losing strength quickly.

"Oh Sabaoth, please forgive me," Amina breathed.

Once she had the map, she ran back to Paxton to check on him. He was still breathing. Amina hooked her arms under Paxton's armpits and painfully dragged him.

It wasn't uncommon for there to be violence or suspicious activity these days, but Amina was still cautious with every corner she turned. Eventually she made it back to open land beyond the city limits. Amina found a nearby abandoned office building and gradually lumbered to it. She felt the growing weight of Paxton's limp body. She needed to put him down before she collapsed.

Inside Amina released Paxton. He flopped like a ragdoll and Amina did the same, wincing at the excruciating pain in her chest. Black specks obstructed her vision and her head was in a fog. She felt as if someone were pulling a blanket over her head and then everything went black.

Amina hadn't even realized she blacked out until she was waking up again. Her head was pressing in on her and it took her a moment to regain her senses. As her head cleared, the events of the night flooded back and her heart raced as fast as her mind. She looked around the empty room. Paxton must've left.

Amina heard a noise from behind her and whipped her head around to see Paxton standing there holding a water bottle. She winced again in pain from moving too quickly but tried not to show it.

Paxton sat beside Amina and handed her the water bottle. "I was trying to find a first aid kit. All I found were some old water bottles, an ace bandage, and a roll of paper towels."

Amina glared at Paxton. She was trying to give him a menacing look but it felt like she was failing. If anything, her look was of complete hurt and betrayal. She should have known he was a liar.

When Amina didn't respond or take the water Paxton continued. "I know. I'm sure you have a lot of questions. And if you'd let me, I can explain."

Amina tried to move to find a more comfortable position but winced and let out a small whimper. Now that the adrenaline of the previous events had worn off, the pain overpowered her senses every time she moved.

"You really should let me attend to that."

"Why? It's a bruise and maybe some broken ribs. There's nothing you can do."

Paxton grabbed the ace bandage off the desk he had been leaning against. He sat back down and held out the bandage. "At least let me help you wrap it."

Amina grabbed the ace bandage from him. "I can do it myself." Amina unrolled a little of the bandage and held it gingerly to her left side with one arm. She slowly attempted to unroll the bandage around her lower ribcage, but when she had to lift her right arm to move the bandage around her back she let out a cry and stopped.

Paxton tried to help but she stopped him. She took a few shallow breaths to muster the courage to try again. This time she got a little further around her back, but tears of pain welled in her eyes and she dropped the bandage. It was useless.

"Please, Amina. Let me help."

"No. I'll be fine without it." Amina leaned against the wall and closed her eyes. How could she let this happen to herself, again? She had started to let him in. She wanted to believe that he was who he said he was. That he was someone she could trust, but she was wrong. So very wrong.

Amina spoke quietly. "So I was right about the Myriad. They are trying to get in so they can kill us all, aren't they?"

Paxton lowered his head to avoid eye contact with her. "Yes, and I was sent into the field in hopes that one of you would find me and let me in."

"It was a good plan. Our people are quite caring. The whole good Samaritan parable coming to life. Only in that story the man wasn't actually a spy trying to kill their rescuer."

"I had to do it. I needed the money for-"

"It always comes down to greed, doesn't it?"

"For some."

"For you."

"No, the money wasn't going to be for me, it was going to be for my dad and grandmother back home. When I got to know everyone, I tried to back out of it. I didn't want to keep helping the Myriad. The only problem was they told me if I didn't do it, they were going to kill my family."

"So we mean nothing to you?"

Paxton shook his head. He tried to take Amina's hand, but she pulled away. "You mean *everything* to me. I've been wracking my brain trying to figure out how to save both your family and mine. I tried to lie to them. That night we were at the restaurant, I met with my handler and I tried to convince him that I hadn't been taken. He didn't believe me for a second, and then he showed me a surveillance photo of my family in their home. They know where they're hiding and they won't hesitate to hurt innocent people. At that point, I had to give him what I knew. I set this meeting up and I told him I'd give him the map and any other information he needed. The raid was set to happen one week from tonight."

Amina sat quietly trying to process what he was saying. She wanted to believe the good in Paxton, that he really was a compassionate person who cared about the Notzrim, but she couldn't. "You're a coward." She breathed, letting her anger simmer. "A heartless coward."

Paxton moved closer again and touched her arm. She flinched and moved away. How could he act so kindly, as if he cared? People who care don't stab others in the back.

"I won't tell anyone if that's what you're wondering. I can leave this city and run far away." He sounded so genuine it was tempting to believe him.

"How can I trust that? After what you tried to do, I can't trust anything you say."

"I may have hidden my reasons for being in the tunnels, but I didn't hide who I am. Everything else I've ever told you has been true."

"I call your bluff." Amina slowly pulled herself off the floor and crossed to a window. As she looked outside the sun was just barely starting to light the sky with a soft white glow. She had to get back underground before it was too late and she'd be stuck the rest of the day waiting in this abandoned office space. "You made it crystal clear who was more important to you when you chose to give us up for your family." Amina clenched her fists tightly, feeling her nails digging into her palms. "I can't say I completely blame you, since I'm willing to do anything for my family." Wasn't she doing the same thing as Paxton by sacrificing everything to save them?

Paxton didn't respond.

"Are you even a Hebrew?"

"No."

"So you're one of them, a Myriad soldier?"

Paxton nodded.

That answer determined her next move. Amina searched around the office, through each and every drawer and cabinet. Paxton didn't move.

Eventually, in a supply closet down the hall, Amina found duct tape and some heavy-duty zip ties. She grabbed the items and walked over to Paxton.

Paxton's eyes grew wide as he scrambled to his feet. "What are you doing Amina?"

Amina calmly moved closer to him with her makeshift handcuffs. "Get over by that pole and sit down." She snarled, nodding her head toward a pole just behind him.

"Please, I told you I won't tell anyone."

Amina shook her head. "I can't trust that. Now sit down before I make you." Amina snatched a large metal paperweight off a desk and held it ready to strike him.

Paxton threw his hands up in surrender. "Okay. I don't want to fight you. I care too much–"

Amina threw the paperweight near Paxton's head; he ducked

out of the way. "Shut up, just shut up!" She couldn't stand to listen. It was too hypocritical. Her eyes burned from the dust mingled with tears. "I don't want to hear any more of your lies!"

Paxton closed his mouth and sat down with his back against the pole. Amina roughly grabbed one wrist after the other and moved his arms around the other side of the pole to secure him tightly. She took another large zip tie and tied his neck to the pole but made sure he had enough slack to breathe. Next, she zip-tied his ankles together as well as his legs. She didn't want to take any chances.

Pulling off a piece of duct tape, she knelt in front of Paxton and stared at him for a long moment. His eyes were full of pleading heartache. Or was it fear she saw? Her emotions were too blurred to be able to read him.

Paxton's voice was soft when he started to speak, "I'm sorry. I really-"

More lies. Amina secured the tape over his mouth.

She walked out of the office and back toward the field. She had to keep moving forward and not allow this set back to thwart her plan.

Chapter 10

Safely back inside the tunnels Amina aimlessly wandered from one tunnel to another. People were expecting her to leave today with Paxton. They were counting on her. She couldn't let anyone know what really happened. She had enough to deal with on her own and she didn't need the judging eyes of anyone else. Two things were certain: she needed her things and she needed a new way to find the Hebrews.

She made her way through the tunnels, avoiding the occupied common areas as much as possible. Thankfully it was still early so there weren't too many people awake.

When she made it to her dwelling, she quickly came down the ladder and bolted behind a tent. Moving from one tent to another, she made her way to her own without being seen by some of the early risers. Inside she grabbed her gear that had already been packed for the journey and then quickly rushed back to the tunnels.

Amina had no clue how she was going to find the Hebrews now. She was starting from scratch, but hopefully, the books she pulled off her shelf would help.

Amina made her way back through the tunnels toward the far east exit when she suddenly remembered the library. Inside the elders' chamber was a highly coveted collection of books.

No one was allowed to use them except the elders, and even then, they only touched them when absolutely necessary.

Amina had to get into the chambers. Surely there was a book in there that could give her the information she needed.

Amina quickly turned and headed toward the elders' chambers.

As Amina rounded the final corner, she saw a light coming from the elders' chamber. They must be in session for a prayer meeting, but for how long?

Amina found a small alcove nearby and waited. It wasn't long before she heard the echoes of footsteps and voices get closer and then fade away. She waited for the sounds to disappear. Then she waited again until she heard the single footsteps of Jade.

Once she was certain everyone was gone, Amina quietly headed into the chambers. First, she went over to the secretary's desk and found the keys. Not much security in this place if the keys were just left hiding under a false bottom of the top drawer. Amina unlocked the door and slipped through it, not making a single noise as she closed the door and locked herself inside.

It was so dark she couldn't see a thing. Amina grabbed the flashlight from her backpack and flipped it on. Searching along the walls she found a panel with a breaker that switched on the lights like a Christmas tree. Amina squinted and blinked as her eyes adjusted.

Quickly Amina spotted the row of old dilapidated looking bookshelves with even worse looking books. She gingerly thumbed through the books that mostly seemed to have some degree of fire or water damage.

As Amina skimmed the spines of each book on the shelf,

she came across a collection with titles that seemed to be referencing the Hebrews. Titles such as *Myths of the Hidden*, *Sabaoth's Chosen Race*, *Where Did They All Go?* and *Stranger than Fiction: The 10,000 who Disappeared*.

Amina grabbed a shirt out of her backpack and laid it on the ground. She then proceeded to take the books and carefully wrap them in the shirt, hoping this would help protect them during her travels.

Just as she was zipping up her bag, the lock on the door unlatched. Amina's heart stopped. She scanned the room for a place to hide, but it was too late, the door opened. There was a startled yelp as Amina stood by the bookshelf like a possum.

Paul grabbed his chest. "Goodness Amina, you startled me. What in the world are you doing here? How did you even get in? And what happened to your face?" His eyes were wide with surprise as he approached.

Amina's muscles relaxed, at least it was only her uncle. She touched her tender cheek remembering the beating she took. "It's nothing, a kickboxing accident," she lied.

"You should have that checked out. Now what are you doing in here?"

"I wanted to inform you that Paxton and I are good to go. We have everything we need and will be leaving now. It should only take us about three days to get there so I should be back in slightly more than a week with your proof. I want to make sure that you will be ready here for my return. Once I have the proof, we won't want to waste any time." At least that was what she assumed. If Paxton was right, the Myriad wanted to attack soon. She prayed that their plans had been thwarted enough to buy the underground a little more time, but she couldn't be sure. In any case, if Amina couldn't find the Hebrews in three days, she would come back anyway with fake proof of some sort and convince them all to leave no matter what.

Paul seemed a bit taken back, as if he had forgotten the mission. "Oh yes, of course, of course. I will pray for you both while you are gone."

"Great, thanks," Amina said, shifting uncomfortably. "I should go."

Amina started for the door, but Paul stopped her. Had he noticed something was missing?

Paul put his hand on Amina's shoulder and gave her a fatherly look. "Be careful out there. I want you back in one piece."

Amina tried to smile, to reassure him that she had it handled, but truthfully, she didn't know what was going to happen. The stress of having to find the Hebrews without a guide was daunting, but Paul was relying on her and she didn't want to let him down. "Don't worry Uncle, I'll be fine."

At the east entrance Amina gave the tunnels one last look around to ensure no one was nearby. She then walked to the security camera monitor and scanned the area for Myriad soldiers. She hated having to go above during the day, but she couldn't stay in the tunnels.

Once she was sure no one was above ground she climbed the ladder, unlatched the lid, and climbed into the open air.

It was a bright and warm morning and Amina had to immediately cover her eyes to help block the sun. She had forgotten how bright it got in the day.

She gave her eyes a minute. They seemed as if they would never adjust and Amina didn't want to wait any longer. She re-latched the lid and headed toward the hills.

As the sun continued to rise, the earth warmed into the

scorching desert that it was. There was no beauty to it. Small trees stood leafless and dead, tumbleweeds and rocks littered the scarred earth.

Amina felt herself dragging as the sun warmed the clay dirt. The foothills were much further away than expected, and she wasn't used to walking this far with so much heat. Sure the tunnels' air was hot and muggy, but it was nothing like the dry scorching sun that wanted to sear her flesh.

There was a small tree nearby with a tiny bit of shade. Amina squatted under it to help relieve her weariness. She pulled out a canteen and took a swig of water as a gentle breeze wafted over her caramel colored skin. She closed her eyes to rest, but as she did, images of Paxton's handler flashed before her. The struggle between the two of them, his large fist pounding into her, the feeling of the knife as it dug into his flesh, and the look-that was the worst part-the look on his pale face as he staggered backward and fell.

Amina opened her eyes, quickly wiping the thought from her mind. There was nothing she could do about it now, what was done was done.

Amina stood and continued her journey toward the mountains. She was too exposed in the open field, and she didn't like it. Although she was miles away from the highway, what if a Myriad patrol or drone could spot her? Amina did her best to keep close to rocks and trees, hoping they'd camouflage her. She could see off in the distance more trees, but they looked so far away.

As she trudged forward, she tried to stay focused on her goal, but thoughts of Paxton and the soldier kept resurfacing. She had been so lost in her thoughts that Amina hadn't noticed when she reached the foothills and the trees. As she ventured into the brush and the trees, the temperature, and it was the coolness of the shade and the breeze brushing across her sweat that made her shiver and realize where she was.

Amina let out her breath, relieved that she was no longer in danger of being sighted from the highway nor in the direct heat.

Deeper into the forest and up the mountain, she pressed. It was a gradual incline, but still steep enough that Amina was breathing heavily. She prided herself on staying in shape while in the tunnels, but this challenged her stamina, which was something she now realized was lacking.

She had always been physically fit, and always enjoyed hiking or bike riding. Every summer she and Aiden would pack a lunch and take their bikes to the foothills. They would ride until they reached some unknown destination to stop for a picnic.

Sometimes they'd talk about silly things such as school or if there was a zombie apocalypse what would they do, or the latest movie they wanted to go see. Other times they'd talk about more serious issues of life, deep philosophical questions that neither of them could ever seem to fully answer or understand. But it didn't matter. They only cared about spending time together.

They would take the whole day and return home just before dark. And every time they went, it was a new unknown adventure. They discovered some pretty amazing locations that way.

Now Amina was on a new adventure, but this time it was alone. She had a direction, she knew the final destination, but she didn't know how to get from point A to point B. She felt lost already, but she wasn't going to give up. Her keen sense of direction and courage to face uncertainty bolstered her confidence. Plus, the books had to have something in them to help her along her way, right?

The sun was already making its decent, but Amina kept walking. She headed east, until the sun was low in the sky. Amina's stomach grumbled and her legs were weak. It was time to settle in and make camp for the night.

Amina walked a little further until she found an open clearing and a couple of sturdy looking trees to hang her hammock.

She set to work hanging her hammock, gathering logs and kindling for the fire, doing all the things she knew had to be done to keep her warm and comfortable over the course of the night. Eventually, she had everything put together and she was heating a can of baked bean over the fire. She sat on a large rock and felt her entire body release the tension of the day. Her mind was still racing, but her body was ready to shut down.

As Amina listened to the crackling of the fire and the chirping of the crickets, she realized those were the only two sounds she could hear, and it was eerie. It had been a long time since she spent a night in such a still location. In the tunnels she was always surrounded by people and noises, even late at night.

A chill ran down her spine, but she ignored it and tried to focus on the sounds she could hear. Amina closed her eyes and let the crackling of the fire and the warmth of the heat calm her. It was a soothing reminder of home.

Amina grabbed her backpack and pulled out the pile of books she stole from the elders' chamber. Carefully she unwrapped the books and set them beside her on the rock.

The first book she decided to look through was a thin water-damaged paperback titled *Myths of the Hidden People*. It was more like a magazine or a collection of articles, blogs, and chat rooms all dated nine years ago, just after the Hebrews disappeared.

Amina skimmed page after page of hypotheses, eyewitness accounts, and rumors of phone call conversations saying where they were going.

Nothing was extraordinarily helpful, although it did bolster Amina's confidence that she was at least in the right area.

There was one particular chat room conversation that intrigued her the most. It was the earliest entry in the book, dated seventeen months before the destruction began:

> MightyQuin268: Where will you be?
> FireStar*: Somewhere very far from here, a valley in the wilderness, but I cannot say more.
> MightyQuin268: Can I come visit?
> FireStar*: No. It would be too dangerous.
> MightyQuin268: Then I'm coming with you!
> FireStar*: You can't come, you are not one of us and you know it.
> MightyQuin268: Will you at least have a computer or cell phone so we can still talk?
> FireStar*: I doubt we will have any sort of technology. We'll be too far away.
> MightyQuin268: I don't want to lose you.
> FireStar*: I will always be with you. Please know, I will be safe. The rocks are high and the caves are deep. We will be protected from what is about to occur.

Amina stopped. Her dream flashed through her mind and she re-read the last entry again. The person was describing a

CHAPTER 10

location, the same location Amina had dreamed about. It had to be a clue.

Amina rummaged through her other books and pulled out an atlas. She flipped through the pages until she came across her current location. As she searched all along the page for the different terrains, she spotted one particular area where the elevation dropped drastically and there was a lake in the center. It was the only place on the map that made any sense.

Amina's eyes flashed with excitement and she smiled.

Between scavenger raids, cleaning crew, and self-defense classes Aiden was exhausted, but he finally finished the music box and took it to his aunt and uncle's place. Emily was over the moon when she first listened to the music box. She exclaimed that it was the greatest music box in the whole world. Aiden laughed because it was far from extraordinary, but he was pleased with himself. The song it played was nothing known and yet familiar. Aunt Mo was also pleased. She loved music and singing. She insisted she was going to create a song to go with the music box. After visiting for a while, Aiden said his goodbyes and heading back to his tent.

Inside, he found another note on the floor just inside the tent flap. He quickly read it: D6-2A-P. Another cryptic code and this one was different from all the others. He knew from the order of the previous ones that it was location, time, topic: Dwelling Six, two AM, and what else? Aiden didn't give it much thought. He crumpled the paper and shoved it in his pocket. He wasn't sure he wanted to go. After confirming that this group was in fact an illegal operation, he started second guessing his devotion. Was doing what he thought to be right worth the risk of getting arrested? Can't the coalition protect the underground without this militia's help? Aiden shook his head. Of course they could, but the militia's mission was so much bigger than defense. It was to attack, to weaken, and to intimidate the Myriad, and Aiden hungered for that. So long as their missions stayed above ground.

As the meeting drew closer, Aiden headed to Terrance's tent in Dwelling Four. He assumed that's where they were meeting based on the note.

Inside the group was much smaller than he expected. In the center of the room stood a round table with papers sprawled all over it. Around it stood Terrance, Jared, Seth, and one other person he recognized from training: Tessa.

Tessa was a short and feisty woman who kept herself in great shape and wasn't afraid to show it off with her cropped tank tops and tight black leggings. Her black hair was pulled into a ponytail and her soft facial features made her very attractive. She was also a brilliant electrical engineer.

"What are you doing here?" Jared asked looking up from the table.

"I asked him to come," Terrance interrupted giving Jared a look. Jared seemed to silently argue back, making Aiden feel even more uncomfortable. He was ready to turn around and leave, but Terrance eventually won the silent argument and then continued by saying, "Now let's get started."

"What's going on?" Aiden walked toward the table to get a better look at the papers. They appeared to be blueprints.

"It's time to break into the weapons vault," Terrance explained. "We had a few guns for training, but we need more."

"Break in?" Aiden looked from Terrance to Jared. "Why would we do that? Jared's in the coalition, can't he just check them out?"

The group laughed at a joke Aiden wasn't getting.

"You're joking right?" Jared asked. "What makes you think this was approved by the coalition?" Jared threw his hands out, palms up.

"I didn't, but I also didn't think we'd have to steal from our own people."

Terrance stepped closer to Aiden. "I need you as part of this tactical team, you're the best I know at picking locks. Don't throw a spanner in the works, man."

Seth spoke this time. "Come on Aiden, this is our chance to do something that matters. Your sister believes that we're under threat and is doing something about it, don't you want to also?"

"Yes, I want to." This was a way to defend his community and keep them protected. A way to show the Myriad that Notzrim are strong warriors they shouldn't provoke. "I just don't like breaking the rules."

Seth grabbed Aiden's shoulders, almost shaking him. "Aiden wake up, being Notzrim is illegal, not taking Teivel's mark is illegal. Sometimes rules are meant to be broken."

The others voiced their agreement, then Tessa spoke. "Living in hiding and stay passive has worked until now, but it's not going to keep working. It's time to stir the pot and show the Myriad we won't go down without a fight. Don't you believe that?"

"I do." Aiden nodded and he meant it. He took a deep breath and let it out. They were all right. Aiden had been breaking the law for the last five years when Teivel outlawed the Notzrim faith. It hadn't felt like breaking the law because his conviction of faith was so strong. So this shouldn't feel any different.

This was the right thing to do and he was going to do it. "Okay, what's the plan."

Tessa and Terrance smiled while Seth patted him on the back. The group hovered over the table as Jared explained the plan. They would carry out the plan in three nights, after everyone from the coalition had gone home. "There's a laser- sensor security system with a keypad here." Jared pointed on the hand drawn blueprint. "Tessa needs to disarm that. After that, Aiden you'll need to pick the lock.

"Once inside it should be a piece of cake to load up and carry out all the weapons and ammunition, lock the safe, reset the security system and get out undetected. Any questions?"

"What do you want me to do?" Seth asked looking a bit disappointed.

"We're taking a lot of weapons, you need to help carry them out. You also need to write down what we take and give that to me so I can change the inventory list. I'm going to be on lookout so I can't do it." Seth nodded.

"What sort of circuit are we talking about here?" Tessa asked.

"It's a PIC via a transistor," Jared responded. "It should be a piece of cake."

"Do you have schematics I can study?"

Jared lifted the blueprints and pulled out another large sheet of thin paper. He carefully rolled it and handed it to Tessa. "It's all yours, just don't ruin it, I need to return it when we're finished. Something else I forgot to mention, once the alarm is disarmed you will have ten minutes to get in and out before the alarm resets itself."

"What kind of lock will I be picking?"

Jared looked over his blueprint and pointed at a note jotted down. "It's an Abloy padlock." He glanced at Aiden. "Is that a problem?"

Aiden's stomach dropped. He had picked a lot of locks in his day, and if there was anything he had learned, it was that the government-issued Abloy padlocks were one of the most difficult. "Why can't we just cut it off?"

"Because our goal is to get in and out without anyone suspecting anything. Plus, they somehow built it into the door, so you can't actually get to the shackle."

Aiden closed his eyes and breathed slowly. He really was going to be sick this time.

When Aiden didn't respond, Jared spoke, "Can you do it?"

Aiden opened his eyes. Everyone was staring at him expectantly. "Yes, I can do it, but I'll need practice and I need a special picking tool that I don't have. Those locks aren't easy and if you want it done in "

"Under two minutes," Terrance cut him off.

Aiden's eyes widened. "Right."

"Then it's a good thing I have an extra one for you to practice on. Better get working." Jared handed him a practice lock.

"Is this the exact lock they have on the vault door? The configuration of disks matters."

Jared shrugged. "You're lucky I was able to find a spare Abloy lock."

Aiden grabbed the lock and looked it over. "What about my picking tool?"

"You'll have to find or make what you need, we don't have anything," Jared snapped, clearly annoyed at all his questions.

They were not making this easy for him. How was he ever going to find the picking tool he needed and practice opening the lock in time?

Terrance moved on, finishing his instructions, but by that point Aiden was too focused on the lock. He flipped it around in his palm, held it to his face to examine the shaft. This was not going to be easy.

Chapter 11

The long days dragged on for an eternity. Amina was only halfway through the second day of traveling, but she felt like she was going in circles. On the map she knew where she wanted to go, but when she looked at her surroundings it was hard to tell if she was getting any closer. *So much for my keen sense of direction.*

The only solace was the thriving mountains. Birds chirped and flitted around as the squirrels played chase in the trees. Amina even saw a few rabbits scurry off when she got too close to them.

Wildlife still existed here, and it struck Amina as strange how this area seemed nearly untouched by the destruction that wreaked havoc upon the rest of the earth: asteroids, drought, water poisoning. And yet, here the trees grew tall and thick. The air was pure, and the animals were alive and healthy.

As she journeyed deeper into the mountains, Amina was at peace. She felt her fear and stress melt away. This was where she wanted to be forever. She focused on the beauty of the nature that Sabaoth had so graciously designed, which in turn reminded her of better times, when her faith was strong and her love for serving others flourished.

Amina had a typical childhood. She grew up on a cull-de-sac

with three other families who had children around her age, and they got along great.

Amina didn't have a care in the world besides wondering when she could go out and play again.

That's how childhood was supposed to be. But when Amina was eleven, the stock market crashed and times were tougher on her family financially. Her father lost his job and when he couldn't find another one quick enough, they were forced to foreclose and move in with Amina's Uncle Paul and Aunt Mo. It was a small, cramped two-bedroom apartment, with barely enough privacy to go to the bathroom.

Amina's mom had a part-time job working at a convenience store, but without a high school degree, it was hard for her to find anything better. And although her father was constantly looking, he just couldn't get a job that would make enough money to find them a home of their own.

After five months, Amina and her family stumbled upon a soup kitchen run by a group of Notzrim. While they weren't homeless, they certainly were in need.

The people at the kitchen not only fed them but clothed them, gave them new blankets, and a bag of groceries to take.

Before sending them on their way one of the women invited Amina's family to come back Sunday morning.

They agreed and that Sunday they heard the most amazing message of their lives. The leader spoke of a god who was full of hope and forgiveness, and that through him one could be given a new life and be taken care of forever.

Amina was immediately hooked. She wanted to know more about this so called Mashiakh, Sabaoth's son, who was willing to put his life in danger for his enemy and save them.

Amina insisted they go back. Week after week Amina soaked

in all that the leader had to teach them about Mashiakh. She even obtained one of their free Sacred Books so she could read during the week.

No longer did Amina feel desperate and afraid. She fully put her trust in Mashiakh and knew he would save them from their demise.

From that moment on Amina devoted herself to Mashiakh and serving with the Notzrim. She attended weekly studies, served at the soup kitchen, and led a community cleanup day in the city. She did anything and everything she could to give back to the church and Sabaoth for the incredible gift she had been given.

She finally felt that there was peace back in her life and a purpose. She felt strong and excited too. There was finally a future in sight for her beyond just finding a job to survive; now she could thrive and help others to do the same. She had freedom to dream and this god, Sabaoth, had given her that.

As time went on her family also came to faith and experienced the change in their hearts that Mashiakh promised.

As Amina's father became more involved, he made friends with one man who owned a small business. He ended up offering Amina's father a job, which he gladly took.

Another family in the church had a small vacant apartment in their basement and allowed the family to move in for free until they could afford a place of their own.

Amina was enveloped in love shown by this new family of Notzrim and she never wanted to leave. She wanted to be as selfless as them and live for something greater than herself.

But as Amina harshly learned, no good thing lasts long. Just nine years after putting her faith in Sabaoth, the Great Desolation began, the church fell apart, and that was just the beginning of Amina's nightmare.

Her faith was being tested, and as long as she had a few close friends and her family, she thought she could stay strong. But as time went on, people started to disappear and it became more difficult to stay strong. Deep in her heart, Amina knew she still had some faith, some hope that what she had put her trust in years ago was still true. That's why when the vision came to her, she jumped at it. She was so convinced that it was Sabaoth speaking to her, but then Paxton turned out to not be who he said he was. So was her entire dream a figment of her own subconscious?

The sun rose high as the dense foliage trapped the moisture in making the air thick. Amina's head swirled as if she were floating. She had to sit down and drink some water before she passed out.

The water felt cool as it trickled down her throat and filled her belly. She imagined what it would be like to jump into a cool refreshing pool or eat ice cream that gave her brain-freeze. Just the thought helped her feel cooler, even if it was only in her mind.

Amina sat and leaned against a nearby tree. Closing her eyes, she forced her body to relax. The less energy she used, the faster she could cool herself off.

Against the tree, not moving, the forest felt absurdly still. She wasn't used to the stillness. She tried to focus on a sound, any sound. She heard nothing; chills ran up her spine. Usually if she listened intently she could hear birds, but there was nothing.

A twig snapped to her left. Amina didn't move, she didn't want to startle the animal.

There was a quiet rustling in the bush and then movement.

CHAPTER 11

Still Amina didn't move. Depending on the animal she assumed staying still would be her best bet, make them think she was no threat. Time seemed to stop and Amina's muscles tensed. Her fingers twitched. The animal let out an unusual grunt, almost un-animal like. It was, in fact, the clearing of a man's throat.

Amina drew in a sharp breath, someone was watching her, hunting her. Without opening her eyes or turning her head, Amina slowly edged her right hand down the side of her leg and into her side cargo pocket where she had a knife.

She listened again. Whoever was behind the bush was still there, but they weren't moving.

She had one chance. If they had a gun, and she wasn't fast enough, she'd be dead. Swiftly, Amina rolled to her right putting the tree between her and her enemy. No gunshots went off. Amina jerked her head looking all around her to see if she could spot others. No one. There was just the one person.

"I suggest you leave before I hurt you," Amina warned, trying to be brave.

No reply.

Amina strained to hear over her own heavy breathing. Nothing. *Where'd they go?* Amina slid toward a rock and peered at the bushes. Whoever was there wasn't visible. She had to think quickly before they made the first move.

She crept her way back behind the tree and toward her bag to grab a larger knife, the person spoke.

"Amina." It came from behind her.

Amina quickly spun around and held out her knife in defense. Her chest constricted and her body was rigid, but she was ready to fight.

Paxton stood in front of her with his hands up in surrender.

Amina blinked. Lowering the knife she straightened but still couldn't find any words.

Finally, although still bewildered, she found her voice. "What are you doing here?" Amina had been certain there was no way Paxton could get out of that office alone.

"I want to help." Paxton stepped forward in a gesture of good will, but Amina quickly stepped back and held out her knife again.

"You need to leave. I don't want you here." Her blood boiled as she tightly gripped the knife—the knife he had given her—the knife that had already killed one person.

"I know you're upset with me, but I want to make things right. I want to make sure that you get the underground to a new hiding place before the Myriad find them."

She wanted so badly to believe him but people lie. "How do I know you aren't on some new mission to find the Hebrews and have them killed too? How do I know you didn't go back and tell the Myriad where my people are? For all I know they could be dead already."

"If you really believed that, you wouldn't be out here aimlessly searching for the Hebrews. Please, let me help you."

Amina scoffed. "That's not happening."

"Look, you don't have to trust me, but you do have to admit that I could be useful."

Amina tilted her head, intrigued with his new spin. If anything, he was persistent. "How's that?"

"I have both survival and combat training. I have great tracking and hunting skills."

Amina crossed her arms and glared. He was starting to sound more convincing. Traversing the mountains was proving to be more difficult than she anticipated. Having the extra help

CHAPTER 11

reading the land would be useful. Amina shook her head. What was she thinking? This man gained her trust and then betrayed her. He was working for the enemy. How could she let him come?

"No. I don't believe you're here to help. You need to leave, now," Amina snapped.

Amina grabbed her bag and took off at a brisk pace. She wanted to put as much distance between her and Paxton as possible.

It wasn't long before Amina heard footsteps. She glanced over her shoulder. Paxton was following.

Amina rolled her eyes. "What are you doing?" she asked, still walking.

"I told you, I'm coming. I want to prove to you that I've changed. I have no interest in helping the Myriad ever again."

"What about your family? They mean nothing to you now?"

Paxton chewed on the side of his cheek. "I have to trust that my dad is a smart man and can take care of my grandma and himself. And maybe," he let out a deep breath, "Sabaoth can protect them?" He didn't sound confident, but he was hopeful. Amina was intrigued but didn't say anything.

Amina forged her way through the bushes and over the rocks for many miles not knowing where she was going. She knew she was heading northeast based on the direction of the sun's movement, but that was it. There was nothing else on her map that gave any indication that she was heading in the right direction. She just had to trust her research and her gut.

As Amina kept moving forward, she noticed the temperature drop and her feet sunk into the muddy ground. She stopped and listened for a long moment until she heard it. Amina smiled with relief as they both declared in unison, "There's water nearby."

Paxton chuckled while Amina scowled and quickened her pace.

Soon Amina could hear the sound of rushing water while the bugs buzzed and swarmed until finally she broke out of the bushes and saw a glorious stream. It wasn't very large or wide, but it was moving and that was most important.

Amina stopped at the edge and knelt down. From the Great Desolation, she knew that much of the world's water supply had been contaminated with either blood or wormwood, and yet, this water seemed to be crystal clear.

Grabbing her bag, Amina pulled out a water test kit and scooped a small test sample into the clear tube. She waited, watching to see if the water changed colors. If it turned orange, it was contaminated, but if it stayed clear, it was clean. The water didn't change.

Amina smiled as she quickly took off her boots, hiked her pants up and waded into the water with her canteens in hand. Once she was knee deep, Amina proceeded to chug the last of her water and then refill her canteens. It was refreshing to let the cool water whirl around her legs. Amina couldn't recall the last time she was in fresh water.

Paxton kicked off his boots and waded into the water beside Amina. He moved much slower than Amina had and as he got closer she could see goosebumps on his neck and arms.

"Cold?"

"Frigid," he chattered. "How are you able to stand in this without your feet feeling like pins and needles?"

"Years of practice. Hot water is not a luxury we have in the tunnels." Amina recapped her last canteen and headed back to the shore.

CHAPTER 11

Once Paxton was back on shore, Amina handed him a small chalky tablet. "Put this in your water. It'll purify it in case there's still wormwood or any other poisons my test didn't catch."

"Thanks." Paxton dropped the tablet into his canteen and it sizzled like Alka-Seltzer.

They sat in silence putting on their shoes. When Amina stood, she felt muscle fatigue settling in, but there were still hours of daylight she didn't want to waste. Amina pulled her arms through her backpack and started up the hill.

"I don't know how you were able to bear living down there for all these years. Having to hide in the dark, always in fear of being found." Paxton spoke as he followed behind. "That would drive me crazy."

Amina narrowed her eyes, annoyed that Paxton was trying to relate to her as if they were friends. She had no interest in letting him in, not after what he did.

"Honestly, until a few months ago, we were never really in danger. The Myriad had no clue where we were and we felt safe. Thanks for changing all that." She kept climbing, her legs felt weighted down like sandbags. She could hear Paxton breathing heavily behind her. It was nice to know she wasn't the only one exhausted.

"You know, Paxton, things would be-" Amina started to speak, but Paxton quickly shushed her. Amina turned, ready to snap at him, but she noticed his eyes closed as he listened. Amina did the same. She realized there was an unnatural sound in the distance and slowly growing louder. A sort of thumping noise. Her eyes shot open wide. It was a helicopter.

Amina looked at Paxton suspiciously. *Did he tell them to follow?* They had to hide and quickly.

"We've got to move, now!" Amina sprinted up the hill, her eyes scanning the area as fast as they could process her surroundings.

Fire shot through her legs and she wasn't sure she could keep going. If it weren't for the threat on her life, she would stop.

"Over here!" Paxton shouted. She saw Paxton standing beside a pile of rocks with a small entrance barely large enough to fit a person through, but it was something.

Amina bolted to Paxton and got on her stomach. She began army crawling into the rocks, but her bag wouldn't fit. She felt Paxton yank her backpack off with urgency. All she could focus on was getting inside that hole.

The helicopter drew closer. It would soon be above them. *What if this was a trap? What if they already knew where they were?* Amina shook the thoughts away.

Amina squeezed inside. The rock pile was actually a small cave and once inside, she was able to sit up, albeit hunched over. She waited, expecting to see Paxton come through next. A drum pounded in her head and she could no longer tell if the noise was her or the helicopter.

Desperately she tried to slow her breathing so she could listen and watch for Paxton. *What was taking him so long?*

Finally, she heard scuffling of dirt and rocks moving. A bag pushed its way through the tiny entrance. Amina quickly grabbed and yanked the bag free and hugged it. Next came Paxton. Once inside, he shoved his arms back into the entrance hole and grabbed his own bag.

Neither of them spoke. They sat in the darkness, straining to hear what was going on outside. The helicopter seemed to hover above the area for an exorbitant amount of time.

CHAPTER 11

Amina closed her eyes and whispered a prayer. She didn't feel worthy of asking for protection, and she wasn't sure if Sabaoth would listen to her, but in that moment, it was the only thing she could do.

The minutes crawled by and she wasn't sure the helicopter would ever leave. Could they see them through the rocks? Did they notice Paxton before he got inside? Maybe there were Myriad on the ground searching for them and it was just a matter of time before they were found and killed. Amina's pulse quickened and she grew short of breath. She hated just sitting there doing nothing. She felt helpless.

Suddenly, Amina heard movement outside their tiny hiding place. She froze as her heart skipped a beat. Her eyes locked on the entrance as she waited, listening. Slowly, like molasses, she set the bag down and pulled out her knife so she'd be ready.

Amina listened to boots shuffling in the dirt. Bushes swished around. Amina guessed there were at least two soldiers.

A radio chattered directly outside the cave. Amina desperately tried to hear what was being said, but she couldn't make out any clear words.

There was a beep and then the solider outside spoke. His voice clearer, but Amina's ears were full of cotton. She wasn't sure if it was the rocks or the fear that made it hard for her to comprehend.

A second beep sounded and more talking. This time Amina understood him.

"That's a negative. If he's in these mountains, he's gone a different direction." *So they are looking for Paxton?* "10-4. I'll head south. We'll find the traitor and make him pay."

Amina heard the soldier's footsteps fading away and she let out the breath she had been holding as quietly as possible. The helicopter also faded in the distance. They were finally gone. Amina leaned forward, toward the entrance but a hand gently pushed her back.

"It's too soon." His voice barely audible. "The soldiers might circle back."

Amina leaned back against the cold rock. They were going to have to wait.

Chapter 12

Hours passed and Amina noticed the light growing dim. There had been no movement or sound coming from outside their hiding place for quite some time, and Amina believed they were safe. Amina looked at Paxton sleeping. She nudged him on the shoulder, but he didn't move. She shook him harder, but still nothing. Amina rolled her eyes as she swiftly elbowed him in the ribs, and he woke with a start.

"I think it's clear now," Amina whispered as she rolled her shoulders and tilted her head from side to side. Her muscles and joints felt stiff like the tin man and took extra energy to move.

Amina started to scoot her way toward the entrance, but she and Paxton were in such tight quarters that she couldn't get past him without making contact.

"Maybe I should go first," Paxton breathed. They were inches away and she could feel his warm breath against her cheek. Chills ran up and down her arms and she felt flushed.

Fixed against Paxton, Amina didn't move. Eventually she spoke. "Okay, sure." Amina slowly moved back to her spot so Paxton could make his way out.

Once Paxton was through the small tunnel entrance, Amina

grabbed the backpacks and shoved them through.

As she belly-crawled out of the cave, no longer filled with adrenaline, she noticed how jagged the rocks were as they scraped into her shoulder blades like barbed wire.

When she finally pushed her way out of the hole, she stood rubbing her shoulder blades since they stung. She was certain they were bleeding. Amina grabbed the bottom of her shirt and wiped the dirt and sweat off her face, tasting the tiny rocks mingled with sweat on her lips. She caught Paxton's gaze.

Amina let go of her shirt, heat rising into her face. She clenched her fists into tiny balls. It was him, he must've led the Myriad here. Without realizing what she was doing, Amina charged Paxton and shoved him against the rock pile. She held her forearm tight against his neck. "It was you, wasn't it? You led them here. You wanted me to get caught!"

Paxton tried to shake his head, but Amina's arm was choking him. "No, I swear. I didn't," Paxton coughed out.

"Don't lie to me!" Amina pressed in hard upon his throat and looked coldly into his eyes. She wanted desperately to believe him, but once a liar, always a liar.

Paxton squirmed his arms between them and shoved Amina away. She stumbled backward, feeling a sharp pain in her chest. He had pushed right on her bruised ribs. Amina breathed sharply.

"I'm not the enemy." Paxton straightened, rubbing at his throat.

"I should have never let you follow me. It's because of you I'm even in this situation."

"Don't blame this on me. I was following orders from an organization who was threatening my family, but I was also trying to protect yours. I didn't give them accurate information."

"What?" Amina's face twisted in surprise and confusion.

"Yes, I gave them a map and some of the information I gave was true, but not everything. That map was not accurate, not completely anyway. I was trying to buy us time."

"Us?"

"You and me, so we could get your people out before the Myriad attacked. I had a plan. Everything was going to work out and then . . ." He trailed off, looking flustered. He ran a hand through his dirty blond hair and let out a sigh.

"And then what?"

"You didn't have to follow me. You didn't have to find out."

"But I did." Amina could feel the heat rising in her face. Why was he playing games with her? *What he's saying can't be true, can it?*

Paxton didn't speak again for a long time. She tried to study his face, determine if he was being sincere, but she felt her own emotions were hindering her judgment.

Paxton took a step toward Amina and spoke tenderly. "I'm here now to *help* you."

He might have been telling the truth, but something led the Myriad to their location. They were looking for him.

Amina charged Paxton and started patting him down. She went over every inch of his clothing and ran her fingers along his neck and arms, checking for implants. Once satisfied, she grabbed his backpack and started tearing through it. There must be a tracker on him somewhere.

Catching on, Paxton helped. After dumping everything out, Amina found nothing. No hidden tracker, no GPS device, nothing that looked like it could give away their location.

Amina threw the backpack with frustration. "How? There's

nothing here!" Amina stood, wild with fear and frustration.

"I don't know, but I swear to you, I did not lead them here."

"If they show up again, we're done. You leave and you don't follow me anymore. Got it?"

Paxton nodded.

Amina grabbed her bag and walked off.

As night fell, Amina stopped at a clearing and set her backpack down. She instantly felt lighter. "We'll camp here for the night," she said curtly before setting to work creating another firepit for the evening. "I hope you packed food because I only brought enough for one."

"I have food." Paxton placed his bag on the ground and sat. As Amina brought over pieces of wood Paxton stopped her. "You can't do that."

"Do what?"

"Build a fire."

She gave him a look. "Yes, I can. I've done it before, I know how." Amina continued stacking her wood.

Paxton shook his head. "I'm sure you know how, but it's not safe right now. We don't know if the Myriad are still nearby. They might double back, especially if they see smoke."

Amina stopped. "Oh, right." Amina dropped the sticks and turned to grab her back.

The sun serenely set bringing forth the stars and stillness of the night. By then Amina had hung her hammock, eaten a bag of nuts, and was staring at the night sky until she drifted to sleep.

Amina stood in the middle of Main Hall Dwelling. All around

CHAPTER 12

her people sprinted past. Horrified faces screamed. They were trying to escape, but they were trapped. Amina spun around, searching for the source of dread. That's when she saw them. Terror ripped through her as she watched Myriad soldiers file in with guns drawn. Scanning the dwelling, she found a tiny opening unguarded. Amina screamed with all her might, trying to get people's attention, but no sound came out. Desperate, Amina tried to move, but her feet were cemented to the ground. She had to stand and watch as the Myriad moved in and opened fire. She had to watch and do nothing as her family fell dead at her feet. Amina tried to look away, but the scene was all around her. Her eyes wouldn't close. Deafening gunfire echoed, but the maddening screams and cries seemed to drown it out. Something warm splattered on her face. Amina flinched. She touched her cheek and felt the sticky blood. When would this nightmare end? She heard a thud and felt something fall across her foot. Amina didn't want to look, and yet something pulled her head down. Slowly she peered into the dead cold eyes of Aiden.

Amina woke in a sweat and breathing heavily as her hammock rocked back and forth. It took her a moment to remember where she was, but then she saw her backpack and Paxton asleep on the ground across from her.

She took in a deep calming breath and slowly let it out. *It was just a dream. It's not real.* She tried to convince herself. But was it just a dream, or another vision? *No, Sabaoth wouldn't give such a horrific vision if there was nothing she could do about it.* If anything, it was a warning. If Amina didn't find the Hebrews soon, that would be her family's fate. Amina tried to lay back down and sleep but couldn't, she was too rattled. She needed to call Aiden and reassure herself.

Amina rolled out of her hammock, and her legs felt shaky. She pulled the cellphone out of her backpack, but then remembered Paxton. She didn't want to wake him. In fact she didn't want him around at all. The only thing he'd brought to the table was more trouble. She assumed the Myriad must be tracking him somehow and that made him dangerous.

Looking to the sky she could see just the tiniest hint of the night disappearing and day taking over. Amina decided to gather her things and leave before Paxton woke.

As she walked, Amina pulled out the map from her backpack. She wanted to make sure she was still on the right path and determine how much further she still needed to go.

There was no telling if the Myriad would return and she wanted to reach the Hebrews as quickly as possible.

Scanning the map she was able to identify the river she was certain they had discovered yesterday.

As she followed the river up the map, she noticed it led into the same valley where she believed the Hebrews lived. So that's what she would do. Follow the river. That seemed easy enough, and it was a good way to ensure she had enough water to stay hydrated.

Once Amina found the river, she flipped open the cellphone, pressed one and then send.

The phone was quiet for a long time. Amina started to wonder if it was even going to work, but then it started ringing. Her eyes welled with tears. Why was she so emotional?

Eventually the ringing stopped, and Amina heard a voice on the other line.

"Amina is that you?" Aiden asked with concern. "Is everything alright?" Amina was choked up. She didn't know how to answer and if she did, she was afraid all that would come out would be gargled words drenched in tears. "Amina. Amina, what's wrong?"

Amina shook her head, even though she knew Aiden couldn't see her. "Nothing." Amina took a deep breath trying to pull herself together. "I had this horrendous dream and– It's just good to hear your voice."

Amina heard Aiden laugh a little on the other end. "You too, sis. I'm glad you're okay. What was the dream about? Did it have to do with us here?"

"Yes." Her voice was thick. "The Myriad had found and killed everyone."

"Oh geez, I'm sorry sis. It was only a dream, we're okay here. There haven't been any attacks or even sightings above ground since you've left."

Amina wiped the tears away with the back of her hand. "Thanks."

There was a moment of silence between the two before Aiden burst with excitement. "And how cool is this that the phones actually work? It's unbelievable!"

Amina laughed. "You should give yourself more credit, you're a smart guy."

"Thanks. So, did you find them yet? Are you with the Hebrews?" His voice grew with excitement. "Should I go get Uncle Paul and tell him? Oh, they're going to be thrilled!"

Amina interrupted Aiden before he got carried away. "No, not yet. I think I'm close though." Amina bit her lip. "Have they figured out an escape plan in case there's a breech?"

"Yeah, I think so. Hey sis, I'd love to chat, but I've gotta go. It's cleaning duty time. You're okay right?"

"Oh yeah, I'm fine," Amina lied. "You go, do what you gotta do. I'll be back soon I'm sure."

"I look forward to it. I love you, Amina."

"I love you too, Aiden." Amina pulled the phone away and pressed end before shoving it back into her backpack. Her brother was alive, everyone was safe, so why did she still feel so uneasy?

Chapter 13

Amina wearily followed the river, wondering if it would ever take her to the valley. It was almost midday and she didn't feel any closer to her destination.

Amina watched the water bounce and race across the rocks, tree roots, and anything else that came along its path. It had direction and it had a purpose, something Amina wasn't so sure she still had. Her hope was waning and her uncertainty was starting to convince her to turn around and go back home.

As she continued along the river, she came around the bend and saw two deer drinking from the water. Amina stopped and squatted down behind a nearby bush so she could watch them and not spook the creatures. It was such a rare sighting. Especially for such docile herbivores.

Most of the animals had been killed from all the devastation and those that were left seemed to have become even more vicious and dangerous than before. They were starving and they were contaminated from the water, which made them extremely dangerous.

However, these deer looked to be at ease. Amina smiled as she watched the two sip the water. Once the deer had had their fill of water they nonchalantly wandered back into the trees and disappear. Amina smiled to herself as she stood and continued on her way. The forest had a way of calming her and bringing peace.

As the day continued, the walk became more laborious. There wasn't a clear bank for Amina to walk along so she was forced to climb over rocks and fallen trees. It was also starting to slope steeper and become muddier, which made it difficult to keep her footing. She had wondered if the river would soon find its way into a steep ravine making it impossible for Amina to follow. Amina looked at the hill and wondered if there was a trail that paralleled the river. If so, she could follow the water without walking in so much mud.

Amina started to make her way up the steep hillside, using tree branches, roots, and rocks to help keep her footing and also have something to hold. It felt as if she was climbing straight up.

Amina took a step in a muddy spot and felt the ground slide underneath her. She slid down the hill on her knees several feet before slowing in the sludge. Annoyed that she was now covered in slimy mud, she let out an exasperated groan before continuing up the hillside.

The hill seemed to go on forever and muscle fatigue was starting to set in. She looked behind her, back toward the river, but could no longer see it. It had disappeared into the mob of trees and bushes. She had hoped there was flatter ground above her, but that was proving to be futile. *Maybe this wasn't such a good idea after all.*

Her body lagged forcing her to stop and sit on a rock barely large enough. She pulled out her canteen and took a swig of water. To continue up or to go back down, that was the question, wasn't it? Down below was the river she knew she had to follow to get to the valley, but she risked reaching a dead end with cliffs and river only. She didn't have a flotation device and her raft-building skills were nonexistent.

To continue up meant maybe she'd eventually reach flat land, but how far away from the river would it take her and would she be able to continue on the right path if she couldn't see the river she needed to follow?

Eventually, Amina determined to work her way slowly back down the treacherous hillside and deal with the river. The river was the key to the valley, she knew that and she had to trust it.

She kept as low to the ground as possible and held on to as many sturdy looking branches as she could find. It was slow and tedious, but eventually, covered in mud, she found her way back to the river.

Amina took a moment to clean the mud off her hands in the icy water before continuing.

The river continued for the next five miles. The bank of the river narrowed, and Amina had to trudge along the soft sandy shore as the river lapped over her boots. Her boots may have been steel-toed and thick, but somehow the water found its way in and soaked her socks.

Even when the bank disappeared and the rocks grew taller beside her—forcing Amina to walk along the shallow edge with her feet submerged—she pressed on. She may have had a temporary moment of doubt earlier, but she'd come too far to turn back now.

Amina continued, despite the water levels rising to her shins. She kept on marching, but for how much longer?

The water was getting deeper and eventually she wouldn't be able to walk anymore. *She needed the mystical boat from her dream.*

Looking around, Amina spotted a rock ahead that she could

climb. She waded forward and hoisted herself onto the rock and pulled out the map one more time.

Everything on the map was starting to look the same. She knew she was following the river and that the river would eventually empty out into a valley, but how far?

Amina scrunched her eyebrows together, trying to look at her surroundings to see if there was a marker or something she saw that also appeared on the map. There was nothing. She was walking blind.

Amina shoved the map back into her bag. Looking up, the cliff didn't look too high. At this point climbing to the top and following from above was her best bet.

After tightening her shoelaces and making sure her backpack was secure, Amina determined a place to start the climb. Small divots in the rock would allow her to get a good grip as she began her ascent. She had never been rock climbing outside of a gym and she definitely had never climbed without ropes.

Slowly, one move at a time, Amina climbed the cliff. Thankfully, the rock had several ledges and openings where she could easily place a hand or foot, but the cliff was sandy and who knew what was living in those holes.

Amina pushed the thoughts out of her mind and kept climbing, praying the entire time for Sabaoth to not let her fall.

Her arms started to shake. She had never been afraid of heights, but climbing a cliff with nothing to catch her was enough to make the adrenaline ignite through her body like pins and needles.

As Amina reached up to the available spot on the rock and stood herself taller, her foot slipped slamming her knee against the jagged rocks and causing her to almost lose her grip. She yelped as she tightened her grip and quickly placed her foot in a small crevice.

Amina closed her eyes and let out a slow breath trying to stop the shaking in her entire body. *Oh please Sabaoth, get me up this rock.*

Amina could see the top almost in reach. Determination surged inside and propelled her forward, but her movements stayed slow and methodical. She didn't want to let the excitement make her overconfident and cause her to slip again.

Amina climbed, taking her time until finally, she was able to pull herself over the edge and flop onto the solid ground. She lay on her stomach with her eyes closed, breathing heavily. She made it. She was alive. *Thank you, Sabaoth.*

She didn't allow herself to rest for too long. There was still a lot of day left.

Amina pulled herself up and looked at her new surroundings. Shockingly the top of the cliff was nothing like the surrounding forest below. Instead Amina found herself surrounded with a plethora of large rocks. The bushes were sparser and the trees appeared stunted.

She was relieved that she didn't have to fight with bushes and trees, but she was exposed now to the heat, as well as any possible helicopters flying overhead—that is if the Myriad hadn't given up their search.

For the rest of the day, Amina followed the cliff's edge and periodically checked to make sure the river was still down below. It seemed as if it would never end. No matter how far she walked, the land just kept going. It was endlessly flat, and she needed it to slope into a valley.

Chapter 14

The sun sat low in the sky. A few clouds hung painted with the orange and pink hue of the setting sun. Amina's body ached from the climb hours before and was ready to rest for the night. She hoped she wouldn't have to do anything that strenuous again, she wasn't sure her body could take it. After wandering a little further, she scoped a small clearing perfect to make camp. Amina dropped her backpack on the ground, and she plopped down beside it, feeling the sweet relief immediately.

As the sun dropped below the horizon, Amina lost her light. She grabbed her backpack to pull out her flint rock, then stopped. Was it possible the Myriad were still looking for them? Amina didn't want to risk it. Instead she rummaged around and pulled out a glow stick. She cracked and shook it, allowing the glowing liquid inside to illuminate. After shoving a few rocks around to make it stand, she found the half-eaten bag of nuts she acquired at flea market day. That day felt like eons ago. Could it really have been only five days ago?

The night enveloped her, but she could make out shadowed outlines of bushes, rocks, and a few trees. Amina debated about hanging her hammock. She was tempted to sleep on the ground, but she also knew the danger that it could bring. Eventually safety won the debate and Amina pulled out her

CHAPTER 14

hammock. Despite most of the trees being short, she did manage to find a few taller and sturdier looking trees for her hammock.

As she slowly stood, her stiff muscles aching with each move, she heard a noise behind her. Amina turned and there, staring right at her, was a wolf. Amina froze, her body rigid. The wolf was strikingly beautiful with its light brown coat speckled with white and gray, and its onyx eyes that stared intently at her, studying her. At the same time she knew how dangerous a wolf could be. At any moment the wolf could attack and take her out in one vicious leap.

Remembering what her father taught her about wolves, Amina lowered her eyes so as not to pose a threat. Slowly, she grabbed her backpack and held it above her head in hopes of making herself look bigger. From her peripheral, she continued to watch the wolf. The wolf lowered its snout, narrowing its ferocious eyes at her, watching knowingly. It continued to stand just outside the clearing, at a safe distance. It seemed odd that this wolf was alone. Why would this wolf leave its pack? What were they trying to prove? Or was it pushed out because of its domineering attitude? Amina empathized with the loneliness of the wolf. Wolves are meant to live in community. They never worked alone, and they accepted help freely. Amina had never come across one before and she certainly never intended to do so, and yet there was a providential connection she felt with this one. The wolf let out a low menacing growl, knocking Amina out of her thoughts. She felt her luck might be running out. She had to think fast.

"Ha!" Amina let out a loud cutting shout, hoping it came off braver than she felt. Maybe if she's big and loud the wolf will think rethink its prey. "Ha!" The wolf flinched but didn't back away. "Ha! Ha!" This time it took a small step back baring its teeth. *Oh Sabaoth, please make it leave.* Her body was now trembling, but she did her best not to flee.

Suddenly Amina heard a noise behind her. Her body went rigid as she drew in a sharp breath. So the wolf wasn't alone. This was it. Amina was outnumbered. If she didn't do something, they would. *Think, think, think! What else am I supposed to do?*

"Amina." Paxton whispered from above. Amina nearly jumped out of her skin. Where did he come from? "Amina," he whispered again, "climb the tree." His voice was quiet but sharp.

Like a snail Amina slid her way toward the tree, still keeping the wolf in her sight making sure it wasn't about to lunge at her. Her back bumped into the hard trunk. To climb meant she had to take her eyes off the wolf, but she didn't trust herself to climb faster than the wolf could attack.

"Come on, Amina, I'm watching her. She's not crouched, you're good to go."

Mustering her courage, Amina turned and started to climb as fast as she could. The tree had several branches close together, making it easy to climb, and for that she was thankful. As she climbed higher, a howl echoed in the night. Instinctually Amina turned to look at the wolf just in time to watch her run away. She was safe. Amina rested her head on a branch. Closing her eyes, she started laughing.

"What's so funny?"

Amina shook her head. "I don't know. I think I'm just relieved."

Paxton smiled. "Me too. Now come up here. I think we should sleep here tonight just in case they come back."

CHAPTER 14

Amina finished ascending the tree until she stopped at one thick branch. She sat on it and leaned against the trunk. Paxton handed her a rope. She wrapped the rope around her waist and handed it back to Paxton who proceeded to tie it to the tree. He too was tied to the tree, that way if either of them lost their balance while sleeping, they wouldn't plummet to the ground.

Amina sat staring at nothing in particular. "How did you find me?"

"I never left you." Paxton admitted almost sheepishly. "I woke up as you were taking off and I've been following all day. I wanted to make sure you were safe."

Amina cocked her head, baffled at his loyalty. She has been nothing but awful to him and yet he continued to watch after her, like a puppy dog. It was endearing and Amina found her heart softening toward him. Was it possible he was telling her the truth? Maybe he truly did regret his previous actions. Amina rested her head on the tree and closed her eyes. "I'm not getting rid of you, am I?"

"Nope."

"Thank you."

"You're welcome."

Paxton reached his hand out and took hold of Amina's dangling fingers. She flinched but didn't pull away.

The next morning, Amina and Paxton rose early, shimmied down the tree, and began their journey side by side.

"So where to boss?"

"Boss?"

"Well yeah, you're the one with the plan, so you're in charge."

She shook her head, but then explained, "We follow the river. I believe it'll eventually lead us to a valley."

Paxton walked to the cliff's edge and peered down to the river below. "And that's where the Hebrews are?" he asked, looking back at her.

"I'm pretty sure."

They spent the morning in silence. Amina kept her eyes focused on the terrain ahead and the river below. She had noticed that as they kept marching forward, the desert-like terrain gave way to more luscious foliage, and the rocky ground slopped downward. They continued their way down the hill and rocks, helping each other when necessary.

By the time the sun reached its peak, Amina and Paxton were only three feet above the water, and when she listened carefully, she heard the water roaring in the distance. Amina felt a sudden flare of excitement as she sped up. This was it. This was what she had been searching for. The valley was within reach. Her mouth curved into a smile. She was now sprinting.

She could hear the roaring of a waterfall. Twenty feet, ten feet. She could see the steep drop off, how the earth just seemed to cut in half. She could see out in the distance how it continued. Five feet. Butterflies swirled in her stomach. And then she was there, standing at the edge of the cliff. The river dropped, launching itself into the open valley below and misting Amina's face.

The valley was a vast open field blanketed with a rainbow of wildflowers. Encompassing the open field was a plethora of towering trees, thick with leaves. They seemed to create a natural barrier around the valley, hiding it from outsiders. From the waterfall, a pool of water opened to a stream that continued on as far as she could see. Flecks of sunlight reflected off the water like tiny diamonds.

CHAPTER 14

It was absolutely breathtaking and even more amazing than the vision of the valley in her dream. At least something from her dream was right, and it was no wonder Sabaoth chose this place for his people to hide. It was a second Eden.

As Amina gazed upon the extraordinary valley, an old passage came to mind,

> *Sabaoth is my shepherd,*
>   *I shall not want.*
>   *He lets me rest in green meadows,*
>   *he leads me beside peaceful streams.*
>   *He renews my strength,*
>   *he guides me along the right path, bringing honor to*
> *his name.*

This was certainly a place where the Hebrews could be restored and at peace, but where was the village? Where were the people who were supposed to be living there? This was the valley from her dream, so why was it empty?

As Amina's eyes scanned the valley, she couldn't find any hints of a settlement. She was so certain that this had to be the place spoken about in the book. The place prophesied to be the hidden Eden, but as Amina's eyes scanned the length of the valley, there was nothing.

Amina felt as if someone had socked her in the stomach making her feel queasy. Hope seemed to drain out of her. They were gone. Even if this had once been where they lived, they didn't anymore. Something caused them to leave or, even worse, she had been wrong the entire time.

Paxton whistled as he looked down to the bottom of the cliff. "That's quite a way down. Is that where we have to go next?"

"I–" Amina started but couldn't find the words. Amina felt her legs weaken and she allowed them to give out from under her.

As she crumpled to the ground Paxton's strong arms caught her and slowly guided her.

"This was supposed to be it," Amina mumbled more to herself than to Paxton.

Paxton sat close beside her. He looked at her with empathy and uncertainty in his eyes. "What do you mean? Aren't they in the valley somewhere?"

"I thought so, but I don't see anything down there."

"They could still be down there, hidden. Aren't they under a protection spell or something?"

"Maybe." Amina tried to recall the conversation she had read in the book. Was there another clue that she had missed?

Amina frantically pulled open her backpack and started pulling out all the books she had taken. There had to be more. She had to have missed something. She hadn't gone through everything before because she was so certain that what she had found was the answer. But now, she needed to comb through every resource she had. Amina was so lost in what she was doing that she had forgotten Paxton was sitting beside her.

She looked at him, wide eyed and desperate. "We need to find a clue."

He tilted his head, pulling his brows together. "What kind of clue?"

"Something to tell us where they are," Amina explained. "I thought the clue I found earlier was the answer. It's what had led me to this valley, but I must've missed something. There must be another clue. We need to find it." Amina handed one of the books to him and then continued looking through her

CHAPTER 14

own book.

Chapter 15

Amina sat and stretched. As she yawned, she tilted her head from side the side to get the kinks out of her neck. When had she fallen asleep? She was still sitting with a book resting on a rock in front of her. There was a new water stain on the paper. Amina brought her hand to her chin and wiped away the drool. Across the way, Paxton sat with a book in his lap and a boyish grin.

Amina smiled as she watched him. There was something about his deep devotion to helping her and his genuine concern about finding the Hebrews that softened her a little toward him.

"What are you smiling about?" she questioned suspiciously.

Paxton sheepishly pointed at her. "Your- uh- hair."

Amina brought her hand to her head and felt the matted knot that had to be wildly sticking in every direction. She pulled her ponytail out and used her fingers to comb out the tangles. Pulling her hair back into a ponytail, Amina walked over to Paxton. "Find anything?"

"Still nothing."

Beside him Amina noticed he had pulled out *The Wizard of Oz*. Odd, she didn't remember putting that in her backpack.

CHAPTER 15

Amina bent down and picked up the book. She sat beside Paxton as she ran her fingers across the tattered cover. As a child, she loved reading this book out loud with Aiden and her father just before heading to bed each night. Then she would drift off to sleep, dreaming about the magical land of Oz.

Amina started thumbing through the pages gingerly. The cover and pages were so worn that many were held together with pieces of tape, and even those were becoming torn from wear. This book had to have been passed around so many times and held in so many hands, it was a wonder it was still intact. There were pencil markings, pen markings, and even some highlights littered throughout the pages.

One highlighted sentence really stood out to her. She read it quietly aloud. "If we walk far enough, we shall sometime come to someplace."

Paxton looked from his book and over toward Amina. "Is that significant?"

"I don't know." Amina absentmindedly replied as she followed the hand-drawn arrow on the page. There in the bottom margin, written in light pencil, read: *Some places are not as they seem. What once seemed lost was never really missing.*

It was an odd comment to write in such a book. Sure the whole story was about a dream Dorothy was having that taught her the value of family, courage, and love but this was a written note. It seemed to have significance to someone.

"What do you suppose it means?" Paxton asked, breaking the silence.

"Beats me." Amina put the book aside and grabbed another to look through for the third time.

Out of the corner of her eye, she spotted Paxton holding a bag of Doritos. "You want some?"

"Where did you get those?"

"I raided a convenient store before coming after you. Do you want them or not?"

She grabbed the bag from Paxton and started munching on them. She hadn't realized how ravenous she was until she took her first bite of the cheese-powdered chip and her stomach began to rumble.

As Amina combed through the book, her mind kept floating back to the note in *The Wizard of Oz*. Why would someone write that? Was it some hidden message? Before the Hebrews disappeared and the Notzrim went into hiding, it wasn't uncommon for them to send messages to one another through books just like this. It was easy to carry classic books around and pass them along without suspicion.

Amina picked up *The Wizard of Oz* again and opened it to the inside cover to see if there was a name of an owner. What she found wasn't the owner's information but rather a note:

To my dearest Ruth, may this book help you find your way home. Love, mom.

Well of course they'd write something corny like that. The whole book was about Dorothy trying to make her way home, but what struck Amina was the date. It was dated the same day as the disappearance of the Hebrews. *Coincidence?* Amina didn't believe in those. Was this a sign? Was is possible this book was left behind for a Hebrew daughter to find? Amina imagined a daughter being separated from her family, desperate to find them again.

For a moment Amina pitied the girl to whom the book was meant because in all likelihood they never found it, which meant she never found her family.

Then again, maybe Amina was reading into it too much.

CHAPTER 15

Maybe she was just so desperate to find the Hebrews that she was willing to project her own hopes into something that wasn't really there.

Amina leaned and showed Paxton the note in the book. "Hey what do you make of this?"

Paxton quietly read it, his mouth moving silently. He looked at Amina. "It sounds like a mother who wanted her daughter to come back home. Maybe she ran away or moved out without her parents' consent. An estranged relationship. I don't know."

"Look at when it was dated."

Paxton stared blankly. "Okay. So?"

"That was the same day the Hebrews disappeared. Just up and left everything. And Ruth is a very Hebrew name.

"So, you think the mom gave this to her daughter just before they left? For what reason?"

"To help guide her to where they were going to be hiding."

"Why didn't she just tell her? Or make her come with them?"

"I don't know." Amina looked down at the book and flipped through the pages hoping to find more of this woman's cursive writing. "Maybe she couldn't. Maybe the mom left it at their home hoping her daughter would find it. Times were very difficult and uncertain back then. They still are."

Paxton sat silent for a moment. Amina could see the wheels turning in his brain. "Okay, so let's assume these people are Hebrews and that the daughter was somehow separated from them. They make this plan to disappear into hiding, but she can't tell her daughter, so she leaves a coded message in the book."

"Which means there's probably more clues in here." Amina stopped on another page that had a passage underlined and the same writing in the margin. "Look here's another one." Amina read the passage aloud, *"The cyclone had set the house down gently—very gently for a cyclone—in the midst of a country of marvelous beauty. There were lovely patches of green sward all about, with stately trees bearing rich and luscious fruit. Banks of gorgeous flowers were on every hand, and birds with rare and brilliant plumage sang and fluttered in the trees and bushes. A little way off was a small brook, rushing and sparkling along between green banks, and murmuring in a voice very grateful to a little girl who had lived so long on the dry, gray prairies."* In the margin the note read, *A new home always provides safety surrounded by deep beauty.*

Paxton's quickly grabbed a pen and paper out of his bag. "Read that again. I want to make a list of all the clues we find."

Amina did as she was told. Page by page they studied the book and began putting together a list of all the clues. Amina was filled with hope that she was getting closer to knowing where she was supposed to go. And she felt her heart soften just that much more toward Paxton for his eagerness to help her solve this puzzle. He was like a little boy on Christmas morning playing with a new toy. Or at least before their lives were upended and they had to hide in the tunnels eking out an existence. Amina let out a small laugh that was louder than she meant it to be.

Paxton looked at her confused. "What's so funny?"

Amina shook the feelings away and tried to cover it up. "Uh, nothing. I just . . . I've had this book for a while and I never thought it would be the key I was looking for." Amina looked back at the book before Paxton noticed the heat flushing her face, but out the corner of her eye she saw Paxton crack a smile of his own.

CHAPTER 15

By the time they finished going through the book and writing down every quote and note that went along with it, they had compiled fifteen clues.

Paxton shook out his hand and massaged the muscles in it. "Man, I couldn't tell you the last time I had to hand write that much."

"I'm surprised you still know how to write." Amina jabbed at him playfully as she grabbed the pad of paper and started reading through the different clues, trying to decode their meaning. Some made more sense than others. And the ones that didn't make sense seemed to be references to experiences and details that only the mother and daughter had shared.

"I'm not exactly sure, but I think we are in fact in the correct place," Amina admitted, looking down at the empty valley.

"So then why is there no village below? Are there more clues to take us beyond this point?"

Amina shook her head. "The only one that gives any clue to a direction is the first one we found."

"Read it again."

"*If we walk far enough, we shall sometime come to someplace.* And the note written says, *Some places are not as they seem. What once seemed lost was never really missing.*"

Paxton repeated the sentences quietly to himself a couple of times. The more he repeated it the more emphasis he gave on certain words, which started to jog Amina's brain.

Amina inspected the empty valley. Could it be possible? "What if it *is* there, but we can't see it?" Amina asked still staring down at the valley.

"Like a giant invisibility cloak is hiding the whole village?"

"Yeah . . . something like that. Sabaoth is powerful, he could do it." Amina looked at Paxton. She was hoping he didn't think she was completely out of her mind. She certainly felt as if she were talking nonsense. But then again, never in her life did she expect to see rivers turn to blood, plagues of locusts, or stars falling from the sky.

Paxton's face didn't show any signs of derision, only support and hope. He started putting the books back into Amina's bag. "Then let's get going. It's worth a try."

After gathering their things, Amina and Paxton walked to the cliff's edge and looked down. It was a long way to the bottom and there didn't seem to be an easy trail.

Amina looked at Paxton and was taken back. His eyes were wide and his face went white. She thought he was going to be sick. "You okay?"

Paxton let out a slow breath. "Yeah. I'm just not a fan of heights, but if the Hebrews are down there, I'll figure it out. Fear is just a mental state, right?"

"Right." Amina scanned the top of the cliff, deciding where to start.

She spotted a few feet away an area where the cliff seemed to have a narrow animal trail zig zagging its way back and forth. It was barely wide enough to stand with both feet together, but it would have to do.

Amina walked over to the trail and cautiously followed it down with Paxton following behind.

There were moments the trail would disappear and then reappear a couple feet below, and there were few shrubs or trees to hold for extra support. They pressed on cautious of their footing. One misstep and they could slip off the cliff face.

Periodically Amina would stop and wait for Paxton who was walking slower than a sloth, overly concerned about every placement of his feet. "Could you go any slower, seriously?"

CHAPTER 15

"I'm not about to go falling to my doom because you're in a hurry. This is new territory and seriously this path looks like it could crumble under my feet at any second, so relax. I'll get down on my own timing."

They were about halfway when Amina stopped.

"What is it?"

Amina was looking around in all directions. "The path disappeared again."

"It's probably below us somewhere hidden by a rock or bush like before."

"If it is, it's extremely hard to see." Amina kept looking, her frustration slowly mounting. "The goats had to get up this cliff somehow. They didn't just fly here."

Amina and Paxton strained to see any sort of hidden pathway, but they saw nothing in reach.

Amina spotted a slick steep rock and the narrow pathway that seemed miles below them. "You know, if we scale down that section over there," Amina pointed, "I think I see another path about fifteen feet down, give or take."

Paxton tensed. "One small slip and we're goners. No thank you."

Amina turned to Paxton and crossed her arms. "Then what do you propose?" She stared at him, waiting for a response, waiting for a plan that he clearly didn't have.

Paxton let out a deep breath. "Okay, fine."

Amina went first. *Okay, this is just like climbing the cliff by the river, only down instead of up. You can do this.* Sitting on the edge of the trail she swung her legs and dangled them over the edge. She rubbed her hands several times on her pants and then in the dirt before rolling onto her belly. Slowly, she lowered herself down the edge of the cliff. Inching lower until it was just her hands gripping the ledge. She felt the rocks scraping along the front of her shins, her knees, her chest, until her foot stopped. She had found her first foothold. Amina confirmed that it was strong enough and then found her second footing.

She looked up for a moment and found Paxton watching her. He smiled nervously and said, "You've got this."

Amina's stomach fluttered. Paxton's confidence in her gave her confidence. Amina closed her eyes for a moment, clearing her head of any uncertainty.

One at a time, Amina reached her hands down as low as she was willing to go. This was it, there was no turning back.

As she descended, she made sure every foothold, every hand grip was sturdy enough to hold her weight before she continued. She knew that Paxton was watching each move she made, noting her exact placement so he could mimic her. It may only have been fifteen feet to the next ledge, but if either of them fell, the ledge below would not catch them.

Amina reached the ledge; solid ground felt good. Amina rubbed her burning forearms and flexed her cramped fingers as she peered at Paxton. "That wasn't so bad." Amina tried to encourage him. She knew he must be shaking worse than she was. "You've got this, Paxton."

Paxton nodded, but didn't move. He wiped his hands on his pants and then in the dirt just as Amina had in order to keep the hands dry during the descent. Then, he followed the course Amina had taken.

With every movement Paxton took, Amina could feel her own muscles tightening and the adrenaline pulsating.

Inch by inch, Paxton descended the side of the cliff. He was doing great.

CHAPTER 15

He stopped for a moment and Amina panicked. *What was wrong? Did something happen?* "Is everything okay?" Amina shouted.

"Yeah, fine." He sounded winded. "I just need a moment."

"There's a good foothold under your right foot about two inches, if you're looking for a place to go."

"Thanks." Paxton saw the spot, then he proceeded to slide his foot cautiously down and to the right. He was like a starfish clinging to the glass of an aquarium.

Suddenly, Paxton's left foot slipped from its spot. Amina cried out. Thankfully, Paxton reacted fast, grabbing with his right hand a root sticking out of the cliff's crack in front of him. He started to swing out to face away from the cliff, but he pulled with all his might back toward the cliff and found a new footing.

"Are you okay?" Amina desperatcly called. She could see him visibly shaking.

Paxton rested his head on the rock. "Yep."

She could only imagine how terrified Paxton was feeling right now, which was likely draining his energy faster than the actual climb. "You've got this Paxton. I know you can do it."

"I know. You're right." Paxton moved lower. Soon he was at the bottom, standing next to Amina.

He leaned back on the wall and closed his eyes.

Amina was relieved. "See, I knew you could do it." Before she even realized what she was doing, Amina grabbed Paxton and pulled him into a hug.

It took Paxton a moment to respond, but he placed his hands on her back and accepted the embrace.

After a moment, Amina let go, quickly feeling awkward at her outburst of affection. She was surprised at herself.

Paxton avoided looking at her by staring at his hands. They were scratched all over and bleeding in a few places.

"Right, well um, we should keep going," Amina spoke.

The rest of the way down the path stayed visible and it even started to widen so they could walk without feeling like they were on a tightrope.

When they finally reached the bottom, Amina was relieved they had survived the cliff. She had been on edge during the perilous descent and hadn't realized until the two of them stopped and sat down on a fallen tree trunk that she was shaking.

Amina looked around. They had ventured away from the waterfall on their trail down, but she could still hear it. She saw nothing but trees and berry bushes blocking her view of the valley.

Paxton pulled out his canteen and took long gulps. He offered Amina some when he was finished, and she gladly took the canteen and drank.

"So," Paxton said, putting his canteen away, "if the village is here in this valley, just hidden, how are we going to find it?"

"I figured we could start at the lake and make our way out from there, following the river. They would want to be close to a water source."

Amina and Paxton made their way toward the lake at the bottom of the waterfall. A flute like song drifted to Amina's ears. It was a pleasant song, but it didn't sound like that of a bird. Amina turned, about to make a comment about the music, but Paxton quickly held a finger to his mouth. Amina closed her mouth and looked around. He must've heard it too.

They stood, unmoving, silent. The music continued to play softly.

CHAPTER 15

Amina looked to her left. There, hiding in the bushes, was a pair of ferret-like eyes staring at her. Suddenly Amina felt a sharp stab in her neck and then warmth spread into her face and down to her chest. Amina slowly reached up to the sting and pulled out a small dart. She looked at Paxton and he too was holding a dart in his hand.

The world began to spin and blur until eventually there was only darkness.

Chapter 16

Aiden stood outside Terrance's tent hesitantly. Everything within him was jumping around with uncontrollable anxiety and excitement. Tonight was the night of the raid. Aiden had been practicing and was confident in his skills to pick the lock in ninety seconds, less than the amount of time he was told, but he wasn't so confident about everything else. What if they got caught? What if someone got hurt? There were so many unknowns.

As Aiden mustered the courage to walk in, he felt a soft hand rest on his shoulder. Aiden jumped out of his skin and nearly yelled, but quickly caught himself before alerting any sleeping dwellers.

Tessa was standing next to him trying not to laugh.

"Goodness, you startled me."

"Sorry about that." Her expression turned serious. "You ready for this?"

Aiden nodded, wiping his sweaty palms on his pant leg. "As ready as I'll ever be."

"Good." She swiftly patted his back and then walked through the tent flap as Aiden followed.

Inside Terrance and Seth appeared relaxed. Aiden tried to look calm too, but he felt like a duck floating in a lake, calm on

CHAPTER 16

the outside but frantically kicking underneath.

Terrance handed Tessa and Aiden each a pair of gloves and a ski mask. Aiden put the gloves on. They were a bit on the small side, but he liked that. It would make it easier for him to use his picking tools when the time came.

The group went over the plan one more time, discussed all possible scenarios, and double checked all their equipment to make sure they had everything they needed. Terrance picked up the walkie-talkie that had been sitting on the table and radioed Jared. He made sure he had the night shift so there would be no one else at the coalition office.

"Just a minute. There's a loiterer. I'll see if I can get them to leave." Jared's voice sounded raspy.

Aiden sat on a nearby stool. Soon his knee started bouncing rapidly. He took a deep breath and placed his hands on his knees, trying to calm himself.

"Nervous?"

Aiden saw Seth staring at him. "Maybe a little."

"Don't worry, Aiden, you've got this."

"Thanks."

The radio beeped and Jared's voice spoke again. "All clear."

"Ten-four." Terrance set the radio down. "It's go time. We've got twenty minutes."

The team made their way through the tunnels toward the coalition office. Even though it was late and everyone was most likely asleep, Aiden kept waiting for someone to stop them around each corner. When they reached the office without any obstacles, Aiden's muscles relaxed.

Jared met the team outside the office and led them to a side door. Inside was a ladder that they would need to climb to access the weapons vault. The vault was in fact on the level above the coalition and unknown to most of the community. The elders insisted it be kept a secret and only used in case of an extreme emergency, but they still kept it secure in case of intruders.

Aiden was the last in the team to climb the ladder. On the level above, he found himself squeezed into another small closet.

Still on the ladder, Jared spoke in hushed tones. "You're on your own. If it's not safe to come back down, I'll let you know by making two clicks on the radio. You do the same when you're finished." He disappeared below.

Tessa flipped on her flashlight and lead the way down the dark tunnel. It amazed Aiden that there were so many areas he didn't know about in the tunnels. Tessa slowed in front of a small fuse box and popped it open. While Terrance held a flashlight and Tessa went to work, Aiden closed his eyes.

The only sound Aiden could hear was the drumming in his ears. He ignored the sound and concentrated on his job. He replayed picking the lock in his head. All that mattered was picking that lock. The process seemed simple enough, but what if the lock they had was different from the one he'd practiced on? If he trusted everyone else to do their job, then he could stay calm and focused.

"Done," Tessa whispered.

Aiden opened his eyes wide with fear. He didn't move. What if he couldn't do this? He was going to blow it.

"Aiden," Terrance snapped, pushing him from behind. "Hurry up."

Aiden felt his body moving forward, but his mind was whirling. At the vault door Aiden pulled out his first pick from his pocket and took a deep breath. *You can do this. You know what you're doing. Just trust yourself.*

He felt all eyes on him. Sweat trickled down his forehead and into his eyes. He rubbed his eyes as he let out another slow breath. *Step one, done.* He put the first pick away. His hands were shaking. As he pulled out his second pick—a universal disk container lock pick that Mitchum helped him weld together—it slipped out of his hands, clattering to the floor. *Shoot.*

"What was that?" Seth asked.

"My pick, it fell. Help me find it." Seth backed away, extending the light's perimeter while Tessa dropped on her hands and knees. Aiden desperately searched. Even with the flashlight it was hard to see.

"Hurry up, we're going to run out of time," Seth barked.

"Here, I found it." Tessa handed him the long thin piece of metal.

Aiden wiped the sweat off his forehead again. His hands were now shaking almost uncontrollably and he wasn't sure he could stop them. Tessa must've noticed because when he went to grab the pick from her, she held on to his hand with both of hers and squeezed as if to say *It's okay, you've got this.*

Aiden quickly inserted the pick into the lock, closed his eyes, and allowed the feel of the metal against the disks to be his eyes. He moved from one disk to the next, slowly jiggling them into their appropriate gates. The whole process was muscle memory, and although the combination of true and false gates was different from the one he practiced, it didn't slow him down. Without having to really think about it, Aiden did exactly what he needed to do. There was a click and a release of tension on the metal picks. Aiden smiled.

"It's open." Aiden stood, expecting applause or praise.

Instead, Seth pushed him out of the way. He turned the giant wheel and yanked the door open.

Feeling deflated, Aiden followed inside. Already Seth was at work opening crates and jotting down everything he wanted them to take.

After Seth would mark an item, Tessa and Terrance would fill the duffel bags. There were a few containers Aiden had to pick open. Compared to the Abloy these were a cinch.

They were more than halfway around the small room when Aiden heard a small high-pitched beeping noise.

That was their cue. The two-minute warning. Seth finished noting the weapons in his current crate. Tessa filled the duffel bag and closed it while Aiden rushed to relock the previous crates. They re-closed the vault door. Aiden spun the wheel until he felt a click and ran down the hallway after the others.

When Amina finally regained consciousness, her head was pounding. She rubbed her forehead and between her eyes trying to make the headache subside. Opening her eyes, she found Paxton sitting across from her with legs drawn to his chest and his arms resting on his knees.

The place they were in had no lights, just indirect sunlight beaming from the entrance. The walls were solid rock, jagged and unpolished. Most likely a cave turned into a prison cell.

"What happened?" Amina asked.

"Tranq darts."

Amina was trying to make sense of everything. "What? By who?"

"Definitely not Myriad. I'm thinkin' it was the Hebrews."

Amina's heart skipped a beat. She tried to stand but whatever

CHAPTER 16

they had drugged her with made her dizzy and unsteady.

Paxton reacted quickly and came to Amina's side. "Careful, with your size, I don't think this stuff has completely worn off you yet."

Amina clutched Paxton's jacket and leaned her head on his shoulder shutting out the spinning world. She breathed deeply and smelled the smoke and pine that had soaked into Paxton's jacket. She found herself relaxing into his support, finding that she was wanting to unravel in his arms.

Quickly, she brushed the thoughts aside and pushed away from him to move toward the barred entrance. "You really think we found them?"

"I don't know who else would be living in this valley."

Amina looked outside. It was dusk and there didn't seem to be any sign of life. There wasn't even a guard. How easy would it be for them to break out?

Amina caught motion off to the side. A young woman, about sixteen, was walking toward them. She was short with long dark brown hair that waved and twisted as it cascaded down her back. Her skin was dark from the sun and she looked fragile. In her hands she held two bowls.

When the girl caught Amina's eyes she stopped several feet away, wide eyed. "You're awake."

"Yes, and we have journeyed very far in-"

"I am not the one you wish to speak with. I will make a request for you to have an audience with the chief." She warily came forward and set the bowls on the ground just outside the gate, then quickly stepped back, out of Amina's reach. "I have brought you soup."

"Thank you." Amina bent down and took the two bowls, careful not to spill anything as she slid them through the bars.

Amina earnestly looked at the girl and implored, "Please let them know we're not here to hurt anyone. We came seeking help."

There was a long silence. Amina wasn't sure if the girl believed her or not.

"I will let the chief know this." With that she turned and quickly walked away.

Amina sighed and turned toward Paxton. "Dinner time." Amina took a big whiff of the soup letting the smell of fresh fish and barley invade her nostrils. Inside the broth also floated small orange cubes of carrots.

Amina sat beside Paxton and handed him his own bowl. He smelled it and he smiled with euphoria.

Amina's mouth watered, excited to eat a freshly cooked meal. She couldn't remember the last time she ate a cooked and prepared meal that wasn't from a can or a freezer. Her stomach rumbled and churned.

There were no utensils so Amina brought the bowl to her lips and slurped the soup. Her mouth watered as her taste buds were overloaded with flavor. "This is the best thing I've had in a long time." Amina took another sip as Paxton did the same. Paxton slurped his soup down so fast he couldn't have possibly tasted it.

"Geez, slow down there, tiger or you'll get a stomachache."

Paxton wiped his mouth with the sleeve of his jacket. "I must be hungry."

Amina looked around their barren cave, realizing that their bags were gone. "Do you have our bags?"

Paxton shook his head. "They probably confiscated them to make sure we didn't have anything dangerous."

"Probably, but I could really use my jacket right now. It's

chilly in here." Amina rubbed her arms, feeling her goosebumps.

"I noticed over in the corner an old firepit with some wood and tinder."

"I don't have my flint to help start it. Do you know how to start it with just sticks?"

Paxton smiled proudly. "I'll show you."

They made their way to the old firepit. Paxton gladly took on the role of teacher as he walked Amina through the science of starting a fire with friction.

It took Amina and Paxton several tries to get the fire started. There were many close attempts where they were able to get the wood smoking, but they couldn't keep it going long enough for the tinder to catch fire. Once they got it going, they were able to build the fire into a reasonable size.

Paxton and Amina sat beside one another leaning against the cool cave wall and staring into the fire's mesmerizing flames.

The dance of yellow flames flickered into the air and kissed it before disappearing while other flames calmly swayed and swirled together in a rhythmic dance.

Amina closed her eyes and listened to the crackling and popping of the wood while she smelled the smoke that had a twinge of sweet cedar.

It took her back to the times when she and her family would go camping. Every summer they went to the lake and camped out for a weekend. She loved roasting hot dogs or marshmallows in the fire while her dad would invent all sorts of adventure stories about pirates, or ghosts, or even mice.

No matter what story he told, it was different every time and it always captivated Amina and Aiden. Their father was an amazing storyteller and a wise man. Amina wished she could talk with him now.

Amina slumped her shoulders forward in disappointment. This was not how she imagined her adventure story going.

She took a stick in her hand and poked at the fire to keep the oxygen flowing through.

"What's going on in that head of yours?" Paxton asked, breaking through her thoughts. He was staring at her intently, examining her.

"Huh? Oh. Just that, this feels like we've failed, and yet, we haven't."

"You're right, we haven't. We found them."

Amina went back to poking at the fire. Somehow it was easier to talk to Paxton honestly when she wasn't looking at him. "You know, I was so zealous to find the Hebrews and bring my people back to them that I never once thought about what I'd say once I was here. What am I going to say to them? How do I convince them to allow seven hundred strangers into their safe haven?"

"You don't." Amina looked at him, puzzled. He continued talking. "If I've learned anything while being in the tunnels, it's that your people have an inconceivable amount of trust that Sabaoth is the one in control. If that's the case, I say you need to ask him to convince the Hebrews, instead of you, right?"

Amina put the stick down. She knew he was right. Hadn't Sabaoth been guiding her all along? The dream of the valley, the book from Lilly, and the order from Paul. None of those events happened because of something Amina did.

Amina walked to the cave entrance. Away from the conversation, away from the revealing fire that would show the tears streaming down her cheeks. When did she stop relying on

CHAPTER 16

Sabaoth and try to do everything on her own?

Paxton cleared his throat and made Amina jump. He had walked up beside her. "I know what it's like to have no hope and feel like your entire life is swirling out of control. You start grasping for anything around you to control, anything that can help you feel stable while the rest of your circumstances come crumbling down around you. That's when you question everything about your purpose in life. It's then that you have to come to terms with the fact that life is not in your control. Sure we make a lot of decisions in life, but in the end, we can't control everything. We can only control how we respond to everything around us."

Paxton stood, watching Amina, waiting for some sort of reaction. But how was she to react to that? She knew she needed to pray and trust, but right now, that seemed easier said than done.

Out in the distance, Amina saw a fire bobbing up and down as it came toward them. She took a step back. "Someone's coming."

Four men came into view, each holding a torch or a gun. They all had long curly hair; some had it pulled back into ponytails while others had it flowing down their shoulders. Their garb was simple linen pants and shirts girded with multicolored sashes.

None of the men smiled, and none of them seemed friendly.

The man at the front of the group held a handgun in one hand and a set of keys in the other. He was taller than the rest and had a long face.

Amina swallowed hard when she saw the guns. The man with deep-set eyes scowled at Amina as the light of the torch beside him revealed a nasty scar running from his forehead, across his eye, and down to his chin.

"Our chief would like to meet you now. Put your hands through the bars. We must bind them before we let you out."

They did as they were told. Amina felt dizzy with excitement. Or was it nerves? Either way, she started playing through her head what she wanted to say to the chief. How she would approach him. She wasn't good with words, but she was passionate. Hopefully, her passion would speak for itself.

The sun had completely gone down at this point and the sky was clear and black as they walked the short distance from the cave to the village. A cool breeze blew over Amina and gave her the chills.

Soon Amina could see several tents. The tents were clustered together in small circles of about four or five each and those clusters seemed to spiral inward.

In the center of each small cluster was a blazing fire. There were a few people here and there sitting around the fire chatting. As the group walked by the spectators stopped and stared. They didn't try to be discreet and they certainly didn't hide their worry.

In the center of the village, there was a large wooden cabin towering over the tents. That's where they were heading.

Inside, lanterns lined the walls, giving the room a flickering glow. The cabin was one giant room lined with benches. At the front was a small platform with a podium and a small table. There was nothing memorable about the place.

They stopped when they reached the front of the room. Amina felt a firm pressure in the back of her knees sending her down to the ground.

Amina's chest tightened and it was hard to breath. They were there to talk with the chief, right? Amina looked at Paxton, kneeling beside her, and there must've been obvious fear in her eyes because Paxton gave her a reassuring look and mouthed, *It's going to be okay.*

Footsteps echoed, and Amina lifted her head toward the noise. Coming toward them was a slender man with a graying beard. He wore a turban rimmed with gold ribbon. He wore a long white linen tunic and beautifully embroidered sash of gold, purple and blue. Just above his bushy gray eyebrows, was a shimmering blue mark of the Hebrew star. Paxton was right: the Hebrews did bear the mark of Sabaoth on their foreheads.

He stopped in front of Amina and Paxton, towering over them. Folding his hands in front, he looked down at his two prisoners. There was a long uncomfortable silence as he examined them, as if he could burrow into their minds with his eyes and extract the information he wanted.

The whole time Amina did her best to hide the trembling she felt. She took a slow breath. *Keep calm, Amina. He just wants to talk. And if not, you know how to fight.*

"So," he spoke, his voice reverberating in every direction. "Why should I let you live?"

Amina sat back on her heels as her body trembled.

"Sir, please," Paxton spoke first. "We pose no threat to your people, but rather we come as family, seeking your assistance."

The man remained stoic. "You, family? I highly doubt that. My only family are those who bear Sabaoth's mark, I see no such thing on you."

Amina cleared her throat. She went to stand, but quickly felt a firm hand on her shoulder. The chief motioned for the guard to let Amina stand.

Amina spoke softly yet confidently. "We are one, united by

the same hope, the same Sabaoth who has brought you here to be protected. And while the Notzrims and the Hebrews have their differences about Mashiakh, we are still family. We come before you now asking for your help." Amina tried to pull her sleeve to show the mark. It was proving to be quite difficult while still bound and Paxton had to help her. Once visible, Amina held out her arm for the chief to see.

He stared at the incandescent marking on her left forearm, stoic. He took a step toward her and took her arm to get a closer look.

The chief looked at Amina and then to Paxton. If he tried to look at Paxton's arm, this whole thing could go south very quickly. Amina held her breath waiting, praying.

Then the chief turned around and walked back onto his platform. The guard took that as a sign to force Amina back down to the floor.

The chief spun back around to face them and cracked the smallest of smiles. "Very well then, I will listen to your story."

Amina let out a breath and her body relaxed. *Thank you Sabaoth.* She then proceeded to lay out her entire story, doing her best to emphasize the urgency. She may have hyperbolized a few details, but she did what she had to do in order to convince this man. This was it. Her one shot and she wasn't about to blow it.

When she came to the end of her story, she concluded by saying, "We are family and we would be forever grateful if you would welcome us into your village."

The chief stood with one arm crossed and his hand cupping his chin. The silence was driving Amina crazy. He seemed to enjoy making her wait.

He looked to Paxton and then to Amina. "How do you plan

to bring them in safely? Without the Myriad following you?"

"For the past nine years we have lived in the shadows, we know how to be invisible. And if need be, we have the training to fight off attacks."

The chief was silent. Contemplating. The wheels turning in his mind, processing this request and the risk it would have for his village.

He tilted his head to the side and his eyes softened. "I don't know if I can grant this request. I will need to converse with the other leaders before making such a consequential decision. Our resources are limited and people are extremely wary of outsiders. I'm not sure it would be good for our unity if you came." Amina opened her mouth about to protest, but he quickly put a hand up and continued. "I will speak with the others and let them decide." The chief addressed his guards. "Take them back. Be sure to give them blankets and enough wood for their fire. The nights can get unbearably cold here." The chief turned to leave.

The guards lifted Amina and Paxton off their feet. Amina felt flustered. While she was thankful for his willingness to consider, it would be difficult to wait too long for a decision. She already felt time was quickly running out back home, and she wanted to expedite the process. "Why don't you call them now?" Amina suggested, trying to hold back the uneasiness in her voice. "You can have your meeting tonight, and I can explain it to them. I don't want to wait too long. We have to get back-"

The chief spun around with a stern look in his eyes, speaking sharply. "How dare you? You are in no position to make suggestions to me. You will wait until we are good and ready. If this is meant to be, then Sabaoth will protect your people until it is time. Get them out of here."

The guards yanked hard on Amina's arm. She tried to resist. She wanted to stay and plead with the chief, but he was already leaving the room.

"Amina, let it go," Paxton warned. "If you keep pushing this, he's going to decide not to help us before he even meets with the others."

The guard pulling on Amina leaned close to her ear. "You should listen to your boyfriend, sweetie. Our chief has a low tolerance for the unruly. Do what's best for your people and shut up."

Amina stopped resisting the guard's pull and let him guide her back to their holding cell.

Chapter 17

Back at the cave, the fire from earlier was now extinguished and the cold from the cave walls weighed on them like the chief's icy warning, shrouding them in a damp and uncomfortable chill.

Amina stormed to the back of the cave, pacing in part to keep warm but also because her anxiety wouldn't let her stay still.

Paxton put one of the blankets around Amina to warm her. She stopped and turned to him. "I blew it, didn't I?"

"What do you mean?" Paxton squatted beside the dead fire. "He hasn't said no yet."

"Maybe not, but I should've said more. I'm not sure he was convinced. I'm not sure he's going to say enough to convince the others."

There was shuffling outside the cave and then clanging on the bars as the guard tossed wood through the bars. "This should be enough to hold you till the morning." He left before either of them could say anything.

Paxton gathered the scattered wood. "Maybe not, but it's in Sabaoth's hands now."

Amina plopped down and watched Paxton start the fire. It didn't take very long to get it going this time, and with the wood they were given, the fire filled the back of the cave. No way this one was going out tonight.

As the two sat in silence with their blankets wrapped around them and the fire warming their faces, Amina's mind drifted back to the tunnels. Were they even aware of everything she was doing for them? Did they even understand how serious their situation was?

Amina felt her eyes watering. The stress and pressure she had put on herself were welling inside and threatened to burst forth. Instead she did what she did best, shove it back down.

"You know, it's okay to be scared." Paxton's quiet voice was just loud enough to be heard over the fire. He was looking at her.

"What?" Amina shook her head, trying to brush away the few tears that started to seep out. "Who said I was scared? I'm not scared, I'm just impatient. I have to get back before it's too late. We've already been gone way too long."

Paxton was quiet. He stoked the fire and a log rolled over allowing new flames to flare. "Why do you do that?" he asked, looking at her.

Amina shot Paxton a critical look. Where was he going with this? "Do what?"

"Push everything away."

Amina crossed her arms defensively. "I do not."

"You're doing it right now." Paxton shook his head. "I'm just trying to understand you. Understand where you're coming from. You're always so closed off Amina, even when people are kind to you and care about you, you don't see it. It's like you refuse to see the good in people."

"Well maybe I have a good reason not to trust people or believe in them. Maybe I've been betrayed too many times in my life."

CHAPTER 17

Paxton scooted closer. "What happened?"

Amina looked away, trying to hide the hurt and the scars that were haunting her. She didn't want to think about the painful memories she had of her family. They were in the past and that's where they belonged. Drudging them up now wouldn't solve anything and they certainly wouldn't help with her current situation. At the same time, something deep inside her longed to share the hurt and release it once and for all, but she wasn't sure if she could handle the pain.

Paxton placed his hand gently on Amina's. "Please. Let me in. Who hurt you so badly?"

Amina rested her head on the cave wall and closed her eyes. "Can't you just leave it alone?"

"No. You need to tell this story. I really think it'll be cathartic for you."

The tenderness in his voice made Amina's guard melt away. *What was it about him that made her feel this way?*

Amina looked back at Paxton, her obstinance subsiding. She wanted to share the burden with someone else. *And why not him? Wasn't he doing everything he could to redeem himself in her eyes and prove his loyalty?*

Staring at the fire, she spoke barely above a whisper. "My mother turned on us, my father was killed because of it, and I watched it happen." Hoping that was enough to satisfy Paxton's curiosity, Amina stopped talking.

She should have known that wouldn't be enough for him. "What do you mean turned on you?"

Amina bit her lip. *Here we go.* "Before the mark appeared, my family and I would go out and share the story of Sabaoth and his plan for our lives. Strangely it was an encouraging time, there were so many people coming to the faith. My family and

I were growing closer together too."

"Your whole family is of the Notzrim faith?"

"That's what I thought. As the months went on and Teivel rose to power, that meant the persecution of us got worse, but we kept pressing on, but then—" Amina took a deep breath to help keep the tears from coming out. "Teivel passed a worldwide law that all citizens were required to receive the mark. A computer chip that would be embedded into our skin and replace all currency, photo IDs, and any other important documentation. And, as you know, without that mark it's nearly impossible to survive."

"I remember when that law was passed. There were a lot of mixed feelings, but eventually Teivel made everyone realize how good this would be for the world's economy, not to mention significantly reduce identity theft. I know the Notzrim were adamantly against it, but why? It doesn't seem so bad."

Amina shrugged. "The idea of the chip is not bad, but don't you remember the other reason why they required everyone to take the chip? It was to show their sole allegiance to Teivel and his new religion. It would mean we agreed that he was not only the supreme leader but a god. He's not a god. He's evil and an enemy of Sabaoth."

"Okay. That's your right to believe that, but-"

"It's the truth."

"What about all the great things he's done to help this world? We have seen some insane natural disasters all over the world and he's the one holding it all together. He even has healing powers that he's used to help others. How is that bad?"

"Because he's not Sabaoth and you don't know what he's really up to. You only see what he wants you to see."

CHAPTER 17

"Okay, fine. That's not even the point right now and I don't want to argue. Keep going with your story. The mark appeared, is that what tore your family apart?"

Amina nodded, allowing her mind to refocus on that dreadful day. "Yes." As she spoke her voice stayed steady, but there was a twinge of sadness. "We were there at the stadium the day Teivel made his big announcement. We had decided this might be our last chance to share the faith with others because once people took the mark and pledged allegiance to Teivel instead of Sabaoth it would be all over and our ministry would end.

"Aiden and I split up from our parents, so we could cover more ground. I should have never left. I should have stayed, then maybe-" A lump caught in Amina's throat and she stopped.

Paxton took Amina's hand again. "Okay, so you went to the rally. You shared your faith. That must've been dangerous. Persecution of Notzrim is legal. You could've been arrested or beaten."

"It was a risk we were willing to take. There was only a handful who came to faith. Most ignored us. A few tried to call the Myriad on us, but we were able to get away before being arrested. Anyway, when we were finished, we went to meet back with our parents. That's when I saw my mom walking toward the stadium.

"I made Aiden go ahead of me and jogged over to my mom. I had to find out what was happening. Just as I approached, she passed by a Myriad soldier, toward a tunnel leading into the stadium. I called out to her. Immediately she turned, there was so much guilt in her eyes. She said she was sorry, but that she had to go. That she had to take the mark so she could be safe.

"I heard what she was saying, but I didn't understand. I kept begging her to come back. At some point the soldier tried to push me back and get me to leave, but I refused. I wasn't going to leave without my mother. But when my mom came back, practically yelling at me to go, telling me she disowned me and never wanted to see me again, I just. . ." Amina stopped again, her eyes burning with animosity. All the hurt and disappointed came flooding back, and the complete rage she felt from her mother's betrayal. It was enough to make Amina want to erupt.

"Then what?" Paxton frowned. He knew there was more.

Amina's lower lip trembled. "My father came and tried to get me to leave. So much of it is a blur to me, I don't really know what else happened. I think my father tried to get my mother to leave, but she refused. There was a lot of yelling.

"I think the Myriad soldier figured out we were Notzrim. That's when he lifted his gun. I panicked. My dad pushed me and yelled at me to run, and I did." Amina stopped herself for a minute and swallowed hard. Paxton squeezed her hand, encouraging her to keep going. The tears were now freely rolling down Amina's face and she let them. It felt good to let it out. She continued, trying to force the words out. "The next thing I knew I heard a gunshot go off. Without thinking, I turned around in time to see my father crumple to the ground. I started to go back, but Aiden tackled me to the ground to ensure the soldier didn't shoot me too. I don't know where he came from, but I tried to fight him off. All I wanted was to run to my father and check on him, but Aiden pulled me away. I never even got to say goodbye."

Amina couldn't talk anymore; the gut-wrenching tears were coming hard and she could barely breathe. That's when she found herself burying her face into Paxton's chest and letting him hold her as she sobbed. She wasn't sure the tears would ever stop.

Still holding Amina and stroking her hair Paxton whispered, "Your father did what any father would do. He protected his daughter whom he loved very much. You shouldn't feel guilty for that. You cannot control what other people do. Not your mom, not your dad, and certainly not that Myriad soldier."

"I know, but I blame my mother for her actions," Amina spoke through broken sobs. "If it weren't for her cowardice, my father would still be alive. It's her fault he's dead."

"I'm sure your mother didn't mean for any of you to get hurt." Paxton stroked Amina's hair. "I'm sorry you had to go through such a horrendous event and that your father isn't here anymore. But I hope you also know that not everyone is like your mom. Not everyone leaves."

Amina appreciated Paxton's comfort and his words, but it didn't change what she knew was true.

Chapter 18

Amina stood at the cave entrance, soaking in the morning sunlight that trickled in. The air was cool but not as uninviting as it felt last night. It was crisp and fresh. She could smell the wet dirt and noticed the leaves were covered in droplets of water. It must've rained last night.

Off in the distance Amina watched two birds flit around from branch to branch. She smiled at their carefree lifestyle. They didn't seem to have stress or big life-altering choices to make. They could fly freely and live life peacefully. If only Amina felt the same way. If only there was a way for her and her people to live peacefully. That, however, felt like a far-off dream, a hope that dissipated as quickly as vapor.

Another movement caught Amina's eye. The young girl was returning, this time holding a tray full of food and drink. The girl placed the tray down and quickly scurried off without even looking at Amina. She thought it was funny how scared this girl was of her simply because she was a prisoner.

"Thank you," Amina called. If the girl had heard her, she didn't acknowledge.

After taking a moment to pull everything through the bars, she repositioned the food and drink on the tray and brought it to Paxton.

CHAPTER 18

Amina kicked the bottom of Paxton's boot. "Wake up, food is here."

Paxton rubbed his eyes and sat. On one side of his head, his hair stuck straight and kinked in unnatural directions and his eyes were heavy.

Amina passed him some food and a cup of water. They ate in silence, knowing the guards could reappear any minute. Amina's stomach knotted. She couldn't eat much, but she forced something down anyway.

Time seemed to pass slowly and it felt like hours before someone finally appeared back at the cave entrance. The contrast between the bright sun and the dark cave made it difficult for Amina to tell who was at the entrance. Only when he spoke, did she realize it was the chief.

"I have your answer." His orotund voice echoed to the back of the cave.

Amina and Paxton looked at each other with a mix of hope and fear. They both rushed to the cave entrance.

Amina placed her hand on the bars. "Well then? Can we go and bring them back?" She sounded more desperate than she wanted.

"No."

"What?!" Amina and Paxton both cried out. Amina had been punched in the gut. It was such a letdown.

Paxton stepped closer. "What do you mean no? We have done nothing but plead for your kindness and hospitality. How can you turn away family?"

"*We* are not family." The chief shot back. His severe glare cut deep. "*You* are a liability. I have been entrusted to keep my people safe until the proper time and the only way I can do that is by not allowing in outsiders. It is clear that if we were to bring more people into the valley there would not be enough resources. Plus, if you were to be followed by the Myriad that would be catastrophic. I cannot have that happen."

This time it was Paxton who snapped. "Coward!" he shouted. "You selfish, uncaring coward! You would let innocent people die?" His face turned crimson and his whole body shook. "Let me out of here and I'll show you how vulnerable you are."

Amina gently touched Paxton's arm. "Paxton, calm down."

"No, I will not calm down!" His brows drew together and he pointed his finger at the chief. "You will let us go. *Now*!"

Amina was shocked. What had gotten into him? Usually he was the more reasonable of the two, but this time Amina was too crushed by failure.

The chief stood, unphased by Paxton's outburst. "I'm sorry, but you cannot leave, ever."

Amina's heartache quickly disappeared. It was her turn to voice her outrage. "You can't do that. We have done nothing wrong."

"You're right, you haven't, but the leaders do not trust you. *I* do not trust you. Your knowledge of our whereabouts is dangerous and we cannot risk you telling others where we are."

Amina shook her head. "We won't tell anyone. We wouldn't do that to you." Amina tried to reason with the chief, but he would not budge.

"My mind is made up." The chief took a step closer. "You will stay here. We will ensure you are not mistreated, and if, one day, we find you amiable, we will let you out of the cave and allow you to live among us. Until then, you will stay in here."

Amina lunged forward and tried to grab hold of the chief

as she let out a yell, but he was too fast and moved out of her reach.

G"I'm going to rip your head off! You can't do this to us!" The chief turned and started walking away. "et back here!" Amina let out another yell as she pushed away from the bars and headed back to the firepit. The chief was sorely mistaken if he thought he could hold Amina prisoner. Amina started rummaging through the firepit until she came across a bone skinny enough to fit into the lock. She then grabbed the small safety pin and stormed back to the gate.

"What are you doing?" Paxton looked concerned.

"We've got to get out of here. If we stay, then everyone in the tunnels will be dead. We can go back home and bring everyone here. He won't say no to that. He can't be that heartless."

Amina started working at the lock, trying to line up the key pins so she could get the plug to rotate and open.

"Now let's rethink this Amina. We should figure out a game plan. A way to bring everyone here that we can then share with the leaders, reassuring them that it'll be perfectly safe to bring everyone here. We can talk-"

"Do you honestly think they'll listen? No, I'm done talking. I'm done waiting." Amina twisted hard on the lock and the bone snapped in half. "Dammit!" Amina chucked the bone to the ground and then went back to the firepit to find something else. Something stronger. She found another bone and started back to the entrance, but then stopped when she saw a woman standing on the other side.

Amina stared at the woman curiously. She was tall and slender with dark sun-kissed skin. Her face was worn from the sun and showed her age around her eyes.

She smiled cautiously.

Slow as a lion approaching its prey, Amina crept forward. Paxton turned to see what had startled Amina and he saw her standing there with her long black hair framing her slender face and vibrant green eyes. In her hands she held two familiar backpacks.

Amina's face lit up. "Who are you?" Amina stopped a foot away from the bars.

The woman pursed her lips together before speaking. "My name is Salome and I am one of the leaders." Amina tried to speak, to let her know how she felt about the leaders, but before she could Salome held up a hand and continued. "I am on your side. I tried to convince the others to let you and your people come stay with us, but I was outnumbered."

Paxton also approached the bars. "Then what are you doing here? The chief told us your decision and about our lifetime membership to your happy village." Paxton's voice oozed with sarcasm.

Salome stepped forward. "I want to help. Your people don't deserve to die. I believe Sabaoth can protect us all. And I couldn't live with myself if I knew that hundreds of innocent people died and I could've done something to prevent it."

A spark of hope flickered in Amina. She smiled. "What's your plan?" Amina asked feeling a lot friendlier toward Salome.

Salome reached into her pocked and pulled out a large rusty skeleton key. "Well first, I'm breaking you out."

With Salome leading the way, they moved from one small bush to the next with stealth until they reached the cliff with the waterfall. Salome knew she had to be quick about it and get back to the main hall before her absence was noticed. Part of her felt completely crazy for deciding to help these two strangers, and yet, she was certain the conviction in her heart was from Sabaoth. All night she had tossed and turned, her mind distraught with their decision not to help these two strangers and their clan. It felt too condemning, too unloving. That was not who they were as a people.

Salome stopped and looked at the two strangers, they were so young. "If you continue along the cliff for another five hundred feet, there is a rock formation, almost like a staircase that you can climb to get you back to the top. Once you're at the top, find the river and follow it until it forks, then head north until you reach elephant rock. After that turn west again. If you keep heading in that direction it will lead you out of the mountains and to a highway. Follow the highway away from the mountains until you make it back to the city, but be careful of patrol units."

"Wait, you're not coming with us?" Paxton asked. Deep lines of concern creased his forehead.

"There are some things I have to take care of here. You will be fine. Just follow my instructions. Now go, before anyone realizes you are missing."

Salome suddenly found Amina's thin arms wrapped around her. She was taken back by the warmth of this stranger, but she quickly returned the hug, welcoming the kind affection.

"Thank you," Amina spoke.

"Don't thank me just yet. We still have to get everyone back."

Salome turned to leave.

"Wait!" Salome looked at Amina again, questioning. "We need proof that we found you. Our elders won't agree to come unless I bring something back."

Salome thought for a moment, then grabbed the cord around her neck and took it off. Hanging on the end of the cord was a small pendant of a six-pointed star with an abalone sphere in the center. "Will this work?"

Amina took it gently and looked it over as if it were a precious commodity. "I think so. It's beautiful."

"Please, take care of it." Salome was hesitant to allow them to take such a cherished heirloom, but she trusted Sabaoth that she would see them again and be reunited with her necklace.

Amina put the necklace around her neck and tucked it under her shirt. "I will. See you soon."

The three parted and headed in their separate directions. Salome's mind soon turned to her next mission. It wouldn't be long before the elders realized the prisoners were missing and she would need to be there when they did.

Back in the village, Salome slipped in through a side door of the great hall and crept her way along the wall until she was a part of the group. She sat on a bench and listened. The chief and other leaders were discussing what to do with their new prisoners. Although they had decided to keep them from leaving, they also knew it was inhuman to keep them locked in the cave.

Salome didn't understand why it was such a difficult decision for them. Salome stood and walked to the front of the group. Looking the chief straight in the eyes she spoke with a firm yet calm voice. "You need to let them go."

"Excuse me?"

"You heard me. You need to let them go. They are not enemies. They do not work for the Myriad. They are not trained soldiers or terrorists. They are scared, desperate people who want nothing more than to protect their family. So let them go."

Salome heard the others laugh around her, jeering and stabbing her with their contentious looks. She stood her ground.

"And if they are caught and tortured for information?"

"That's on them. We have to trust that Sabaoth will protect us as he promised. Or have you forgotten his words? Have you forgotten that he never backs down from a promise?"

A voice spoke from behind Salome. "That may be so, but that doesn't mean we're undetectable. We still must use wisdom and it is unwise to take such a risk."

Salome spun around to face the broad-shouldered man, with the scar across his face, staring her down. "And who's to say that it is not wise to help others, Aryeh? Does not Sabaoth help those in need when they cry out to him? These people are crying out to us for help. It is selfish and unholy of us to shun them." Salome could feel the heat rising in her face. Her throat tightening along with every muscle in her body that wanted to start trembling with anger.

"I've heard enough." The chief stepped toward Salome and gently put his hand on her shoulder to provide some sort of solace. "I know you want to help them, and I commend you for it, but we must look at the larger picture. If we let them go and something happens, it could be disastrous for our whole valley."

Salome's eyes bore into the chief. She was too upset to say anything else. If she spoke now, she was certain she'd say something she regretted. Taking a deep slow breath, Salome closed her eyes and lowered her head. "Very well."

The chief looked at the others. "Now, how long do we give them before we try to incorporate them into the village? I don't want them thinking they can be freeloaders here."

The chatter of the others seemed to fade until it was a dull muffle. Salome's thoughts swirled around her. Her fight was not over yet.

Salome had a seat on a bench nearby. She had an obligation to stay.

Suddenly a young woman, the same young woman who had been bringing food to the prisoners, burst into the hall out of breath.

The leaders stopped their conversations and stared at her with confusion and annoyance.

Aryeh was the first to speak. "Can't you see we're in the middle of a very important meeting. Get out of-"

"But-" the girl had her hands on her knees and was trying to catch her breath. "The prisoners-" she continued between gasps of air, "they're not- they're gone."

A pin could've dropped and been heard clearly when they heard the news. No one moved, no one spoke. They were stunned. It only lasted a moment before they burst into raucous debate about how the prisoners escaped.

Salome let a small smile slip, but she quickly wiped it away and turned her face away from the group.

It took the chief several moments of shouting and pounding on the nearby table before everyone settled down. "Instead of arguing, let's work together to find them."

Salome raised her hand as if asking permission to speak. She didn't wait for anyone to acknowledge her before mentioning, "So is this Sabaoth's way of telling you you were wrong?"

Aryeh stormed toward Salome, his face red. He got in her

face, hoping to intimidate her, but she didn't back down. Instead, she stood ready to defend herself.

"It was you, wasn't it? You had something to do with this."

"What if I did? It was the right thing to do whether you can see that or not. I don't regret my actions."

"You will when you are cast out of the village and left to fend for yourself."

"You'd like that, wouldn't you Aryeh, to get rid of me? Well it's not happening."

The chief walked over and looked at Salome. The deep lines in his face said it all. He was hurt. "What have you done?"

He looked betrayed. Salome felt sorry for hurting him, but she didn't regret what she did. She frowned, her voice soft. "Papa, don't look at me like that. You were willing to let hundreds of innocent people die. I won't have their blood on my hands. Not if I can help it."

"They'll be the death of us." Another voice called out from behind them.

Salome spun around. "We will make it work. When they return we will figure it out. There is plenty of land to farm. Sabaoth always provides, trust in Him."

"Have they already left?" the chief asked.

"Yes."

"Then you must go with them." His fatherly voice was rather stern and there was no hint of compassion. "You must ensure that they are not caught, that our location is not compromised. Do you understand? They are your responsibility and if something happens to us, *your* family, our blood will be on your head."

"Yes papa, of course." Salome turned to leave, but not before her father spoke again.

"Oh and Salome, when you return," he let out a breath, as if he was struggling to speak the next words, "we will discuss your consequences."

Salome's eyes closed as the words pierced her heart. She was certain he was only saying that because the others were there and it was law to banish anyone for insurrection. But her own father wouldn't allow his only daughter to be banished, would he?

Sweat trickled down Amina's face and back. She took another swig of her water, trying to keep herself hydrated. It was an excruciatingly hot day and the vegetation made air flow almost non-existent.

It was day two of their journey back to the tunnels, and they had been walking for half the day already. Amina was ready for rest. She stopped by a fallen tree and plopped down, using her shirt to wipe the sweat off her forehead.

"All I want right now is an ice bath."

"You're telling me." Paxton sat beside Amina and pulled out his water. "Today is awful."

"It wouldn't be so bad if we could just get a stinking breeze." Amina screwed the lid back on her canteen. So far they had followed every instruction Salome had given. Amina wasn't fully convinced that the elephant rock they found was in fact the one Salome was referring too, but Paxton's persistent confidence caused Amina to give in. "We've been walking downhill for the past hour so I feel like we should be approaching the highway soon."

"What are we going to do when we reach the highway?"

"What do you mean?"

CHAPTER 18

"There's not really a whole lot along that highway to keep us covered."

"We'll wait till night, of course." Amina stood, feeling slightly light headed as she did. She pressed her hand to her temple and rubbed, trying massage away the dizziness.

The two were about to start moving again when they heard movement behind them. They both stopped and looked at each other warily. Amina moved her hand down to the knife she kept in her side pocket. Paxton reached for his own knife in his bag. When they both had what they needed they spun around pointing their weapons at the bushes.

Amina immediately relaxed and lowered her knife, relieved and excited that it was Salome.

"What are you doing here? I thought you weren't coming?" Amina asked, putting her knife away.

"Change of plans. I'm coming with you to ensure you get there and back safely."

Amina narrowed her eyes suspicious of the change in plans. "What happened?"

Salome innocently looked at her. "What do you mean? Can't a person change their mind?"

"Yeah but you seemed so certain of yourself before."

Salome sighed and her face drooped. "They made me come. They know I helped you escape and they know you're planning to come back with everyone, and they're not happy." Salome continued, telling them everything that had happened back at the hall. How she tried to reason with them, but they refused to listen. How she ensured them that this was the will of Sabaoth, but they wouldn't budge.

As Amina listened to the story, she felt indebted toward this woman. They were complete strangers and yet she was willing to help them. She risked her own life for them. Amina was floored when Salome explained how she might never be able to return because the chief and leaders might banish her.

"You did all that, for us?" Amina asked. "Why? Why would you help us? You could lose everything and you don't even know us."

Salome gave a motherly smiled. "This is true, but I've always been a nurturer. I've also had this need to help others and you remind me so much of my daughter. Strong, passionate, and very stubborn. I wasn't able to help her, but maybe I can help you."

"What happened to her?" Paxton asked with genuine concern.

"When the chaos started, she was living in the dorms at the college. She tried to get home, but our people had already set the date and time to leave and there were no exceptions. I tried to leave her a note as to where we'd be, a sort of code so that if others found it they would just think it was a gift from a mother to her daughter." Salome lowered her eyes. "I don't think she ever got it. I don't even know if she's alive."

Something sparked in Amina's memory. She didn't know why, but she had a feeling *The Wizard of Oz* book she had was the gift. Amina pulled the book out of her backpack and handed it to Salome. "Was this your gift?"

Salome gleamed with recognition as she slowly took the book. She opened the cover and ran her fingers along the note written inside. Pressing the book to her chest she let a few tears trickle down her cheeks. "Yes," she whispered. "How did you find this?"

Amina shrugged. "It was given to me. Somehow it found its ways into our community. Your notes are how we found you."

CHAPTER 18

Salome closed her eyes and let out a few silent sobs. Amina shifted uncomfortably, not sure what to do or say.

Paxton immediately went to her side and put a reassuring hand on her back. "She may have never gotten the book, but she could still be safe. It's possible she found somewhere else to hide. Stay hopeful."

Salome wiped her tears and sniffled, recollecting her emotions. Handing the book back to Amina she walked past them. "We better get going if we want to reach the highway before the end of the day."

Chapter 19

The highway emerged before them lonely and ominous. It stretched in both directions as far as the eye could see and still there was no sign of a city nearby.

On either side of the highway were several abandoned vehicles, trash, tumbleweeds, and dirt. A whole lot of dirt. It was a ghostly sight and yet familiar to Amina. It was highways like these that Amina and the others used to travel and find abandoned places to rummage for food.

It was dusk and the shadows of the dimming day were growing.

Salome placed a hand over her mouth. "What happened to this place?"

"War, natural disasters, famine, plagues, what hasn't happened?" Amina stated flatly. "Be thankful Sabaoth rescued you from all this."

"I am, but I am also heartbroken for everyone who has to live this nightmare."

"There's something I've gotta ask," Paxton blurted out, looking back and forth between the women. "Why the Hebrews and not the Notzrim? Why two different people but one Sabaoth. I don't get it."

"It is our birthright," Salome replied. She wasn't arrogant

CHAPTER 19

in the way she said it, but Amina hinted a bit of pride. "From the beginning of time, Sabaoth created his own chosen race, the Hebrews, to be his people. And it was decided, long before any of us were born, that Sabaoth would protect his people from the Great Desolation."

"As for the different faiths," Amina pipped in, "we have two different views on Mashiakh's role in our religion."

"So, they're like two sects of the same religion."

"Sort of." Amina looked at the sky and decided to sit. It was going to be a while before it was dark enough for them to venture out. "Anyway, we better eat and rest. We have a long night ahead."

Salome and Paxton joined Amina and they each pulled out food from their bags. No one spoke much. While Amina was full of curious questions to ask Salome, she also wanted to rest. The sun had drained a lot of her energy and she was going to need every bit she could muster if they were going to make it through the night.

As the sun faded and the dark took over, Amina also faded into a heavy sleep. When Paxton had to shake her hard to wake her, Amina flailed her arms, smacking Paxton in the face.

Embarrassed, Amina threw a hand to her face. "Sorry."

"I'm fine, really," Paxton responded through his cupped hands. "It's time to go."

Amina stood and put on her backpack. They crept their way to the trees' edge and checked for Myriad patrols before venturing out onto the highway, moving from vehicle to rocks to piles of trash.

They made sure they were never too far away from a place to hide in case a Humvee came rolling by on patrol.

They were able to make it three miles before they heard a

car motor. Quickly they dove into a nearby sedan and ducked as low as they could get, crushing themselves on the floor between the seats. No one moved for a good five minutes after they stopped hearing the motor. Then Paxton popped his head up to look around. When he was certain the coast was clear he stood, and the others followed.

It was another five miles before Salome stopped, listening carefully. Amina listened too as she heard the fluttering noise growing louder. Amina knew immediately what it was.

"A drone. Quick!" Amina frantically searched for somewhere nearby to hide that would protect them not only from the sight of the drone's cameras but also the infrared. There were plenty of places to hide, but nothing to block the infrared. The closest thing she could find was an old convenience store that might have mylar thermal blankets. It was a long shot, but they had to try. "This way!" Amina ran to the building and the others quickly followed.

Amina could see the drone coming into view above them. She ran as fast as her legs could go but they felt like lead and didn't seem to want to move fast enough. Sweat trickled down her face and into her eyes blurring her vision. She wiped it away, they were almost to the door.

"Stop! This is the Myriad and you are breaking curfew. Stay where you are!" A loud recording boomed from the drone overhead.

They'd been found. *No! We're too close to home!*

The recording continued. "You are breaking curfew, stay where you are. Foot patrol is on its way!"

Ignoring the warning, the three of them darted into the store.

"We only have about three minutes before they show up.

CHAPTER 19

What's the game plan?" Paxton said, trying to catch his own breath.

Amina drummed her fingers together, but she couldn't think She was out of ideas. This was it. The end. There was no way out of this one. "I-" Amina tried to speak but couldn't. Fear gripped her mind.

Paxton paced around the liquor store, but suddenly stopped. Staring out the window he suggested, "What if we drive?"

Amina looked at Paxton who was staring out the window with a goofy grin on his face. "What?"

"That black Dodge looks in good condition. I can hot wire the car, and we drive out of here."

"That is if someone hasn't siphoned all the gas out of it. Besides, we'd still have the drone following us."

"So, we shoot it out of the sky."

"With what?"

"With. . ." Paxton looked around at the shelves, there was nothing useful, just a bunch of empty looted shelves. "I'm sure we could find something in here."

It seemed ridiculous, but what was their other option?

"You better be fast, we don't have much time," Amina said.

The three split up and raked through the store hoping to find something useful. Time was running out and the store seemed completely useless. Eventually Paxton walked from the back holding a flare gun. Before Amina could say anything, he ran outside. With one impeccable shot, he hit the drone. It sparked into flames and went plummeting to the ground as the three of them sprinted to the car and got in so Paxton could get to work. It took Paxton longer than Amina had thought to get the car started, but eventually he did and the engine roared to life. All the lights, indicator bars and the radio jumped on.

Salome jumped from the loud metal music blasting through the speakers. Amina turned the music off as Paxton put the car in drive and hit the gas.

He took off down the road with his foot pressed to the floor. The car accelerated and soon they were flying at 100 mph.

They hadn't been driving long before Salome looked through the back window and then back toward Amina. "I hate to say this, but we have company."

Amina turned to look through the back windshield to see a Humvee quickly approaching. "Go faster Paxton, now!"

"I've got the pedal to the floor. It's going as fast as it can."

The Humvee was catching up and soon was beside them. Inside Amina could see two Myriad soldiers dressed in black uniforms and helmets. As the car came closer, it nudged its way into the side of their Dodge, trying to edge them off the highway. Paxton swerved hard to his left to get away from the influence of the Humvee, but they kept on him. The nudge came again but this time harder.

"Come one Paxton, pull ahead!" Amina was now shouting.

"I'm trying."

A third nudge came, harder than the others and rocked the car. Amina grabbed the side of the door and let out a startled yell.

"Slam on the brakes," Salome commanded from the back.

"Are you kidding right now? We don't want to stop. We need to get away from them."

"I know," her voice was as calm as rain. "Slam on the brakes, turn the car around, then punch it again. It'll force them to slow down."

"But then we'll be going in the wrong direction."

"Just trust me."

CHAPTER 19

Paxton took a deep breath. "Okay." He slammed hard on the brakes and as the car started screeching across the asphalt, he cranked the steering wheel hard to get them to go the other direction. The car spun like a carnival ride and Amina thought she was going to be sick. The instant they were facing the other direction Paxton punched the gas again before the car ever came to a complete stop.

Amina looked behind her and could see the Humvee turning around. "We need to change directions again!"

"Not yet." Salome insisted, watching the Humvee gaining speed.

"But they're going to catch up!"

"Amina, shut up!" Paxton shouted. His knuckles were white as he gripped the steering wheel. "I trust Salome, so just shut up so I can hear her."

Amina closed her mouth, gritting her teeth. She didn't see how this was going to work.

"Okay . . . now!" Salome shouted.

Paxton slammed on the brakes again and spun the car around. This time it was much smoother. As he hit the gas again the Humvee flew past him. They were trying to hit their breaks but they had been going so fast that the Humvee flipped on its side and rolled off the highway.

Paxton took off down the highway again full speed, leaving them behind.

"They're not going to give up," Amina stated.

"No, but it bought us some time." Paxton shot back. "We just have to make it to the outskirts of the city. I'm sure I can lose them after that."

Ahead of them, headlights started to bounce into view. Amina braced herself. Paxton swore as he swerved out of the way. He had turned the wheel too hard and the car tipped and started rolling. Amina's body flew around like a rag doll until the car landed on its side. A sharp pain pierced the side of her face. Her eyes seemed to lose focus. Beside her she saw Paxton, moving slowly. She tried to call out to him but her voice didn't seem to work. That's when two Myriad soldiers approached the car, guns drawn, and started pulling them out.

Aiden made his way to the west tunnel entrance. He was feeling more jittery than ever and he thought he would burst from all the adrenaline pulsing through his body.

After proving himself with the weapons vault raid, it was now time for his first above-ground op with a larger team. They had gone over the mission late last night. A team of ten would go above ground to take out and steal supplies off a food truck that was coming their way. How Terrance got the intel, Aiden had no idea, but Terrance had insisted it was good information and that this would be just the hit they needed to not only provide for their community but also shake the Myriad's confidence.

There would be three on lookout, including Terrance. Their job was to take out any drones as well as keep an eye out for unsuspecting Myriad. According to intel, there would be one Humvee leading the way, one at the rear and a drone.

Once the drone was taken out, the attack team would approach the truck, take out the driver and get the truck open. Aiden was on the attack team.

"Where you heading?" Josiah's disembodied voice called.

Aiden stopped and slowly turned around. What was he doing awake? "Just going for a walk," Aiden lied. "I couldn't sleep.

CHAPTER 19

What are you doing up?"

"Follow you."

Aiden let out a thin laugh. "Why would you do that? I'm just going for a walk, like I said." He crossed his arms as his toe tapped impatiently. He needed to meet with the others. They were going above at any moment.

"I know something's going on, Aiden. You haven't been yourself lately. You're always going off by yourself, you've been more tired that usually-"

"I've lost a lot of sleep worrying about my sister, so I take more naps."

"I've also seen you talking to people you don't normally spend time with."

"So I've made new friends. Is that wrong?"

Josiah sighed, exasperated. "No of course not, but I think there's more. What are you up to?" Josiah took a step closer.

Aiden stepped back. "Nothing. Just go home, I'm fine." Aiden gestured for Josiah to turn around and leave, but he didn't move.

"I care about you, Aiden."

"And I appreciate that, Josiah. But right now, I want to be alone." Aiden hated being so dismissive to Josiah, but he knew he'd never understand or approve of what Aiden was doing.

"Fine, I'll go," Josiah finally said. Before turning to leave he said, "Whatever you're up to, just be careful."

Aiden took off down the tunnel away from Josiah and made it to the west entrance just as Terrance recapped the plan, checking that everyone knew what they were to do. Aiden tried to shake away the squabble with Josiah. Now was not the time to be distracted.

Terrance finished talking and then walked to the fuse box

at the bottom of the ladder and disarmed the camera and alarm system. He didn't want any unwanted coalition officers noticing what they were up to.

It wasn't long before the team was above ground and moving into position. Point one was a shallow crater everyone quickly slid into. Guns and weapons drawn, the lookout team took their positions and waited while Aiden and the attack team continued forward. They made their way to a crumbling concrete wall at the edge of the highway.

They waited. The silence felt like the calm before the storm.

Soon, in the distance, Aiden heard a thumping noise. It was the drone. Aiden could see it before he saw the Humvee or delivery truck.

Aiden looked back at the lookout team. Terrance was looking through binoculars while the others either held a sniper rifle or a small rocket launcher.

The drone followed along the road. Behind it, the Humvee appeared. Soon after, the truck followed. It was a sixteen-wheeler with one lone driver inside. This was going to be easier than Aiden thought, that is, until the tank came into view. *How are they going to take that out with their tiny rocket launcher?*

Aiden looked at the lookout team who were pointing and moving around frantically. The window was quickly closing. If they didn't go soon, they'd miss their opportunity.

"What going on? You need to hit now," Jared radioed.

Terrance's voice came over the radio, agitated. "We don't have what we need to take out a tank. It was supposed to be two Humvees."

"Tell Terrance to distract it. I've got a plan." Seth instructed and then crawled over the wall and sprinted for a car in the middle of the highway.

CHAPTER 19

Aiden watched in terror. They were going to see him.

Suddenly, Aiden heard a noise and watched as a flair shot into the air.

As soon as those in the tank saw it, both vehicles slowed to a stop and the drone hovered above them. The tank's turret slowly moved, pointing in the team's direction, looking. Aiden held his breath as he watched Seth continue making his way toward the tank. As he approached, undetected, he pulled something out of his vest and stuck it to the lower front plate of the tank and then disappeared around the side of the truck.

"What is that idiot up to?" Tessa murmured.

Her question was quickly answered when a loud explosion echoed all around and a bright flash pierced the dark. Seth had set off a grenade.

As the smoke began to clear, Aiden could see a head popping out of the cupola.

There was a sudden noise like something ripping through the air, and then the soldier slumped over and toppled off the tank. A second Myriad soldier appeared with his gun drawn.

A second shot went off. It struck the soldier's shoulder. He ducked back inside the tank.

At that same moment, the rocket launcher shot its missile and took out the drone while red team climbed over the wall and ran toward the truck. Aiden sprinted with the others, praying the other soldier didn't attack them. Thankfully, they made it to the truck before the slow turret was able to make its way back in their direction.

Aiden slammed against one of the large tires and waited, breathing heavily. Seth and Tessa went to the front of the truck and pulled the driver out, forcing him on to the ground face first. Aiden could hear the man pleading for his life. Aiden turned away, he couldn't watch. There was still a part of him that wasn't okay with the group's tactics. A shot echoed.

"Aiden, let's go," a voice whispered in his ear as they walked passed him and to the back of the truck. Aiden followed one of his teammates, he couldn't tell which one.

Aiden's teammate had his weapon drawn and stood guard while Aiden went and picked the padlock. Soon the lock was open and Aiden pulled on the door to reveal boxes and boxes of supplies.

More gun shots. Tires screeching. Aiden turned. Blinded by headlights he shielded his eyes. One of his teammates, a guy name Keegan hung his head out the window of a Myriad Humvee and shouted. "Let's load up."

The rest of the team joined as they loaded boxes.

As Aiden moved deeper into oppressive heat of the truck, gunshots rang in the night. Aiden ducked behind a pile of boxes as his throat constricted. His mask was suffocating him. Aiden pulled the mask off. Just outside the truck unfamiliar voices shouted commands. Seth shouted back. Aiden peered around the box just as he heard a sickening crack and watched Seth's head whip to the side as his body hit the ground with a thud.

Aiden scurried deeper into the truck and sat with his knees drawn to his chest. He was trapped like a mouse. With his head down, he clutched at his hair with his cold clammy hands. He rocked back and forth praying to Sabaoth that he wasn't next, that somehow they wouldn't find him.

The truck bounced as Aiden heard boots echo inside the truck. Aiden caught a glimpse of a flashlight bouncing around. He heard the distant chatter of a radio.

Aiden felt goosebumps crawling up his arms. And then he

CHAPTER 19

heard the click of a gun. He slowly lifted his head. Standing in front of him, with a devilish grin, was a Myriad soldier.

The room had no lights on, only the dim glow of the moon coming through a small opening in the ceiling. Amina grabbed her head as she sat. She felt a warm sticky substance and let out an exasperated sigh. "No, no, no, no!" Amina slammed her fist on the concrete floor.

Looking around the room she saw Paxton lying on the floor possibly unconscious or asleep, she couldn't tell, and Salome siting against the wall with her knees drawn to her chest and her head resting on her knees. There were tiny whispers slipping through her lips.

"Where are we?"

Salome tried to give a reassuring smile, but it was lacking. "Some holding cell. The Myriad pulled us from the wreckage and left us in here. They've been gone for at least two hours."

"No," Amina groaned. This was not what was supposed to happen. "So how do we get out?"

Salome shrugged. "Your guess is as good as mine. This place looks pretty solid."

"Nothing these days is solid." Amina stood and glanced at Paxton. He was breathing softly and his face appeared relaxed, although the bloody nose and bruised cheek did not look appealing.

Amina kicked the bottom of Paxton's boot, waking sleeping beauty. It took a couple of kicks before Paxton finally opened his eyes.

"Just five more minutes," Paxton yawned.

"Get up Paxton. We gotta get out of here."

He blinked a few times, sitting and looking around like a dazed puppy. Finally his surroundings registered. "Oh crap. What the- how'd we—?"

"We crashed, remember?"

Paxton closed his eyes and sighed. "Amina, I'm so–"

Amina brushed him off. "It's fine, just help me figure a way out before they come back."

The three searched the room, looking over every beam, every crack in the wall, for something that seemed weak enough to break out. When Amina reached the door she examined it carefully. It was a steel door with a tiny window. The lock was a strange shape she had never seen before, but was certain it was a U-lock, which was impossible to pick. The hinges were also on the outside so they couldn't break down the door.

"I don't think there's a way out," Paxton said, still looking around.

"I can see that." Amina looked at the window and wondered if she could break it. She tapped on the glass a few times and ran her hand across it. Then she let out a loud yell as she punched the glass as hard as possible causing the other two to jump. The glass seemed to bow a little under the impact as a crushing pain spread from her knuckles up her hand and wrist, but the glass didn't crack. "It's Plexiglas."

While Amina examined her reddening knuckles, she heard a light click that sounded like a door closing. Amina peered out the window to see two Myriad soldiers making their way down the hallway. "Two people are coming. Maybe if we ambush them, we can get out."

"It's worth a shot." Paxton went to the door and stood against the wall with Amina and Salome on the opposite side. They waited silently as they heard the lock and door click open.

CHAPTER 19

The soldiers stepped into the dark cell. "Rise and shine my little puppets. It's questioning time." He laughed at his own comment. When no one walked out of the cell, the soldiers were forced to go inside.

As soon as they were just past the threshold, the three jumped out of their spots. Amina kicked the shorter soldier square in the back, knocking him forward. Paxton shoved the other so that he ran into his partner. Then they bolted as Salome slammed the door shut.

Without looking, they turned to run down the hall but were immediately greeted by another soldier and an AR16 pointed directly at them.

"Nice try, but you're not going anywhere. Up against the wall!" The soldier moved forward and the three put their hands up as they backed against the wall to let him pass. The man opened the cell door, never taking his eyes or his gun off them.

The other two soldiers walked out and quickly restrained the prisoners with zip ties. They proceeded to lead them down the hallway to three separate rooms.

The door slammed closed and locked behind Paxton and the soldier with the gun. He was an older man, in his late fifties. Short gray hair and grayish blue eyes.

The soldier looked at Paxton with a grim expression. He moved his jaw around as if chewing on tobacco. Finally he spoke. "Now how in the world did you get yourself mixed up with those two, Paxton?" The soldier lowered his gun and let it hang from its strap. Pulling out a knife, he walked over and cut the zip ties off Paxton's wrists.

"Nice to see you too, Sergeant Ray." Paxton rubbed his red

wrists. "Look it's a long story, but I'm on an assignment given to me by Lieutenant Haddad. You've got to let us go or it'll bust my whole plan."

"Is that so?" Paxton nodded. "Interesting, because I've heard something different."

Paxton gulped and took a small step back. "Oh?"

"I've heard that you've gone rogue and that you're helping the terrorists."

Paxton laughed, trying to mask his discomfort. "That's ridiculous." He could feel the heat rising in his face.

"Is it though?" Sergeant Ray gave Paxton a hard look. He wasn't nicknamed the human lie detector for nothing. "Because I have orders that if you're found, I'm to turn you in to Lieutenant Haddad. They're calling you an enemy of Teivel."

Paxton had to think fast and keep calm or he'd never convince Ray. "That's what I *wanted* everyone to think. I had to do something drastic in order to win the trust of one of the terrorists so she could lead me to something even bigger."

"Bigger?"

Paxton nodded. "I not only now have the location of the terrorists, but I also have the location of the Hebrews."

Sergeant Ray swore under his breath, dumbfounded. "Are you for real right now? Do you know what this means for us?"

Paxton nodded. "But you have to let me go so I can finish my plan."

Sergeant Ray pursed his lips into a straight line and shook his head. "No can do, buddy. You've got the intel, you've brought in two prisoners. I think your work is done. Stay here while I go make a call." With that, Ray pulled out his radio and started talking into it, no longer paying attention to Paxton. He swung

CHAPTER 19

the door open and walked out.

As the door slowly closed, Paxton ran and stuck out his boot to stop the door from latching. He watched Ray make his way down the hallway and out of sight.

Paxton crept down the hallway toward the next door in hopes of finding Amina or Salome alone inside. No such luck. As he peered through the small viewing window of the door, he saw Amina giving her captor a death stare. Paxton smiled. He appreciated Amina's ferocity. She didn't dare let anyone push her around.

Paxton placed his hand on the door and slowly tried to push down on the handle, it didn't budge. Thinking for a moment, Paxton decided to do something bold. He knocked.

The guard jolted in his seat and then turned to see who it was. Paxton quickly moved out of sight and waited.

The handle moved and the door swung open as Paxton heard the soldier complaining about being interrupted.

Paxton stepped in front of the soldier and swiftly punched him in the face. The soldier staggered back, grabbing his busted nose. Paxton kicked the soldier in the abdomen while he was off guard and sent him down.

"Let's go." Paxton motioned for Amina to follow and headed to the door.

"I can't, I'm kind of stuck."

Paxton turned, he hadn't realized she had been tied to the chair.

The soldier was getting up and reaching for his radio, but not before Paxton kicked it out of the guy's hand sending it crashing to the floor. The two men grappled with one another. Paxton was quick, but so was the other guy. The soldier was able to get off a few good punches that rattled Paxton, but eventually Paxton got in one good blow to the soldier's temple, knocking him out.

Paxton rushed to the soldier and found a switchblade that he used to cut through Amina's zip ties. He also grabbed the soldier's handgun and radio. *These could come in handy later.*

"How did you get out?" Amina asked, rubbing her wrists.

"Never mind that, let's get Salome and get out of here before anyone else finds us."

Salome stumbled into the small interrogation room as she was shoved from behind.

"Sit down." The taller of the two soldiers had brought her in. He had a bald head and a long and narrow face like a giraffe. He clenched his jaw as he shoved Salome into the chair and proceeded to tie her to it.

"Is this how you treat all your citizens?"

"Oh honey, you're no citizen, are you?" He gave one last tug on the rope around her waist, she felt it press hard into her abdomen making it hard to breath. "Now." Swinging a chair in front of Salome he sat in it backward. "Let's start with where you're from."

"Here. I have lived here my whole life."

The soldier gave her a look. "Is that so? What's your address?"

"48 E. Blake Street, condo number thirty-two."

"Your job?"

"I work at the market down the street."

"Your identification code?"

"781-562V."

The soldier stared at her for a long moment. His prying eyes ogled her up and down which made Salome's skin crawl, but she held his gaze refusing to be intimidated. The soldier smiled and stood. "Alright, then I suppose you won't mind if I scan your chip."

Salome tried to remain stoic as she felt the breath being sucked out of her. "And why would you need to do that? I gave you all the information you need."

"Because, darlin," the soldier grabbed Salome's right wrist hard. His face was inches away from her own. She could smell his foul garlic breath. "I know you're not really one of us." Salome tried to pull away, but that only made him grasp harder. He twisted her arm to reveal her empty wrist. "See, no chip." He took her other wrist and flipped it, but when there was nothing there either he brushed back her bangs to reveal the imprinted six-pointed star that stretched longer at four points to reveal a cross in the middle of the star. The soldier stepped back, his mouth open. The man swore under his breath as he stumbled out of the room.

Salome closed her eyes, her body trembling. *Breath Salome, just breathe. Sabaoth will get you out of this. Be strong.*

It wasn't long before the door flew open again making Salome jump out of her skin.

However, when she saw Paxton and Amina instead of the guard, Salome closed her eyes and tilted her head back. *Thank you Sabaoth.* Paxton dashed over to cut Salome's restraints as Amina stood watch.

"How did you get out?" Salome was puzzled.

"Never mind that, let's just go," Paxton snapped. He rushed back to the door and checked to see if anyone was in the hallway. Then he silently motioned for the other two to follow.

They made their way down the hallway with Paxton leading

and Salome bringing up the rear. Every minute or so Salome glanced behind them, paranoid that someone was following or was going to start shooting at them. Yet every time she did, no one was there.

At the end of the hallway was a set of stairs to their left and an office to their right. Paxton discretely peered into the office to make sure no one was on guard. The room was empty and sitting on the desk were three familiar bags.

"I found our stuff. Hold on." Paxton tried the handle, it was unlocked. He pushed the door open, crept in to grab the bags, and came back out.

They climbed the stairs, skipping two at a time until they reached the top. Paxton stopped, causing Salome to nearly run into Amina. She braced herself on Amina and could feel Amina's shoulder twitch.

They waited at the top of the stairs for an eternity before Paxton opened the door to the outside. Salome felt so lost. If there was a plan, she had no clue what it was. She hoped Paxton had thought this through. It would be easy for the soldiers to follow them.

Outside the building, they were in an abandoned strip mall on the outskirts of town. In the distance Salome could see the looming cement wall that had been built when the war had started in order to keep those inside the city "safe." At the same time, leaving the city without orders was also forbidden.

Salome continued to follow Paxton and Amina as they sprinted across the parking lot to the closest car and jumped in. The car was a white van with no windows, which made it rather convenient for them to hide out.

"If we start the car, they'll hear us," Salome whispered.

"We're not starting the car," Paxton whispered back. We

CHAPTER 19

just needed a place to stop and figure out where we are."

"Any ideas then?"

Paxton moved toward the front seat and looked out the windshield that was pointing away from the building they had just left. He kept looking from side to side. Squinting his eyes every once and a while as if that would help him see better.

Amina sat beside him while Salome sat in the back. The van wreaked of lemon scented cleaner and bleach. Salome scrunched her nose disgusted. "We must hurry. They're going to figure out we're missing and come looking for us soon."

Amina turned to look at Salome. "It looks like we're about a half mile away from the south tunnel entrance. I think we can make it if we building hop. The next closest hiding spot is that building across the street. We can go through it to the alley in the back."

Salome and Paxton agreed with the plan and they were soon out in the open again, running as fast as their legs would carry them. Paxton and Amina were much faster than Salome. Salome's chest was tight and she had a hard time regulating her breathing. She really needed to do more exercising. She wasn't used to all this running.

They made it into the building safely and Salome had to stop the others so she could catch her breath for a moment. She raised her hands over her head and paced back and forth allowing air to return to her lungs and her heart rate to drop. "Okay. Let's keep going."

They spent the next twenty minutes moving from one building to the next. It was a slow way to move but safe and effective. Eventually they ran out of buildings and all that was left in front of them was an open field.

The sun was now far above the horizon heating the day and

dissipating any sense of stealth the group had left.

Paxton stopped when they reached the last back door. Before opening it.

"What are we-"

Amina held a finger to her lips, silencing Salome's question. She continued to listen carefully. Salome tried to listen too but wasn't sure what she should be listening for.

Eventually, Amina nodded her head and Paxton cautiously opened the door to look outside.

"There are no cars in sight," he confirmed.

"Is the entrance out there?" Salome asked referring to the open field ahead of them.

"Yes. Probably about a quarter mile that direction." Amina pointed out and a little to her left.

"Well then let's go." Salome tried to walk forward but Amina pulled her back before she got out of the building.

Amina shook her head. "Not until we've seen the patrol pass by. They circulate this location often. I don't know when they last came by, but I'm not about to risk anything when we're this close."

"So we wait?"

"We wait."

Paxton closed the door again and they all sat down in the little hallway.

Salome closed her eyes and immediately realized how tired she was. So much had happened that her mind and body just wanted to drift off to dream land. She felt her body sinking as the muscles in her face relaxed and her mind went blank.

Chapter 20

It had been at least thirty minutes and still Amina hadn't heard a vehicle roll by. She was starting to wonder if something else was happening. She glanced at Paxton who also appeared concerned. He was holding a Myriad radio.

"What's wrong?"

"There's chatter on the radio."

"Okay . . . so what?" She didn't like the pitying look Paxton was giving her.

The radio crackled until someone spoke. "Red team has cleared the site and we are in position ready to infiltrate on your command."

The voice on the other end came through clearly and Amina recognized it immediately. She felt her stomach flip and her jaw clench as she listened to the voice.

"Remember, as soon as you infiltrate those tunnels you have five minutes to find their central hub."

"Understood." The radio went dead. Amina expected something else, but nothing came.

Amina's eyes darted back and forth as she stared at the ground. "I need do something." Her voice was shrill. She started looking through her bag. "I have to warn them." Amina found the phone Aiden had given her. She flipped it open and pressed one. As soon as she hit send, the phone buzzed with white noise. "Come on." The phone started ringing, once, twice, three times. Amina stood and began pacing. Her whole body was jittery. Six times the phone rang and no one answered.

"No!" Amina fumed as she stuffed the phone back in her pocket and headed toward the door.

"What do you think you're doing?" Paxton grabbed Amina's arm.

"I have to help them. If I can get to the entrance, I might have a chance to trip the security alarm sooner than they would and give them more time."

"You'll never make it. You're just going to get yourself killed."

"I have to do something." Amina yanked the door open. The bright sun burst into the hallway blinding Amina for a moment. She shielded her eyes until they adjusted. When her vision came back, she was about to head across the street and into the field.

That's when she saw them, dozens of Myriad soldiers, tanks, and Humvees scattered all around. She could see the tactical team lined up directly beside the tunnel entrance.

Amina stared without blinking, her hand covering her mouth. "Oh no." She ran her hand through her hair. *No, no, no, this can't be. This isn't happening.*

Paxton swore under his breathe beside her, his hands on his head.

"Maybe I can reach the other entrance before they go in." Amina tried to take off down the hallway to the other exit, but this time Salome stopped her by grabbing her arm.

"Hun, I don't think there's time."

CHAPTER 20

"I have to try. I can't just stand here and watch this happen. I have to save them. I'm responsible." Tears were running down Amina's face. Tears of fear. It was going to happen again. Everyone she cared about was going to be gone. "Please," Amina begged with every ounce of her being. "I have to."

Paxton turned to Amina, his face full of distress. "It would be pointless, Amina. You'd end up getting killed right along with them. Is that what you want?"

"I don't care, I have to do something!"

Over the radio Amina heard the familiar voice again. "Red team you're a go."

"Affirmative. Blowing the hole now."

Amina heard the deafening explosion from the field and dropped to her knees. She could barely catch her breath as the sobs wrenched from the depths of her soul. She thought someone was tearing her heart out. Salome bent down and put her arms around Amina and tried to sooth her crying, but nothing could soothe her, nothing could stop the pain she was feeling.

Through the tears Amina watched Paxton grab the radio and listen to it. Part of her wanted to hear their interactions as well, but another part of her was too afraid.

Amina buried her face in Salome's shoulder and held tightly. Tight enough that she could feel her fingernails breaking the skin. This was it. It was all over. All her work was for nothing because she was too late.

As Salome stroked Amina's head and rocked her back and forth, she heard Salome whispering something. Her voice had a rhythmic quality to it and was oddly peaceful.

Amina assumed she must've been praying, and at that moment, Amina realized there was only one thing left that she could do: pray. So she prayed from the pit of her soul with every ounce of her being. She cried out to Sabaoth and as she did, she realized she was not only asking Him for protection; she was surrounding herself with Him.

Oh Sabaoth, please stop this. Protect your people. You are the only one big enough to defeat this army. You are the only one who can save. I am too small, too powerless to fix anything. I've tried so much and yet failed. I need you now Sabaoth. Save your people from destruction. I relinquish control to you.

The next twenty minutes were the longest of her life. The radio seemed to go dead, all she could hear was static and her own sniffles. She couldn't understand why they were down there for so long. What was happening in there?

They continued to wait.

Amina stood, her legs felt weak so she held onto Paxton's shoulder and felt his strong arm wrap around her waist as they moved toward the door and peered out the window.

Amina saw movement and audibly sucked in a breath and held it as she watched the team emerge from underground, slithering out like snakes.

Amina carefully examined each person who came out of the hole, but she didn't see anyone other than soldiers.

Where are the Notzrim? Did the soldiers slaughter them all and leave them to rot?

"Where are the others?" Salome asked, just as confused.

"Probably still down there, dead." Amina couldn't hold it together anymore. She had done the only thing she could think of, she had trusted that Sabaoth would take care of it and he didn't. He had failed her.

"It's just me now. They're all gone." Amina turned to Salome emotionless. The shock had sucked it all out of her.

CHAPTER 20

"You can leave. You have no obligation to stay, so just leave me here and go back to your home."

Salome stepped forward and took Amina's hand. "I'm not leaving you." She looked at Paxton and then back to Amina. "*We're* not leaving you."

"Why, everyone else has?" Amina avoided Salome's gaze. She wasn't in the mood to be comforted. "No matter what I do, everyone either gets hurt or leaves."

"Not everyone," Paxton answered as he slid his hand into hers. "I haven't left, and I'm not going to."

Amina had thought she dried out all her tears, but then they came again, dripping down her cheeks like tiny streams.

Suddenly there was a loud beep and static from the radio. Amina jumped from the unexpected noise.

"Red team, report," the woman spat. She sounded agitated.

"The mission was unsuccessful. They're gone."

"What do you mean gone?"

The radio was silent for a moment before the commander of the red team spoke again. "I mean, the place was completely abandoned."

Chapter 21

It was as if her whole body were unraveling. *Gone. They're all gone. But where? And how?*

Amina had to go see for herself. They had to still be down there. People don't just disappear. Amina was about to open the door when Paxton laid his hand on hers.

"We need to wait until they clear out. Then we can go. But not now, it's not safe."

An hour passed, waiting. All Amina could do was play the same scene over and over in her head. They went in, they searched, and they found nothing. Sure the tunnels had protocols for break-ins, but nothing elaborate. And although Aiden was certain they had created a new escape plan, how is it they got everyone out in time? It seemed implausible.

If they somehow managed to hide everyone, Amina still wasn't sure how the Myriad didn't find their hiding place. The tunnels were limited due to some of the massive meteors that hit the earth five and a half years ago leaving massive holes and destroying much of the sewer system.

Amina wracked her brain, trying to figure out all the possible places they could've gone to hide, but nothing seemed secure or hidden enough. The Myriad would've raided everything.

Amina got up and walked to the door again and peered

through the window toward the field. It was empty. Finally, they were gone. Amina opened the door and the heat of the day blew in on Amina's face like a hot oven. The sun was starting to set, but that didn't mean the heat went with it.

She peered down the street in both directions. "The coast is clear." She opened the door all the way and walked out, not waiting for the others. She hurried across the street and made her way through the field toward the now blown open manhole. Amina heard footsteps behind her and knew the others were catching up.

Once the three of them made it to the opening they stopped. Amina peered down into the manhole, shaking her head at the mess the Myriad had created.

Down inside the tunnels Amina walked to the fuse box and flipped the switch that illuminated a string of lights up and down the tunnel. It smelled of sewage water and sweat. Amina wrinkled her nose. It was surprising how unused to the smell she had become after being away nine days.

"Ugh, you live down here?" Salome gagged and quickly put her hand over her mouth.

"Home sweet home."

Paxton took a bandanna from his pocket and handed it to Salome to put over her nose. Looking to Amina he asked, "So if they are in fact still down here hiding, where would they be?"

"I say we make our way to the Main Hall dwelling and go from there. If they chose to hide somewhere, I'm guessing they'll be coming out soon."

Amina led the others through the maze of tunnels. At each turn, Paxton insisted on checking the area with his new handgun just to ensure no danger lurked around the corner. One turn after another, they walked until they reached their destination.

It was eerie how empty it was. The only sound was water trickling from one of the upper tunnels.

Memories flooded Amina's mind of the last time she spoke in this place. When she still had so much stubborn arrogance. Whatever made her think she had to be the savior of it all? That she was the only one capable of such a thing? "Start scanning the place for anything that might be out of the ordinary. A hidden door, a panel, anything that might lead us to a secret hiding place."

The three split up and examined every inch of the dwelling. Amina ran her fingers up and down along the walls. Paxton lifted and overturned anything that wasn't bolted to the ground while Salome climbed one of the ladders. But everything seemed normal.

Where are they?

"Should we move on?" Salome asked.

Amina shook her head feeling lost. "I guess. We can head toward the elders' chamber." Amina led them to the tunnel, and as they jumped into it, Amina heard an odd noise, like that of something scraping. She slowly turned around. When she looked at the far wall, she saw it slowly slide open revealing an opening. Amina was dumbfounded. Hadn't she checked that wall? There were no doors.

Amina, Paxton, and Salome stepped into the shadows of the tunnel just to be safe.

As the door came to a stop, Amina could see shadowed figures, but she couldn't tell who they were. Her fingers tapped vigorously on her thigh with anticipation. Could it really be them? Amina waited until the figures stepped into the light and she could plainly see Paul's face and a few coalition

CHAPTER 21

officers.

Amina couldn't contain herself. She jumped up and down as she gave a fist pump. "It's them, they're alive!" Amina practically shouted she was so relieved. "Uncle Paul!" Amina called, but stayed back in case the coalition officers were trigger happy.

The group was startled and quickly held their guns in defense but no one pulled the trigger. "It's me, Amina." Amina stepped out of the shadow.

"Amina, you're back!" Paul broke away from the group. Amina climbed down the ladder and met her uncle with a huge bear hug. "I'm so glad you're safe. We were afraid something had happened to you."

"I'm okay. Where is everyone? The Myriad were down here, how did you hide from them?"

"We've been working a long time on this extra underground space for emergencies just like this. Unfortunately, we had a breach some days back. This alerted us to raise security, and when one of our coalition officers came across a Myriad radio frequency overhearing their new plan, it gave us time to get everyone to safety."

"Wait, there was a previous attack?"

"Yes, but they didn't get in, it was above ground. What about you? Did you succeed?"

Amina was smiling ear to ear. "We did. It took a while but we found the Hebrews and I brought one of them back." Amina turned around and motioned for Salome and Paxton to come down. "Uncle, I'd like you to meet Salome."

"It is a pleasure to meet you." Paul shook Salome's hand and gave her a warm smile. "I know it's not much, but welcome to our home."

More people started trickling out from the secret tunnel. They were hugging and talking. Feeling both relieved and grateful to be safe.

Paul walked to the guards. "Don't let anyone leave. We are holding a town hall meeting right now. I have good news for them."

The guard nodded and then started directing citizens to find a place in the dwelling to stand and wait.

Amina shook her head, astounded at how Sabaoth protected her family. She watched group after group come out of the tunnel with more smiles than she had ever seen.

But as the dwelling continued to fill, dread crept up her chest and throat, constricting her breathing. Where was Aiden? She needed to see her brother, feel his embrace, and know that he was okay, but the place was almost full.

Amina went to Paul who was now with Mo and Emily. Mo pulled Amina into an instant hug and kissed her on the cheek as she gushed, "I'm so glad you're okay."

"Thanks. I'm glad you're okay too."

"Cousin Amina!" Emily clung to Amina squeezing tightly.

As Amina rubbed Emily's back lovingly she asked, "Uncle, where's Aiden?"

"What do you mean? He hasn't come up yet?"

"No. Was he in hiding with all of you?"

"To be honest I haven't seen him in a few days, but I'm sure he was." Paul looked to Mo. She shook her head, her face painted with concern.

Amina wanted to continue searching for Aiden, but at that moment, Matthias walked over to her with Josiah standing at his side. Matthias had a proud grin on his face and held his arms outstretched. "Amina, you made it back."

CHAPTER 21

Amina knitted her brows together and glanced at him sideways. Why was he suddenly being so nice? Amina smiled back tentatively, but avoided his hug. "It's good to be back sir. I've brought someone with me. A Hebrew who has agreed to help us on our journey to her home."

"Wonderful. Where is she? I want to hold a meeting and tell everyone the good news."

"Sure, but I need to find my brother."

"I'm sure he's around here somewhere, you'll see him later. This can't wait."

Amina gave in and waved Salome over. After introductions, Matthias ushered the two of them up to the elder's platform.

While Matthias worked at getting everyone's attention, Amina leaned over to Josiah and whispered, "Have you seen Aiden?"

Josiah shook his head. "Not for a couple of days. He and I sort of go into an argument and we haven't spoken since."

Amina bit her lip as a sinking feeling settled in the pit of her stomach.

When Amina tuned back into Matthias' speech, she heard him say, "Thanks to the bravery of Amina Haddad, we have found a solution to our distressing plight." Matthias motioned for Amina and Salome to step forward. "This here is Salome, a Hebrew who has been living safely in the mountains under the protection of Sabaoth. She has graciously agreed to bring us back to her home." Cheers and applause arose from the crowd below. It was music to her ears and temporarily took her mind off Aiden's whereabouts. Joy swelled within as she smiled from ear to ear and held her head high. They were going to be okay. Sabaoth had led Amina and Paxton to the Hebrews, He moved the heart of Salome to help, and He protected the

Notzrim from death. *Thank you, Sabaoth. You truly have been looking out for us all along.*

The applause quieted and Matthias continued. "Now my family, we do not have much time. There's no telling if the Myriad will decide to come back. If so, we need to ensure that we are safely in the mountains before they do. So please, pack lightly, and be ready to leave by nightfall."

Amina was floating as she descended the stairs. It had been a long time since she felt such inner peace and she couldn't wait to tell Aiden.

Epilogue

Aiden opened his eyes and blinked the sleep out of them. His forehead pulsed violently. He tightly squeezed his eyes shut and opened them again, trying to focus on his surroundings, but his vision was blurry.

The cement underneath him was cold and pressed on his body in all the wrong places. As he slowly pushed himself up, every muscle in his body ached. It had been three, maybe four, days since he was captured. At this point it was hard to keep track. His tiny cell had no windows and only one small door that let in some light through the viewing slot, but that was it. Otherwise, Aiden sat in darkness day after day. To keep track of time and his sanity, he counted each time they brought food. They'd bring it twice a day, and if Aiden's internal clock was correct, they brought it once in the morning and once in the evening.

When he wasn't eating or sleeping, he was praying and singing hymns to keep his spirits lifted. When confined in the dark with no sound and no light, it was easy for Aiden's mind to wander into the dark places. To dwell on the negative, but so long as he could sing and repeat verses he had memorized over the years from the Sacred Book, he was okay.

When he didn't, fear would slither in like a venomous snake.

It would wrap around him and constrict every part of his body and mind. His throat would constrict, his heart would start pounding in his ears, and his vision would blur making it difficult to focus on what was real and true. When those moments came, it would take Aiden some time before he could finally calm himself and refocus on prayer.

Today, Aiden's body felt weaker than it had before. The lack of movement and conversation was eating away at him. He needed to figure out a way to get out of this hell, but the walls were thick and the door was strong. He had no tools of any sort in his prison and even when they brought food, there were no utensils.

Why were they keeping him alive? What purpose did it serve?

Aiden stood and stretched, trying to work out the kinks from sleeping on a hard floor. He took a slow deep breath in and let it out even slower, taking in the oxygen to help wake his mind and calm his anxieties.

As Aiden continued to stretch, he started to hear footsteps that grew louder and louder. Breakfast, he assumed. Aiden turned toward the door and walked to it. The food always came through a tiny slot at the bottom of the door, but Aiden hoped that today, if he was lucky, when the guard bent down to slide the food in, Aiden could grab hold of the guard's arm or neck or anything that he could dig his nails into and somehow convince the guard to open the door all the way. It seemed improbable, but Aiden was desperate and willing to try anything.

The footsteps stopped and he waited patiently for the scraping of metal as the food slot opened, but that's not what he heard. Instead, he swore he heard keys jingle. Aiden's heart raced and his body tingled. Were they actually opening the door?

EPILOGUE

Aiden took his stance, like a football player ready to tackle. The instant that door opened, he would charge, no matter what.

The door creaked slowly, and light spilled into the room. Aiden squinted at the blinding light he was no longer used to. The change made his head hurt even more as his eyes tried to adjust. Aiden shook it off and waited until he was certain the door was open all the way. Just as he was about to charge he felt hands grab him firmly. Aiden flailed and kicked till he made contact, but he had no strength.

"Don't fight it Aiden, it's no use," the woman standing in front of him said moving closer.

Aiden's eyes adjusted just long enough to see the woman take a syringe and plunge it in to his neck. His eyes flashed with recognition just as his entire body went limp and he blacked out.

A Free Novella Just for You

I hope you enjoyed reading *Searching for Refuge*. The story first came to me as a dream and eventually took shape into a three part series. So thanks for sticking with it and I hope you'll read book two *Searching for Direction*.

Or, for a special read of *The Search Begins: A Prequel*, visit http://bit.ly/3B408qB.

All Amina wants is to keep her brother safe, but how far is she willing to go?

Just six months after losing her parents, Amina's secret life is up heaved by a new government mandate: receive the mark or be arrested. The catch is, taking the mark means giving up who she really is. Determined to keep her brother Aiden safe, Amina determines to find a new safe haven where they can survive until the final days. The only problem is, she doesn't know where or how to do this before the government finds them and rips their freedom away forever.

About the Author

Britney Farr loves to create suspenseful and dangerous worlds from the safety of her home. There's nothing more exciting than watching her characters thrust into impossible situations, forcing them to grow despite the surrounding threats. Through grit and perseverance, Farr challenges her characters to find hope and strength in something greater than themselves—God.

Beyond writing, Britney Farr is a social communications manager at her church in the north metro Denver area and serves as president of the Thornton Community Chorus.

Britney Farr is an avid reader, devout Christian, and former English/Theatre teacher. She loves crafting her creativity and skills to bring readers an emotionally engaging, nerve-wracking, faith-filled story.

Farr has a bachelor's degree in English, but first began creating other worlds and characters as a young girl and she's never stopped. Whether she's building a character through her acting, creating emotion with singing, or putting pen to paper,

Britney loves the creativity. When she's not being creative or watching others' creativity, you can find her enjoying the outdoors. She loves hiking, camping, traveling the world, escape rooms, and enjoying the company of her friends and family.

To connect, discover fun bonus readings, and stay updated on Britney Farr's most recent writing projects, subscribe to her mailing list.

You can connect with me on:
- https://britneyfarr.com
- https://www.facebook.com/BritneyFarrAuthor
- https://www.instagram.com/BritneyFarrAuthor
- https://www.goodreads.com/britney_farr

Subscribe to my newsletter:
- https://landing.mailerlite.com/webforms/landing/h5d1g6

Also by Britney Farr

Searching for Direction
Just as the pieces come together, they're shattered again.

Amina returned home victorious, only to have her world shattered. The Myriad abducted her twin brother, Aiden, and she's determined to get him back.

Amina hands Salome the daunting task of guiding the Notzrim to their new home and to the unwelcoming Hebrew residents. No matter what she does, someone will not be happy.

Meanwhile, Aiden discovers the identity of his captor and the extraordinary lengths they will go to entice him to stay. The only question that remains is whether Aiden will give up everything he believes in for this new and unexpected opportunity.

Made in the USA
Las Vegas, NV
17 March 2023

69236864R00184